HARD ASSET

A COBRA ELITE NOVEL

PAMELA CLARE

WWW.PAMELACLARE.COM

HARD ASSET

PAMELA

CLARE

Hard Asset

A Cobra Elite novel

Published by Pamela Clare, 2019

Cover Design by © Jaycee DeLorenzo/Sweet 'N Spicy Designs
Photo Credit: Nikolas_jkd from Shutterstock.com

Copyright © 2019 by Pamela Clare

ISBN 13: 978-1-7335251-4-5

ISBN 10: 1-7335251-4-9

This book is dedicated to the Rohingya people. May your children, born in refugee camps, inherit a homeland, a future—and justice.

ACKNLOWLEDGEMENTS

A world of thanks to Michelle White, Benjamin Alexander, and Jackie Turner for their unflagging support during the writing of this book. Michelle, your willingness to talk any time I needed to go over this story was a godsend. Jackie, your feedback kept me from jumping off bridges. Benjamin, you did so much in the house and garden to free up time for me to write. I am eternally grateful.

Additional thanks to Shell Ryan for a very helpful edit.

Special thanks to Benjamin Alexander and Christopher Wu for answering questions regarding military operations and firearms.

Thanks as always to my beloved readers, whose enthusiasm keeps me going. You are the best.

1

C onnor O'Neal tossed back his second shot of whiskey, liquor and loud music helping to bring him back to earth. Yesterday, he'd been taking down cartel assholes in El Salvador. Tonight, he was drinking with his Cobra buddies at the Pony Express, their favorite dive bar in Denver, and trying to keep them from getting arrested.

Re-entry was never easy. Before joining Cobra, Connor had served for a decade with 1st Special Forces Operational Detachment-Delta—what civilians called Delta Force and what he simply knew as the Unit. Even so, he still hadn't figured out how to make the transition back to real life. One minute, he was pumped up on adrenaline, rounds flying, life and death hanging in the balance. The next, he was pushing a shopping cart through the grocery store buying toilet paper.

That's when the nightmares started.

He glanced around, taking a quick headcount. Malik

Jones, a former Army Ranger, and Dylan Cruz, who'd left the SEAL Teams at DEVGRU to join Cobra, were shooting the shit and playing pool. Lev Segal, who'd come to Cobra after a legendary career with Sayeret Matkal, was arguing politics with a hipster in skinny jeans. Meanwhile, Elizabeth Shields, an intel specialist who'd worked for the CIA, was trying to teach Quinn McManus, a former operator with the British Secret Air Service, how to line dance, the big Scot picking it up quickly.

Doc Sullivan, one of Cobra's medics, sat beside Connor, beer in hand.

Connor pointed with a nod of his head. "Who would've thought he could dance?"

Doc looked out at the dance floor, grinned. "Do you think he remembers Shields is off-limits?"

"At the moment?" Connor saw the way McManus looked at her. "Hell, no."

"He'd better watch his ass." Doc took a sip of his beer.

"Yeah, he's mostly watching hers." Connor chuckled at his own joke.

Doc laughed, too. "Alcohol and hormones are a dangerous combination."

"Isn't that the truth?"

It was an open secret that McManus had a thing for Shields. So far, he hadn't done anything to get himself fired, though his persistent use of the nickname *Lilibet* for her hadn't gone unnoticed. Cobra International Security, a private military company, owned and staffed by veterans, had strict rules against hookups among employees. Given the kind of work the company did—running security and carrying out a range of covert operations on behalf of the United States, its allies, and non-governmental organizations like the UN—the rules made sense.

When bullets flew, distractions could be fatal.

For all the rules and risk, working for Cobra was a vacation compared to life in the Unit. Connor hadn't known what to do with himself after leaving the army until his buddy and fellow operator Nick Andris had emailed him a recruitment brochure.

Connor hadn't regretted his decision to sign on—not even when he'd taken a round to the gut last November. The hours were better. The pay was better. The gear was state-of-the-art. His fellow operatives were experienced, top-notch fighters and intel specialists recruited from special forces around the world. They even had a new guy, Thor Isaksen, from Denmark's Sirius Dog Sled Patrol.

"What about you, man?" Doc seemed to study him. "What happened to that blonde you were seeing?"

"I wasn't *seeing* her." Connor made it a rule not to get mixed up emotionally with women. It wasn't good for them —or him. "It was just, you know ..."

"Ah. Got it." Doc took another swig. "You ever thought of settling down?"

"Sure, but that was a long time ago."

He'd been new to the Unit and cocky as hell—proud to be an elite operator and drunk on testosterone. He'd met a fancy college girl at a bar, and they'd ended up fucking the sheets off her bed. Soon, they were living together at Mandy's place, and he'd thought he had it made. He was working his dream job and head-over-heels in love with a smart, beautiful woman. It lasted through one deployment.

"What ended it?"

Connor didn't feel like getting into this, so he gave Doc the short, sanitized version. "She didn't like the way I earned my paycheck. How about you?"

"I—"

"Dinnae you touch her, you feckin' piece of shite!" McManus' shout cut Doc's answer short.

Connor looked to see the Scotsman standing toe to toe with a guy in a cowboy hat, his face almost as red as his hair, Shields thrust protectively behind him.

"Hell." *Here we go.*

Connor stood, made his way through the crowd, Doc beside him.

When McManus was shit-faced or pissed off, he lapsed into almost unintelligible Glaswegian—usually just before beating the shit out of someone. At six foot four and as strong as an ox, McManus threw a bone-crushing punch.

Shields tried to defuse the situation. "Quinn, I can handle this. He's drunk. You're drunk. Just drop it."

McManus ignored her, crowding the city cowboy, who glared at Shields, clearly not understanding that he was in mortal danger. "Why do you wear tight jeans like that if you don't want men to touch the goods?"

"You'd best bolt yer rocket, lad, or I'll shove your bawbag up yer arse."

"What the fuck does that even mean?" The cowboy glared up at McManus, his buddies crowding around him, watching his six. "I can handle you, carrot top."

Segal, Jones, and Cruz pushed their way through the crowd to flank McManus, Jones and Cruz still holding their pool cues.

Shit.

Connor caught a glimpse of McManus' fist clenching. He shouldered his way in between the two men. "Break it up! That's enough! McManus!"

Shields stepped past McManus and took on City Cowboy herself. "You're obviously not a smart man, so let me put this in terms even you can understand. You just picked a fight with a military guy who is here with the rest of his team. They just got home from an op and are still pumped on adrenaline. These guys fight for a living, so unless you want to go home in pieces, apologize to me and get out of here."

City Cowboy glared at her and then McManus—and pulled a switchblade from his pocket. "I'm not afraid of him."

"Oh, look, he's got a wee knifey." McManus might have been drunk, but his reflexes were lightning quick. He snatched the knife out of the idiot's hand, examined it as if he'd never seen a blade before. "I could shave wi' this."

Connor met City Cowboy's gaze. "Listen to her. Save yourself some pain."

The bar was now silent, the air thick with tension.

City Cowboy's gaze shifted from McManus to Connor and back again before dropping to the floor. "Sorry."

"Good choice." Shields' contempt was clear. "To answer your question, a woman *never* puts on jeans hoping some drunk loser will grab her butt. The *goods*, as you call them, aren't yours to touch. Women dress to please themselves."

"What the hell's going on?" Evan, the bouncer, pushed his way through the crowd. Big and bald, his forearms thick and tattooed with skulls, he was an army veteran and, more importantly at this moment, a friend.

"City Cowboy here grabbed Shields' butt." Connor stepped back, made room for him. "We were just working it out."

Evan grabbed City Cowboy by the back of his shirt and dragged him toward the door. "You're a fucking idiot, you know that? These guys could flay your sorry ass. You can't treat women like that. Get the fuck out of here, you piece of shit. Don't let me see your face again."

Connor exhaled. "I need a drink."

August 28
The Hague

SHANTI LAHIRI FOUGHT to contain her frustration. "If I arrive with an armed escort, it will discourage survivors from speaking with me. These women were raped by military men. They watched soldiers murder their children, their husbands, everyone they knew."

The first security company they'd hired to protect her had pulled out at the last minute for unknown reasons. Shanti had hoped that meant she wouldn't have one, but Bram wouldn't budge.

"I understand it makes your job more challenging, but I won't send you in without a security detail." Bram's voice was infuriatingly calm, his Dutch accent almost imperceptible. "The camps aren't safe. You know that."

Two British journalists had been abducted from the Kutupalong refugee camp in Bangladesh last month, taken across the border into Myanmar, and then arrested and thrown in jail. Authorities in Myanmar claimed the two had crossed the border illegally and had been trying to steal state secrets. The charges against them were false, of course. They'd been doing exactly what Shanti was about to do— visiting Rohingya refugees in search of the truth about General Naing and the allegations that he had ordered ethnic cleansing, genocidal rape, and the killing of innocent Rohingya civilians.

The reporters had hoped to expose the truth about Naing in the press, but Shanti was traveling there to collect official witness statements on behalf of the International Criminal Court. She wanted to put Naing in prison.

"It's not just Naing's troops. There are reports of sex traffickers and sexual assault—"

"I wrote the brief, Bram. I understand the situation." She'd been working on this case for almost two years.

Bram leaned back in his chair, looked at her through his bifocals. "We will, of course, insist on the greatest discretion. We want to keep your visit as low-key as possible—no press, no public statements, no social media, nothing on the website."

"How is showing up with a team of Rambos discreet?" Military guys put Shanti on edge with their chauvinism, their guns, and toxic levels of testosterone. She knew only too well the devastation they could cause. "Do they have to be armed?"

Bram grinned as if she'd said something funny. "If they're any good, they'll insist on it."

Bram was her boss and a brilliant human-rights attorney, but it had been a long time since he'd met face to face with victims of brutality.

"I don't want the sight of armed men to re-traumatize these people."

Bram's expression changed, his brow weighed down by sadness, his blue eyes sympathetic. "By asking them to recount their stories, you'll be making them relive it all. You know that. I think this is personal for you, and I understand why."

Okay, inconvenient truth there.

Bram changed the subject. "How much Bangla do you remember?"

"I understand a lot, but I can't say much—just basic

things like 'hello' and 'thank you.' Bangla won't help me in the camps anyway. Rohingya is its own language."

That's why she'd asked the UN to find an interpreter.

Shanti had been born in Dhaka, Bangladesh, to a Bengali Hindu father and an American mother. Her parents had met on the campus of Dhaka University, where her father was a professor of economics and her mother studied Hindu literature. They had fallen in love, gotten married against the wishes of both families, and were happily married still.

Sectarian violence had led her parents to relocate not long after Shanti was born. They had ended up in Ithaca, New York. She'd grown up speaking English. Although she had visited her grandparents in Dhaka each year, they'd spoken English to her, too.

Still, those visits had shaped her in so many ways. She'd heard the story of her grandparents' narrow escape during the genocide of 1971. Not all of her relatives had made it. And, although her family was quite wealthy, Shanti had also witnessed unspeakable poverty. That stark inequality, along with her family's tragic history, had driven her to study law.

"Can we at least ask them to wear street clothes and hide their weapons?"

"Ask for whatever you want, but don't expect them to agree to all of it."

≈

Denver

CONNOR GLANCED around the conference room table, head throbbing, cup of coffee in his hand. The only one who didn't look hungover was Shields.

Derek Tower, one of Cobra's two owners, stepped inside, grinned. "Hard night?"

"He grabbed Shields' bum." McManus was clearly still angry.

Tower's eyebrows rose. "Sorry to hear that, Shields. Is he still alive, this asshole? I'm surprised I'm not bailing you all out this morning."

Connor grinned. "We defused the situation."

"Good." Tower sat, turned on the wall-mounted flat-screen monitor. "We've got a last-minute job. Another security team backed out on a prosecutor from the International Criminal Court who is headed to Bangladesh."

A blurry image of a pretty, dark-haired woman filled the screen. Or maybe it was Connor's vision that was blurry.

"This is Shanti Lahiri, a prosecutor with the ICC. She's got dual US-Bangladesh citizenship. Her father is Bangladeshi and a professor at Cornell. Her mother is American and teaches poetry at Ithaca College. Ms. Lahiri studied at Harvard Law and graduated top of her class. She has a brother. Never married. No children."

The image on the screen changed to a man in a green military uniform.

Shields made a face. "Oh, look, it's General Asshole."

Tower pointed toward the screen. "This is General Min Thant Naing. He is believed to be the driving force behind the massacres of Rohingya people in Rakhine State in Myanmar. Shields, can you brief us on the history?"

"Southeast Asia isn't my area, but I'll give it a shot." She took a sip of her coffee. "Ethnically, the Burmese and Rohingya are different—Southeast Asian and Indo-Aryan, respectively. They also speak different languages and worship different gods."

"Let me guess." Cruz stood, poured himself more coffee.

"Despite everything they have in common, they just don't get along."

"Imagine that." Shields told them how, when Japan invaded what was then Burma during World War II, the Buddhist majority sided with Japan, while the Muslims fought with the British. "The British promised the Rohingya an autonomous state but didn't deliver. The Rohingya view Rakhine State as their homeland because they've lived there since at least the fifteenth century, but the Burmese ethnic majority see them as illegal immigrants—unwelcome foreign invaders with a different language and religion."

McManus grinned. "What a pity it is that Lilibet knows so little about it."

Shields went on. "In the early eighties, the government of Myanmar rewrote its citizenship laws and specifically excluded the Rohingya. There have been repeated attempts to drive them out, acts of ethnic cleansing. Two years ago, a Rohingya militia attacked a police station, setting off this latest wave of brutality. Over the past few years, Naing's men have torched Rohingya villages, killing the men and children and raping and killing the women. The number of refugees in Bangladesh is now around a million. The UN calls the Rohingya the 'most persecuted minority in the world.'"

Jones glared at the screen. "Why hasn't anyone gone after this fucker?"

Tower took over. "Ms. Lahiri is going after him—legally speaking—and it's our job to keep her safe. Two British journalists were recently abducted from one of the camps and taken across the border into Myanmar, where they were accused of spying and thrown in jail. They'd been asking questions about Naing in the camps."

Everyone at the table understood. This operation wasn't

just about making sure Ms. Lahiri wasn't mugged. It was about protecting her life from a man who would risk almost anything to stop her from doing her job.

"Shields, I need an intel report by noon. O'Neal, you'll be in command of this operation. You are wheels up at sixteen-hundred hours for The Hague. Shields, Segal, Isaksen—you head straight to Bangladesh with a geek team to set things up. Everyone be sure to check with Doc about vaccines and malaria meds."

Connor's spirits lifted. "All right, guys. Take some aspirin. Coffee up. Get your heads back in the game."

He was relieved to be heading out again.

Being home, pretending to fit in—it was too damned much work.

2

Shanti followed Bram down the maze of hallways, her heels clicking on the dark tile floor. When she'd first come to work at the ICC two years ago, it had taken her almost three months to learn her way around the building. She would have left trails of bread crumbs or paper clips if she hadn't been afraid it would get her fired.

She was glad finally to be leaving for Bangladesh, but she still wasn't happy about the idea of traveling with a security team. "What do you know about the company? Have there been any criminal prosecutions against them?"

The last thing she wanted was an escort made up of men like the one she was trying to bring to justice—men who had butchered innocent people and were little better than war criminals themselves. That would compromise her principles.

"Relax. They're squeaky clean. I've been told they're the best." Bram opened the conference room door and held it for her.

She stepped into what looked like a photoshoot for *GQ*.

Several tall, handsome men stood around the conference table, all of them impeccably dressed in tailored suits.

"Not the Rambos you were expecting, are they?" Bram whispered as he took his seat on her left. "Gentlemen, welcome to The Hague and the International Criminal Court. I'm Bram Meijer with the Office of the Prosecutor, and this is Shanti Lahiri, one of our shining stars."

Shanti willed a smile onto her face, lifted her gaze—and found herself looking into a pair of deep blue eyes. "Thank you for meeting with us."

The words came out without conscious effort, her mind blank, her gaze fixed on the man across from her. He had thick, dark brown hair, his face rugged but somehow also ... beautiful. Full lips and long lashes softened the impact of his chiseled jawline and a nose that looked like it had once been broken. There were hollows beneath his cheekbones. One cheek bore a small white scar.

She willed herself to look away as the men introduced themselves.

"Derek Tower, one of the owners of Cobra International Security." Mr. Tower was hard-edged, his face tanned from years outdoors, his hair a sandy blond.

"Malik Jones." Mr. Jones, a visibly ripped black man, could easily have made it as a model or actor. "I served with the US Army Rangers."

"Dylan Cruz." He looked either Cuban or Puerto Rican with a warm smile that reached his brown eyes. "I worked with the Teams at DEVGRU."

"Ah, yes. SEAL Team Six." Bram chuckled. "You're famous."

"In his own mind," Mr. Jones muttered, making the other men grin.

"Connor O'Neal," said the man with blue eyes, his gaze still focused on Shanti. "I served with US Army special forces."

"McManus, ma'am," said a redhaired mountain of a man, a Scotsman by his accent. "British Secret Air Service."

"O'Neal will command your escort," Mr. Tower said. "We've asked the Bangladesh government for permission to get drones overhead while you're in the camps. We'll also have a helicopter at the nearest airport."

Drones? A *helicopter*?

Shanti gaped at him. "Is all of that necessary?"

"As I'm sure you're aware, the situation in the camps is far from safe. If Naing's men were willing to cross the border to abduct British journalists, imagine what they'd be willing to do to stop a criminal investigation."

A shiver slid down Shanti's spine.

CONNOR SAW the shadow of fear in Ms. Lahiri's amber eyes, her pupils going wide. She was right to be afraid.

"You're paying us to be prepared for any contingency," Tower said. "We would rather have assets available and not use them than be caught with our pants down."

Connor wished Tower had used a different metaphor. The physical reaction he'd had when Ms. Lahiri had walked through the door made any mention of pants awkward. The photo he'd seen during their briefing yesterday morning hadn't done her justice.

Or maybe you were hungover.

She wasn't just pretty. She was ... *hot.*

Dark hair that hung, thick and straight, down her back. Wide amber eyes framed by dark lashes. A delicate nose.

Soft brown skin. That full lower lip. Curves in all the right places, curves her tailored skirt suit couldn't hide.

Damn.

"The organization appreciates your thoroughness, Mr. Tower," said Meijer.

Ms. Lahiri's gaze dropped to her notepad. "Before we get started, I have some concerns I'd like to discuss."

Tower nodded. "Please, go ahead."

In a blink, the fear he'd seen disappeared from her eyes. In its place, Connor saw the confidence of a successful, Harvard-educated attorney.

"The people I'll be interviewing are victims of terrible violence—arson, rape, murder. I'd like to do my job without adding to their trauma. That means no camo or visible military garb and, if at all possible, no guns."

Connor blinked.

What had she just said?

No *guns*?

Connor fought the impulse to laugh, exchanging glances with Jones and Cruz, who were just as surprised as he was.

Seriously. No guns?

Connor had to give Tower credit. The man kept his game face, seeming to consider Ms. Lahiri's ridiculous request.

"Obviously, we want you to be able to complete your mission. We'll wear street clothes. That's not a problem. Most protection details wear regionally appropriate street clothes over body armor, not camo. But I won't send my men into the camps without firearms. That would be a dereliction of duty. I won't risk your life—or theirs."

Damn straight.

Ms. Lahiri's chin went up. "Surely, there must be other options—nonlethal weapons like Tasers or pepper spray."

Connor's gaze met Tower's.

Yeah, what the fuck, man?

Mr. Meijer cut in. "Shanti is concerned that people, particularly women, will be afraid to speak with her if she's accompanied by armed men. Also—I think you should know—she is uncomfortable around soldiers and firearms due to family history."

She didn't deny it. "I know what they can do."

Yeah, so did Connor. He'd been on the receiving end of bullets. Still, most people felt safer with a Cobra team around specifically *because* they were armed.

Tower nodded. "That's good to know. I understand your concerns, Ms. Lahiri. Here's the problem: If anything goes sideways at the camp, the enemy won't be packing Tasers or pepper spray or baseball bats. They'll carry rifles. Of course, you could always decline our services and search for another team."

Whoa. Way to lay it on the line, Tower.

Mr. Meijer shook his head. "No, no. We respect your judgment."

Ms. Lahiri looked anything but satisfied.

Did she expect them to protect her from men with automatic weapons without being able to return fire?

"Ms. Lahiri?" Tower waited, his gaze fixed on her.

"Can you conceal your weapons? The Secret Service doesn't walk around carrying openly, and they protect our presidents."

Tower looked like he was considering this.

Oh, come on, man. No way.

"We might be able to accommodate you on that, depending on how the situation seems on the ground," Tower said after a moment. "However, the point of carrying a weapon is to be ready to use it. They won't do you any good otherwise. We will, of course, do all we can not to impede your work or intimidate anyone."

"Thank you. I would appreciate that."

Tower handed Meijer and Ms. Lahiri each a folder. "Inside, you'll find information about Cobra—who we are, how we operate—as well as a list of precautions we expect Ms. Lahiri to take while we're in the field. I want to go through those now."

It was basic stuff. No unaccompanied excursions. No sharing of travel plans with anyone outside the ICC, UN officials, or Cobra, not even family. No using her personal cell phone while in Bangladesh. No arguing with the Cobra team if they believed a situation was unsafe.

"If we find ourselves in an emergency, we expect you to do exactly as you're told without question. The lives of my men, as well as yours, could be on the line."

Ms. Lahiri nodded. "I understand."

"How do you plan to dress while in Bangladesh?"

The question seemed to catch her off-guard. "How do I plan to dress?"

"Your father is Bengali. You have relatives there. Your social media has photos of you wearing traditional Bengali clothing. We advise against that."

"I want to make the women in the camp feel safe. Dressing like them might make them feel more comfortable and help me blend in."

Connor didn't think Ms. Lahiri would blend in no matter where she was or how she dressed—not with that face and body.

"It's that last part that worries us. If you look like everyone else, it might confuse the sex traffickers and gangs that prey on young women in these camps."

Her gaze dropped. "I hadn't thought of that."

Mr. Meijer chuckled. "That's their job—to think of everything."

It was an almost twelve-hour flight from The Hague to the Cox's Bazar International Airport—not a hardship on Cobra's luxurious private jet. Shanti had never seen anything like it. Bar. Television. Refrigerator. Comfortable seats. Coffee tables.

While the members of her security team played video games, read books, or napped in their seats, Shanti put on noise-canceling headphones and re-read the report prepared by the UN investigator, her sense of rage rising at descriptions of unspeakable cruelty. This was textbook ethnic cleansing with a side of mass rape and genocide.

The government of Myanmar denied the allegations, claiming that the Arakan Rohingya Salvation Army—a Rohingya militia group—had attacked villages that refused to provide them with volunteers. But the government's photographic "proof" of this had been exposed as false. More than that, their version of the story contradicted every statement given by Rohingya refugees UN investigators had interviewed.

She was so focused on her work that she didn't see or hear the team leader until he tapped on her shoulder. She pulled off the earphones, looked up—and felt a jolt of attraction.

Mr. O'Neal stood beside her, looking lethally sexy in butter-soft jeans and a T-shirt that stretched over the muscles of his chest, his blue eyes warm. "I asked whether you were hungry. There's food in the fridge—sandwiches, fruit, sliced veggies, cheese, yogurt, those little sausage things."

"Thanks." She glanced at her watch to see that it was past noon then looked up to find him grinning. "What?"

"You look at your watch to decide whether you're hungry?"

"I just didn't realize four hours had gone by." She unbuckled her safety belt and followed him back to the refrigerator, her new pumps pinching her toes.

He opened the brushed steel door. "Take whatever you want. There's soda, too, and juice. I think Cruz just made a fresh pot of coffee."

"Fresh-ground Puerto Rican beans, man," Mr. Cruz called from a plush chair where he sat with a video game controller in his hands. "Ah, fuck. I'm dead again."

"Give me a good brew," said the big Scotsman without opening his eyes. Shanti had thought he was asleep. "I'll take a cuppa any day over hot bean water."

Mr. O'Neal chuckled. "McManus here has been known to break out a little stove and brew a cup of tea on the battlefield."

"Really?" Shanti couldn't imagine that.

She found herself smiling at their good-natured banter. She had to admit, at least to herself, that these guys weren't what she'd expected. There was no macho bluster, no swagger, no chest-thumping. The way they joked with one another reminded her of her younger brother, Taj, and his friends.

She reached into the refrigerator and chose a turkey sandwich and a bottle of Perrier. She'd just turned to go back to her seat when the plane hit turbulence, throwing her off balance.

Strong arms caught her, steadied her, kept her from falling.

"Careful. The ride always gets a little bumpy over Turkey."

Shanti found herself looking into those blue eyes, awareness burning through her, making her pulse trip. "Thanks, Mr. O'Neal."

He held her for just a heartbeat longer than was necessary, his gaze locked with hers, his body hard and muscular. "Connor—or just call me O'Neal like these jokers do."

"You can call me Shanti."

"Okay, Shanti." He released her, leaving her to make her way back to her seat.

She sat, drew a breath, her pulse still skipping.

What had just happened?

The turbulence had taken her by surprise, and she'd almost fallen.

It was just adrenaline.

Of course. Right. And all those muscles and those blue eyes had nothing to do with the way her heart was beating. Nothing at all.

It was just after eight at night when they landed in Cox's Bazar, an area in southeastern Bangladesh named after an officer with the East India Company. The men put body armor over their T-shirts, clipped on their radios, and disappeared into a back room for a moment only to emerge armed.

Cruz popped in his earpiece. "Longest unbroken sand beach in the world, but do I get to chill and hit the water? Hell, no."

"Says the whiner who left the SEALs because he was sick of getting sand in his underwear." Jones chuckled and followed him through the spacious cabin toward the exit.

"What about our luggage?" Shanti asked.

"It will meet us at the hotel."

Connor did a radio check and then led Shanti down the stairs toward a waiting Land Rover, he, McManus Cruz, and Jones clustered protectively around her. There was no joking now, the four men silent, their gazes searching the area as they moved.

The air was humid, the familiar scents striking a soft place inside Shanti, stirring childhood memories—trying on her grandmother's beautiful silk saris, eating ice cream at the lake next to the Houses of Parliament with her parents, visiting the Dhakeshwari Temple with her grandfather. Monsoons. Humidity. Spicy food.

When they reached the Land Rover, Connor opened the door and helped Shanti inside. He followed, the other men climbing in and taking their seats. He reached for his handset. "The asset is safely off the plane and in the vehicle."

Asset?

Was that what she was in private security slang?

Then it came to her. "Who are you talking to? Your radio set can't reach the United States, can it?"

Connor grinned, a smile that made her belly flutter. "The rest of our team flew straight here to vet the hotel staff and get our operation set up."

"Oh." Shanti had never traveled with a security detail before. She'd had no idea of the scale of such an operation. She had expected a couple of bodyguards. Then again, Bram had told her that Cobra was the best.

Guilt needled her. Had she truly dismissed them as Rambos?

She did her best to make up for that. "Thanks—to all of you. I really appreciate everything you're doing to keep me safe."

But the men's attention was fixed on the world outside their vehicle, and they didn't seem to hear her.

3

_____

Connor escorted Shanti inside the hotel and into the elevator, Jones, McManus, and Cruz piling in behind him. "Cobra has the entire top floor. You've got the suite. I'll be staying in the adjoining room."

The room was intended for an assistant or servant, so it was small. Still, it more than met Connor's needs for this mission.

"Thank you."

"It's what we do."

The elevator stopped, and the doors opened with a *ding*.

Shields was waiting for them. "Welcome to the Longest Beach Hotel, Ms. Lahiri. I'm Elizabeth Shields, part of Cobra's support team. Did you have a good flight?"

"Yes, thank you."

"I'm glad to hear it." Shields handed Shanti and Connor their keycards. "ETA on your gear is about five minutes."

"Ms. Lahiri, let's get you settled." He glanced at the others. "Staff briefing in thirty. Shields, I want an update on the drone problem."

He followed Shanti into her suite. The others had

secured this floor yesterday, so there was no need to clear the rooms.

She turned on the light, set her handbag on a table just inside the door, not reacting to the luxurious surroundings. He knew she came from money, so maybe the polished wood floors, king-sized bed, leather sofas, large flat-screen TV, bar, and other amenities didn't impress her.

Connor had *seen* suites like this before. He'd served on details for dozens of traveling dignitaries—diplomats, senators, ministers of various governments—but he'd never *stayed* in anything this fancy. His paycheck from Cobra was good, but it wasn't *that* good.

"Are you hungry?"

"No, thanks." She stepped out of her heels, a look of relief on her face as she wiggled her toes. "I'd just like to take a shower and change my clothes."

"Your luggage is in the elevator." Connor figured he ought to review the basics. "When you need to order food, you let us know what you want, and we'll order it for you. We'll meet room service at the elevator and bring the food to your door. Don't go down to the restaurants or the bar. If you need a glass of wine, we'll get that, too."

"Got it." She crossed her arms over her chest as if she were cold—or anxious.

He found himself wanting to reassure her but kept his distance. He didn't need a repeat of this afternoon. He'd only meant to keep her from falling, but something had passed between them the moment he'd touched her.

Sexual attraction.

Yeah, well, he needed to put a lid on that if he wanted to keep his job.

"The elevator is set up so that only those with keycards for this floor can get here. The doors to the stairways are locked from the inside. We've got our own surveillance in the hallway." He pointed to the open door that led to his room. "I'll be right in there if you need anything. Just call or knock. You're safe here, Shanti."

"Oh, it's not that." She gave a little shake of her head, looking less like a high-powered attorney and more like an uncertain young woman. "This is the first time I've been the point person for the Office of the Prosecutor. I can't screw it up. It's too important. So many lives lost. So much brutality."

Connor could empathize. He knew what it was like to shoulder a big burden at a young age. His first op had been a hostage rescue. He told her what he'd said to himself that day long ago. "If they trust you to carry this, you must have what it takes. Once you get your boots on the ground and get into the action, you'll be fine."

She doesn't wear boots, idiot.

Shanti smiled, nodded.

Then Shields' voice came over Connor's earpiece, telling him their bags were sitting outside the door.

"Our bags are here." He brought in her luggage first and then shouldered his duffel. "You're welcome to join us in the briefing if you want. We'll be running through tomorrow's itinerary—the foreign minister's visit and so on."

"I'd like that. Thanks."

"See you in the room at the end of the hall in twenty-five minutes." He left her to do her thing, closing the door to his adjoining room on the way out, sorting his gear, and taking a quick shower to revive himself. Twelve hours on an airplane was never fun.

He found the others milling around in the makeshift operations room, shooting the shit, and hitting the coffee hard. "Let's get started. I believe Ms. Lahiri is going to..."

Connor's words trailed off when she stepped into the room, the sight of her like a fist to his solar plexus.

Holy ... shit!

He couldn't stop himself from staring.

Gone was that stiff skirt suit. In its place, she wore a silk sari in hot pink and gold, her blouse a matching pink, her midriff bare, a long fall of pink and gold cloth spilling over one shoulder. Something about the sari accentuated her narrow waist and the sweet feminine flare of her hips, her dark, damp hair hanging down her back.

Good God, she was beautiful.

"Sorry I'm late."

Segal and Isaksen, the only members of the team that hadn't yet met Shanti, stood and introduced themselves while Connor tried to find his tongue.

"Lev Segal, Israeli Defense Force."

"Thor Isaksen, Denmark's Sirius Patrol."

Get it together, dumbass!

"We were... uh ... just starting."

SHANTI ATE BREAKFAST the next morning in her bathrobe, savoring the fluffy *poori* bread and the spice of the potato curry. She'd ordered scrambled eggs as well, something her grandparents, who had been strict vegetarians, would never have made for her. But it was the steaming *cha* that made her moan—hot milk tea with cloves, cardamom, ginger, and sugar.

No one made tea like Bengalis.

The taste filled her head, bringing back memories of meals on the veranda of her grandparents' house, sheltered from the dust and noise of Dhaka and surrounded by the sweet scent of jasmine vines. Those visits had seemed happy and magical, her grandparents and their servants spoiling her and her brother, Taj, rotten. She hadn't known until much later that her grandmother had opposed the marriage and couldn't stand her mother.

While she finished her breakfast, Shanti checked her email. An email from her parents asking her how she was doing. A few emails from Bram. Junk mail. She replied to her parents, telling them only that she was really busy with work this week. Then she took her malaria pill, showered, and dressed, taking care with her makeup, hair, and clothing, choosing a long-sleeved blouse that covered her belly and a more conservative sari in dark blue and gold.

The Minister of Foreign Affairs would be here in an hour for a private meeting. It was just a formality, a courtesy call, the government's way of welcoming a representative of the ICC to their country. Still, there were butterflies in her stomach as she buzzed Connor to ask him to have someone order tea and remove her breakfast tray.

He knocked before entering, the sight of him making her pulse skip. He wore a tailored suit, but he was different from the men she worked with at the ICC. Some of them were handsome, and some wore three-thousand-dollar suits. But Connor was bigger, more muscular, and he radiated a confidence they lacked, a sense of physical power, an air of danger.

His gaze moved over her. "I'm sure he'll appreciate the traditional dress."

"He might not like the fact that I'm not wearing a veil." Except for when she was in the camps, she refused to cover her hair. The majority of Bangladeshis, including Dr. Khan, might be Muslim, but she'd grown up in a secular Hindu home.

Connor picked up her breakfast tray, carried it to the door, and handed it to someone outside before walking over to her once more. "I'd prefer to stay in the room with you. I'm sure he'll have an entourage. We don't know who they are, so we haven't been able to vet them."

She was about to tell Connor that she was sure she'd be safe. The Minister for Foreign Affairs and his staff weren't going to murder her in her hotel room. But some part of her liked the idea of Connor staying with her. No, it wasn't the fact that she found him attractive. It wasn't that at all.

"That's fine."

"If you get the chance, ask him if he can help cut through the red tape around the drone issue. I'd feel a lot better with eyes in the sky."

"I'll do what I can."

Connor paused as if listening to something. "He's on his way up. The tea, too."

Shanti went to stand by the sofa and adjusted the pleats of her sari, heavy silk rustling as she moved, blue and gold cloth spilling over her right shoulder. She clasped her hands together, drew a deep breath, and let all emotion fade from her face.

The face is the index of the mind.

It was an old proverb her father had taught her when she was growing up. She had used it to remain composed through law school, in the courtroom, and at the ICC. It didn't matter how nervous she felt. What mattered was giving the perception that she was in control of herself—and the situation.

"Hey, you've got this." Connor gave her a reassuring smile. "He knows your father, and he went to Harvard just like you did."

Shanti hadn't known this. "Thank you. I was focused on

the case and didn't have time to prepare for this meeting, so that's really helpful."

Connor spoke into his microphone. "Good copy. We're ready."

One of the other Cobra operators—Malik Jones— opened the door to her suite. He was also wearing a suit.

Three men stepped inside—two she didn't recognize followed by Dr. Amir Sadik Khan, an MP and the Minister of Foreign Affairs.

She waited for them to cross the wide room. "Welcome, gentlemen. I am Shanti Lahiri, special prosecutor with the International Criminal Court."

Women didn't ordinarily shake hands with men here, but she'd come as a representative of an international organization.

She held out her hand, and Dr. Khan took it. "Doctor Khan, it's a pleasure to make your acquaintance. I understand you knew my father. Won't you please sit down and enjoy some *cha*?"

"Welcome to Bangladesh—or should I say, 'Welcome home'?" Dr. Khan wasn't a tall man, and he clearly loved to eat, his face round and beardless, his dark hair white at the temples. He smiled, switched to Bangla. "Do you speak our language?"

She answered in English, aware of Connor, who stood silently at some distance behind her. "I know only a few words. My parents spoke English at home."

It was bad manners to go directly to talking about business, so Shanti made polite conversation about the weather, about Dr. Khan's time at Harvard, about his relationship with her father, while Connor and the other two men stood in the background.

"I remember hearing that he had married an American

student against his parents' wishes." His tone left no doubt that he thought her father had done the wrong thing. "In Bangladesh, we are raised to respect our elders."

Shanti smiled. "My grandparents on *both* sides objected to the marriage, but my parents are happy and still very much in love. As my mother says, their happiness together is the best revenge."

"I never met your mother. After you were born, your father left his country and moved to the United States."

"There were pogroms against Hindus that year, as I'm sure you remember. Innocent Hindus were beaten and raped and had their homes and shops burned down. After what happened to my father's siblings during the genocide, my father left his homeland to keep us safe."

Dr. Khan's gaze dropped to the coffee table. "Those were awful times."

Shanti moved on to business. "Thank you for allowing me to enter the country as a representative of the International Criminal Court. My work here must move forward if we are to help the Rohingya people find justice."

"We support the ICC, of course," Dr. Khan said. "But this is a sensitive issue for us. Myanmar is our neighbor. Bangladesh cannot take in all of the Rohingya who have fled here, and so we must negotiate a solution with Myanmar for their repatriation. We cannot do this if our relations with Yangon deteriorate because we assist in your prosecution of one of their military leaders. I regret that we cannot provide you with a military escort."

This discussion had already taken place through diplomatic channels, so nothing he said surprised Shanti.

"I understand the delicate position in which Bangladesh finds itself, and I have no desire to make your job more difficult than it already is. As you see, the organization has provided me with security. I'll be quite safe."

Dr. Khan looked straight into her eyes. "*Inshallah*."

God willing.

~

CONNOR WATCHED while Shanti talked with Dr. Khan, who was clearly nervous about her mission. She handled the pressure well. She sat there, spine straight, chin up, looking more like a princess than a prosecutor.

"I was hoping you could help me with one thing," she said at last.

Here it goes.

"Please, ask for anything. I will do all I can."

"My security team would like to deploy a small observational drone to watch over my location in the camps. They haven't gotten their permit approved yet. I wondered if you might be able to intervene and speed things up."

Khan set his teacup down. "I'm sure you understand that these things take time. The government is very concerned about violations of our airspace, and the regulations are stringent. This is not my department, but I will try."

That wasn't the answer Connor had wanted.

"Thank you. I'm grateful."

Khan stood. "It has been a delight to make your acquaintance. Please pass along my regards the next time you see your father."

Shanti stood, too. "I will. Thank you."

When Khan had gone, Shanti turned to Connor. "I'm sorry. I tried."

"I appreciate the effort. We'll make it work either way."

He glanced at his watch. "We leave for the airport after lunch."

Two hours later, Connor, Shanti, Cruz, and Jones were in the armored Land Rover, air conditioner blasting, on their way to the airport, where the UN project manager, Pauline Montreux, had flown down in a helicopter to take Shanti on an aerial tour of the camps. None of the camps were more than five klicks from the Myanmar border, but they'd be in the air today and not on the ground.

Shanti had changed out of her princess clothes and put on a pair of jeans and a blouse, her hair tied back in a ponytail, sunglasses shading her amber eyes. "I've never flown in a helicopter before."

"No?" For some reason, that made Connor smile. He'd been in more helicopters than he could remember and walked away from his share of crashes, too. "You're going to love it."

Provided it stayed in the air, of course.

Shields had asked about the pilot and had learned that he'd served with India's Air Force for twenty-five years and had been flying missions for the UN for the past five years here in Cox's Bazar.

They found the helicopter ready for take-off when they arrived at the airport, Ms. Montreux waiting for them.

"It's a pleasure to meet you, Ms. Lahiri!" she shouted over the noise of the rotors, her French accent strong.

"Thank you for being willing to show me around!" Shanti shouted back, shaking the other woman's hand.

Alert for anyone who might be lurking outside the airport's perimeter fence, Connor escorted Shanti through the heat and humidity to the helo, Cruz and Jones flanking them. He helped her on board, climbed in to sit beside her, then buckled his safety strap and put on his earphones, motioning to her to do the same.

He spoke into the mic. "Can you hear me?"

"Yes."

The helicopter began to lift, nosing into the prevailing wind, carrying them south. As it gained altitude, the airport and hotels fell away below them, the sand of Cox's Bazar stretching on forever, the deep blue water of the Bay of Bengal unfurling in white waves along the shore.

Shanti smiled the moment she saw it. "Isn't it beautiful?"

"Have you been here before?" Ms. Montreux asked, not pronouncing her "h" sounds.

"No. I was born in Dhaka, but I grew up in Ithaca, New York."

Connor listened to the women's conversation as they got to know each other, his gaze on Shanti. She was different somehow, more relaxed, her face no longer the icy, calm mask he'd seen at their first meeting or with Dr. Khan this morning.

"How long have you been in Bangladesh?" she asked.

"I became the UNHRC project manager nine months ago."

"It must be a big job."

"Yes, but very rewarding."

Ms. Montreux told Shanti about some of the UN's recent advancements here—getting people IDs, vaccinating children, setting up more schools. It wasn't long before the Kutupalong-Balukhali camp complex came into view.

"Holy shit," Cruz muttered under his breath.

"Look at that," Jones said. "How many people live here?"

A sea of small huts made of bamboo poles and tarps crowded together on the hillsides below, bamboo towers placed at intervals, rutted dirt roads connecting the huts to bigger, more permanent bamboo structures—perhaps medical facilities, schools, or food distribution points. People on the ground looked up at them—men, women, children—shielding their eyes against the bright sun.

Some of the kids waved. Ms. Montreux and Shanti waved back.

"The main camp at Kutupalong is home to about twenty-five thousand refugees, but the rush of new arrivals over the past two years left people settling outside the camp," Ms. Montreux answered. "The Kutupalong-Balukhali expansion site is home to more than five hundred thousand people. There are now more than a million refugees spread out between all of the Rohingya camps."

Jesus.

That was *a lot* of homeless people—not just homeless, but stateless.

Connor had learned that Bangladesh had also passed legislation denying the Rohingya people citizenship. No one wanted them.

More than *a million* people with nowhere to go.

That's gotta suck.

"Is sanitation a big problem?" Shanti asked.

"You might think that, but the camps are very clean. We have a very active WASH sector—that's water, sanitation, and hygiene. They take care of any problems that might arise. The residents of the camp do many of these jobs themselves, just like any community."

Ms. Montreux told Shanti that their most worrisome threats were infectious diseases and violence from Bengali gangs and human traffickers.

"There aren't enough water stations, so many young girls are sent to nearby villages for water, only to be raped or kidnapped and sold into the sex trade. People are sometimes robbed and beaten by roving gangs."

"What a nightmare." Shanti shook her head. "These people have suffered so much already, and now they're trapped in a place that doesn't want them, waiting to have a future, waiting for a place to call home."

"It is a terrible tragedy," Ms. Montreux agreed.

"Do those towers help people watch out for gangs?" Shanti asked.

Ms. Montreux laughed. "Those are for elephants. Kutupalong sits on a migratory trail. People have been killed when elephants entered camp and became cornered and afraid. Now, we are organized. If an elephant is spotted from one of the towers, volunteers try to herd it gently back into the forest. It is much better now."

Connor would've been lying if he hadn't just found himself hoping to see an elephant or ten while he was here.

They flew to the southernmost camp—Nayapara—and had turned to head northward again, the women talking about repatriation efforts, when Connor spotted something on the ground, something that shouldn't have been there, something that made his blood run cold.

"RPG! Incoming! Nine o'clock!"

4

Shanti gasped as the helicopter lurched upward and banked hard toward the east, her stomach seeming to drop as if she were on a roller coaster.

BAM!

An explosion behind them made her pulse skyrocket, a shudder passing through the helicopter. She heard Connor speak into his mic, realized she was clutching his arm.

"I say again, we are taking RPG fire. No damage. The suspects are two unidentified males. How copy?"

"Wh-what's an RPG?" Shanti asked.

"Rocket-propelled grenade," Connor answered.

Pauline's face was pale, but her voice was calm. "Have them contact Nayapara security. Maybe we can catch them."

Connor reached for his handset again. "Cobra, Team One. Contact security at Nayapara camp. The males are running east toward the Naf River at the south end of the camp. One is wearing a green shirt, the other a red. How copy?"

"The Naf River is the border between Bangladesh and

Myanmar," Pauline told Shanti. "If they cross the border, no one will be able to touch them."

"Cowards," Malik said, looking toward the ground. "They think they can take a cheap shot at us and run?"

Connor glanced over at him. "Yeah, well, they're right. We're not setting down to pursue."

"Too bad," Dylan muttered. "Assholes."

Shanti struggled to keep up with what was happening, adrenaline making it hard to think. "Did someone just try to shoot us down?"

"Yeah," said Connor, as if this was something that happened every so often, "but they missed."

"Thank goodness for that!"

Connor spoke to the pilot. "Good flying there. Quick reflexes."

"I never thought I'd be getting shot at here." The pilot laughed, a note of relief in his voice. "I'll maintain this altitude until we reach the airport."

"Roger that." Connor turned to Shanti. "Are you okay?"

She willed herself to let go of him. "Yes. Yes, I'm fine. Just a bit ... shaken."

A big hand covered hers, his touch strangely comforting. "I can't blame you for that. They're far behind us now. We're out of range."

"It's a UN helicopter," Pauline said. "Maybe they don't like the UN. Insurgents come in from the tribal areas in the Chittagong Hill Tracts to try to recruit sometimes."

Shanti latched onto this thought. Maybe this wasn't about her case. Maybe it had nothing to do with her at all.

Connor didn't seem convinced. "We won't know who they were or why they fired at us until they're in custody. Have insurgents fired on UN helicopters before?"

Pauline shook her head. "No."

Shanti's stomach knotted.

"We should have flown in our bird. I'm going to need a list of everyone who knew Ms. Lahiri was taking this flight with you today. Can you do that for me, Ms. Montreux?"

"But of course."

The rest of the flight passed in silence, Shanti's gaze fixed on the beach below, where tourists played, oblivious to the hardship, suffering, and violence that was mere kilometers away. She hadn't expected anything like this. She hadn't even imagined it. She'd wanted to believe that no one would dare to strike at a prosecutor from the International Criminal Court.

Then again, why not? Why wouldn't they?

Some stinking mercenary had shot down Dag Hammarskjöld's plane in 1961, murdering him and his entourage, and he'd been the UN secretary-general.

Do you feel better now?

As they neared the airport, Connor was in almost constant contact with the rest of the Cobra team. Shanti saw some of the other Cobra operatives hurry out onto the tarmac near the helicopter's landing pad in full military gear, guns in their hands. As the chopper landed, they dropped to their knees, rifles raised and facing outward, forming a protective perimeter.

The moment the helicopter touched down, Connor unbuckled his safety harness. "We'll go first and then help you out. We've got three vehicles. We'll get you into one of them, and then we'll take off for the hotel."

Shanti nodded, her pulse picking up again.

He turned to Pauline. "Ms. Montreux, do you have an escort?"

Shanti felt a rush of warmth for him. His job was to keep

her safe, but he wasn't going to drive off and leave Pauline. What if those men had been targeting her?

"I drove here with two security guards. I'll be fine."

Connor gave her a nod. "We'll be in touch about that list."

Shanti took Pauline's hand. "Thank you, Pauline. I'm so sorry this happened. I appreciate everything you shared with me today. I hope to see you again soon."

Pauline smiled. "It's not your fault. Tomorrow will be better."

The door opened. Connor, Dylan, and Malik piled out, turning back to help Shanti. They hurried her to the Land Rover, which was now sandwiched between two identical vehicles.

Connor opened the rear passenger door, helped her climb in. He sat to her left, while Dylan sat on her right, Malik riding shotgun. The men who'd formed the perimeter stood and hurried into the two other vehicles.

"Let's go!" Connor called to the driver.

The ride to the hotel lasted no more than five minutes.

"How are you doing?" Connor asked.

She tried to look as calm as everyone else. "You could have all been killed."

"Risk is part of the job." He gave her hand another squeeze. "We'll do our best to find out who is behind this."

CONNOR WAS STUDYING a detailed map of the camps when Segal entered their make-shift ops room.

"I just heard from Nayapara security. Witnesses saw the two men jump into the river. They're in the wind."

Connor pointed to the map. "Nayapara is the camp

closest to the Myanmar border and farthest away from backup at our hotel. If they wanted to hit us and disappear, they couldn't have picked a better spot."

Damn it!

"I wouldn't give them too much credit," Segal said. "Any soldier knows it's all but impossible to hit a helicopter with an ordinary RPG unless the bird is hovering, landing, or taking off."

He had a point.

Shields walked in.

Connor had sent her to check on Shanti, figuring that she, as another woman and an analyst with HUMINT training, would best be able to support her. "How is she?"

"She's gone from badly shaken up to seriously pissed off." Shields poured herself a cup of coffee. "She's on the phone with the foreign affairs minister, Khan, demanding that they speed up the permitting process for our drones."

Connor hadn't asked her to do that, but he sure as hell approved.

"I think I like the lass," McManus said.

Shields passed him without sparing him a glance. "You like all the lasses."

Laughter.

McManus looked like he was about to say something. He apparently thought the better of it and shut his mouth.

"If it makes you feel any better, she trusts you, O'Neal." Shields sat at her station. "She feels safe with you. That came through loud and clear."

That knowledge settled on Connor's shoulders like a weight. *He* was in charge this time, not Tower, not Javier Corbray, not Nick Andris. Whatever happened here was *his* responsibility.

Connor looked around at his team. "I need answers,

people. We're supposed to drive to Kutupalong tomorrow. An RPG might not be able to take down a bird at cruising speed, but it sure as hell can fuck up a vehicle."

"Postpone it," Segal suggested. "Tell Ms. Lahiri that until we have answers, it's just too hot."

Shields shook her head. "Oh, no. Don't even try. Her exact words were, 'If Naing thinks he can scare me into giving up, he's dead wrong.' She is tougher than she looks."

Connor knew there was steel in Shanti's spine. He'd seen it this morning in her meeting with Khan. But being tough couldn't stop a grenade. "Shields, analysis."

"I might have one for you if you hadn't sent me to play therapist." Shields logged into their secured network. "Give me an hour."

Connor looked around at the others. "We don't have a lot of options. We can fly in, or we can drive, and unless Ms. Lahiri is successful and we get that drone permit, we'll be going in blind. I want a plan on the table in fifteen minutes."

He started for the door.

"Where are you goin'?" McManus asked.

"To see if Ms. Lahiri has had any luck." In truth, he just wanted to see her.

He left the ops room and walked down the hallway to where the Dynamic Duo—Jones and Cruz—stood watch.

"Hey, O'Neal," Jones called. "They catch 'em?"

"The bastards jumped into the river."

Cruz swore under his breath. "If I'd had my rifle, I could have taken them out."

"If you had, we'd be up to our necks in shit."

Cobra was in Bangladesh with the permission of its government. They couldn't shoot fleeing enemies in the back. The rules of engagement for private security work were very different from military service.

Connor knocked on Shanti's door, waited.

She answered, cell phone to her ear, and motioned him inside. "You understand that if I am killed, it will bring global attention to my investigation. The fact that Cobra has requested a permit for a small observational drone is already a matter of record. If the government in Dhaka continues to delay, especially after what happened today, some might wonder whose side they were on—the ICC's or Myanmar's."

So, Shanti was playing hardball.

Connor sat on the sofa and watched while she argued with Khan, determination on her face. She must be something to see in a courtroom.

She walked to the refrigerator, pulled out a bottle of water, held it up.

Connor nodded.

She brought it over to him. "Forgive me for being so direct, Doctor Khan, but I wasn't raised here, as you know. When one of my clients is in dire need, I do all I can to help them, regardless of how rude I might seem. Now *I'm* the one in need. If that helicopter had been shot down today, I wouldn't have been the only one killed. The UN project manager was on the helicopter, too, along with my security team and the pilot. What would you have said to my father, to officials in Washington, to the UN?"

She squeezed her eyes shut in frustration, clearly not getting the answer she wanted. "Yes, sir. Thank you. I appreciate whatever help you can give."

She ended the call, sank onto the sofa next to him. "He said he'd try."

"Fingers crossed then."

She shook her head. "You don't understand. My father

says that when a Bangladeshi official says they'll *try*, it's often a polite way of saying 'no.'"

"We're working on this from our side, too, asking our contacts at the Pentagon to put pressure on Dhaka."

"I won't give up and go home." She looked up at him, frustration on her face. "Naing is a criminal. He *must* be brought to justice. If you'd read the reports I've read..."

"We got a briefing. No one is giving up. We'll work it out." He couldn't explain what came out of his mouth next. "Why don't we talk about it over dinner?"

What the hell? Had he just asked a client for a date?

Of course, not! That would be out of bounds and get him fired. No, this was business. Right. Sure. Business.

"I've got a meeting in a few minutes, and then we can order whatever you want and talk through our plan for tomorrow."

She nodded. "What time?"

SHANTI SPREAD her napkin in her lap while Connor poured the pinot grigio. There was no reason for her to feel nervous. This wasn't a date. The fact that she had changed into a little black dress, fussed with her makeup, and put her hair in a perfect messy bun didn't make it a date. It was just dinner with the tall and incredibly attractive man who led her security team, a chance for them to get to know each other like disinterested business associates often did.

He wore jeans with a gray button-down shirt that he'd left untucked, its color somehow making his eyes seem bluer. "Tell me what we're eating."

"This is *chingri malai*—a seafood curry—and this is *ilish macher jhol*—hilsa curry, our national dish. Hilsa is a fish like herring. The fish is marinated in turmeric and chili paste and fried in mustard gravy, so it can be pretty spicy."

He smiled. "Is that a warning?"

Oh, that smile.

It transformed his face from serious and rugged to seriously sexy.

Was it hot in here?

"You can take it any way you like. I thought you could try a bit of each and decide which one you like more."

"Good idea."

Shanti served him a little of each dish, along with rice and naan, and took a bit of both for herself, waiting for him to take his first bite.

He tried the hilsa curry first, moaned, the sound sending a shiver through her. "Oh, that is good."

"Not too hot?"

"I eat raw jalapeño peppers, so, no, not too hot." He took another bite then tried the *chingri malai* and moaned again. "Mmm. This is fantastic."

More shivers.

"I'm so glad you like it." She took a bite of the hilsa, the tastes of turmeric, chili paste, curry, and mustard bright on her tongue.

"Is this the food you grew up with?"

She nodded, dabbed her lips, finding it hard to maintain eye contact. There was something about the way he looked at her that made her feel flustered. "Yes, though I ate my share of pizza, too. There's an Indian restaurant in Ithaca that we went to a lot. The service is awful, but the curries are delicious."

"You told Khan that your grandparents objected to your parents getting married. That must have been tough for them."

"Especially for my mother." Shanti told Connor how her grandmother had prayed every day for her mother's death. "It finally stopped when my mother became pregnant with me."

"Seriously? She prayed for your mother's death?"

Shanti couldn't help but laugh at the shocked look on his face. "Yes. Then I came along. My grandmother was desperate to have grandchildren again after... My mother was always very gracious to her, and they pretended to get along for the sake of the rest of us after that. Enough about that. Where did you grow up?"

"A tiny farm town called Ault in Colorado. My parents grow corn and raise chickens there. I spent a lot of time outdoors and learned to work hard when I was young. It was a good way to grow up."

Unable to eat another bite, Shanti dabbed her lips and set her napkin aside, leaving the rest for Connor. "Why did you go into the military?"

"Farming just wasn't the life for me. My parents couldn't afford to send me to college, and I didn't want to waste away working at the Bean and Feed Store. I signed up without telling them and left right after I graduated from high school."

She wanted to ask him how he made peace with taking human life, but she didn't want to offend him. "Have you ever regretted it?"

"Never." He took a drink of his wine. "My first big action was a hostage rescue. When it was over and the hostages were safe, I knew I was doing exactly what I was meant to do."

Shanti didn't know what to say to that. "Do you have someone waiting for you at home—a girlfriend, a wife, kids?"

He didn't wear a wedding band, but Shanti had read somewhere that military men often didn't wear them in the field.

He grinned as if something about the question was funny. Okay, so, it was a little transparent. She could admit that. "No. No wife. Never married. No kids, either."

Shanti would be lying if she said that didn't feel like good news.

He changed the subject. "Why did you become a human-rights attorney?"

"Oh, that's a long story." It wasn't a happy story, either.

"I'm not going anywhere."

Shanti steeled herself with another sip of wine. "Okay."

She told him how, during Bangladesh's war of independence in 1971, Pakistani troops had moved through the country targeting Bengali intellectuals, killing men and women, dumping their bodies in mass graves. Her grandfather was the owner of a newspaper chain and had advocated for independence. He was high on their list.

"My father was twenty-two and studying at Oxford at the time, but the rest of my family was here. Soldiers forced their way into the newspaper's offices, looking for my grandfather and killing his staff. With the help of friends, he managed to escape with my grandmother to India. But my father's older brother, Abani, and his younger sister, Chakori..." Shanti swallowed—hard. "They were dragged into the streets with their kids and spouses and shot. Their bodies were dumped in a mass grave and never found. My grandmother almost died from grief."

"God. I'm sorry." Connor pressed his hand over hers, his gaze warm with concern, his touch sending frissons of awareness up her arm. "That's what you mentioned to Dr. Khan today, isn't it?"

"Yes. It's also why my parents named me Shanti. My name means 'peace.'" She gave him a sad smile. "After I was born, when the pogroms against Hindus began, my father decided to leave Bangladesh for good."

"I can't blame him."

"I grew up hearing my family's story, seeing the grief in my grandparents' eyes, wondering about the aunt, uncle, and cousins I never met. I decided when I was a teenager that I would dedicate my life to nonviolence and helping victims of genocide."

He drew his hand away. "I can see why you're uncomfortable with soldiers and firearms. But what happens when those who dedicate themselves to violence like General Naing gain the upper hand?"

Shanti met his gaze. "We have to learn to prevent those situations, to stop conflict through peaceful means before it turns to violence."

"For good people like you to build a better world, Shanti, there have to be people like me willing to back you up with force. Otherwise, the bad guys win."

5

Connor watched out the rear passenger side window, HK416 in his hands, McManus riding in the helicopter overhead, giving Connor regular updates. Trees and pools of rainwater stretched along a highway that was busy with tourists in green auto-rickshaws and locals on bicycles. Grazing deer. Seagulls. Pedestrians with umbrellas. The wide expanse of the Naf River, the Mayu Mountains of Myanmar in the distance.

Shanti sat in the middle, sandwiched between Connor and Cruz, her hands folded in her lap, a large handbag holding her camera, digital recorder, encrypted phone, and files on the floor at her feet. She'd worn a long white blouse, brown pants, and boots, a white cotton scarf draped around her shoulders, her eyes hidden behind shades.

She hadn't said a word since they'd left the hotel, and Connor couldn't shake the feeling that he'd upset her. He'd tried to make a point last night. Courts and laws and noble intentions were only as strong as the force that backed them. But the moment he'd said those words, the happiness had faded from her face.

"I understand what you're saying, and I'm grateful for your protection," she'd said. "But too often when government leaders put weapons in people's hands, it's only because they're not achieving political goals by peaceful means. When those goals change, so does the target."

He'd had to fight not to feel insulted by that. He was no politician's puppet.

You sure?

She'd grown quiet after that, almost withdrawn, though she'd smiled and thanked him for his company.

When he'd gotten back to his own room, he'd looked up the 1971 Bangladesh genocide online. Images of bodies had filled the screen—at least three hundred thousand killed and hundreds of thousands more raped and tortured by Pakistani soldiers.

He'd felt like a fucking idiot.

She'd described how soldiers had murdered members of her family, grief on her pretty face, and he'd more or less told her that killing was sometimes a necessary and *good* thing. Not his best move.

What would she think of you if she knew?

Darkness twisted in his chest.

He pushed the thought aside. That had been different. It hadn't been deliberate. Shit happened on a battlefield, and it wasn't pretty.

Corbray and Tower always told them never to let down the professional barrier between them and their clients. Connor had broken that rule this time when he'd asked her to have dinner. Then again, Tower was a fucking hypocrite. He'd ended up sleeping with a Cobra client last year at the compound in Afghanistan. He hadn't even tried to hide it. He and Jenna were getting married soon.

"Team One, this is Helo One." McManus' voice came

through Connor's earpiece. "Two vehicles are sittin' on the side of the road about two klicks ahead. It looks like an accident or a puncture. Copy?"

"Helo One, Team One, good copy." Connor didn't need to relay this information to anyone as they were all listening in on the same frequency. When they neared the two vehicles, the drivers accelerated and shifted into the right lane, giving them ample room.

On the shoulder, two men changing a flat stopped to look up at the helicopter.

Connor turned to Shanti. "How are you holding up?"

Yesterday's grenade had been a first for her, and now she was sitting in a speeding armored vehicle with three men holding military rifles.

Her lips curved in a forced smile. "I'm glad finally to get to work. It's been almost two years since I started collecting evidence."

"You'll get the job done."

She let out a breath. "I hope so."

It was beginning to sprinkle when they rolled into Kutupalong Refugee Camp. The helicopter veered off and headed north toward the airport.

"You two remember your rain gear?" Connor asked Cruz and Jones.

"Hell, yeah," Jones said.

Connor unclipped his HK416 from his harness, Shanti watching. He, Cruz, and Jones would leave their rifles locked in the vehicles with Isaksen and Segal and the others and carry concealed pistols inside the camp.

"I appreciate that. Thank you." She drew her scarf over her hair, draping one end over her left shoulder.

"We'll do whatever we can to support your mission—as long as we can still complete ours." He shouldered his pack

—it held extra magazines, a first aid kit, food, and his rain gear—and stepped to the ground, turning back to help Shanti.

Ms. Montreux was waiting for them together with Shanti's interpreter, a young Rohingya woman named Noor who lived in the camp. The women greeted each other, Noor giving Shanti a shy smile.

"It's a ten-minute walk to the hospital. I'm afraid it's going to rain." Ms. Montreux looked up at the leaden sky. "Did you bring an umbrella?"

Shanti nodded. "It's in my bag. I used to play in the streets during the monsoons."

Connor could almost imagine that—little Shanti playing in the rain.

Ms. Montreux gave Connor a piece of paper. "The list you wanted."

He tucked it into a pocket in his body armor. "Thanks."

"This way," Ms. Montreux said.

"Heads on a swivel."

"Copy that."

SHANTI FOLLOWED Pauline and Noor along a maze of muddy paths that were lined with sandbags, passing countless shelters made of tarps and bamboo poles and heading uphill toward a large white building with a blue roof. "Is that the hospital?"

"Yes. It's not far now."

The witnesses and survivors she interviewed this week risked potential shame and retaliation by sharing their stories. To protect them, she and Pauline had arranged for the witnesses to be interviewed at the hospital under the pretext of seeing a doctor. If anyone asked who Shanti was, Pauline would say she was a trauma therapist. Shanti would record the interviews with a small camera and digital recorder and upload the files to The Hague when they got back to the hotel.

They reached the hospital just as the sky opened up and rain began to fall. Shanti dashed after Pauline, laughing as cold raindrops hit her skin.

Connor was right behind her. "Cruz, take the front entrance. Jones, take the back."

"You got it."

"Copy that."

Shanti followed the two women inside the hospital and down the main hallway to a door marked PRIVATE, Connor behind her.

Pauline turned to Connor. "You'll have to wait here, I'm afraid."

"I'd like to check the room first."

Pauline looked troubled by this but nodded.

Connor opened the door, stuck his head inside, then closed it again. "Is there any other way to enter this room?"

Pauline shook her head. "No."

Connor gave Shanti a nod.

Shanti entered, followed by Noor. She found a young woman sitting on the floor, a veil covering her hair and the lower part of her face. She used the few words of Rohingya she'd learned. "*Assolamu Aláikum. Añár nam Shanti.*"

Peace be with you. My name is Shanti.

The woman watched through brown eyes that ought to have belonged to someone much older. She said something Shanti didn't understand.

"She wants to know who that man was," Noor said.

"He works for me. He is here to keep us safe and make sure no one disturbs us."

Noor sat beside the woman and translated Shanti's words.

The woman seemed to relax.

Shanti sat, too, and took out her files. "Your name is Sareema, right? Thank you for meeting with me."

Noor asked the girl. "She says yes, she is Sareema."

Shanti explained why she had come to the camps, pausing every so often to let Noor catch up. "I need to record this interview so that it can be used in court as evidence against the men who hurt you. I know it will be difficult, but please tell me everything you can remember."

Sareema replied, Noor translating. "She says she understands. She wants these bad men to be punished."

"I will do my best to make sure that happens."

Shanti set up the small camera, making sure it caught Sareema's face, then set it to record. She sat on the floor across from Sareema, her backup digital recorder in hand. "What village do you come from, Sareema?"

"Myar Zin."

Shanti was familiar with Sareema's story, but listening to her tell it over the next hour and a half left her feeling sick.

Soldiers had come to Sareema's village in the middle of the night and forced their way into people's homes, shooting the men and dragging the women outside. They'd killed Sareema's young husband and his parents in front of her. Then four of them had dragged Sareema into her home and took turns raping and beating her even though she was heavily pregnant.

"One cut my breast with a knife. They kicked my belly again and again until I began to bleed between my legs. I passed out."

Smoke had revived her, waking her to a nightmare. All the homes of the village, including her own, had been set on fire, women and children trapped inside.

"She thought she would burn to death. It was hard to walk. She was in so much pain. She broke through one of the bamboo walls and ran into the forest. She could hear women screaming. She recognized her sister's voice. They were burning alive. She wanted to help them, but the soldiers were still there and shooting people."

Sareema's baby boy had been stillborn under a tree the next day. Though she'd lost a lot of blood, she'd met other survivors, some of whom had given her food and water. She'd managed to make it with other refugees to the Naf River, where a fisherman had agreed to take them across in exchange for their valuables.

"They had nothing. The fisherman demanded that one of the women give him sex instead. He didn't want Sareema because she was bleeding."

Sareema had arrived at Kutupalong feverish from post-partum infection and weak from blood loss. There had been burns on her hands and feet that needed treatment, too.

"She has not felt happy since that night. She never got to raise her baby boy. She misses her husband. She misses her parents and her sister. None of them escaped. At night, she can still hear her sister screaming."

Sareema didn't shed a tear as she recounted this horror, but Shanti could see she was trembling. "You are brave, Sareema. I know it must be hard to make yourself talk about this. I am so sorry that you were made to suffer and that your family was killed. What happened to you was a terrible crime. These men should be punished. Are you certain they were soldiers and not border guards or men from another village?"

Noor translated Shanti's words, gave Shanti Sareema's answer. "They wore green uniforms with red patches on their sleeves."

The uniform of the Tatmadaw, Myanmar's army.

Shanti asked her if she would recognize any of the men who'd been part of the attack, whether she'd gotten a good look at their faces.

"It was dark, and I was so afraid, but there was one face. He told the other soldiers what to do. When he stepped out of his truck, the headlights lit up his face. They called him Naing."

Shanti set a folder of photos in front of her—officers who served with Naing, henchmen, and Naing himself. "Can you point to him if you see him here?"

Tears filled Sareema's eyes. She pointed to Naing, answered.

Noor translated. "Yes. It was this man."

CONNOR STOOD watch as three different women met with Shanti to offer testimony against General Naing. The walls weren't thick, so he couldn't help but overhear. He'd seen some pretty sick shit in his time as an operator, but their stories were among the worst he'd ever heard.

Babies torn from their mothers' arms and thrown into fires. Little girls and women gang-raped, mutilated, murdered. Old men left to bleed out, their limbs hacked off. Grandmothers paraded naked in front of lines of laughing soldiers who filmed it on their cell phones before killing the women.

Connor wanted to find Naing and make him eat his own fucking balls.

How strange it was. This hospital was full of volunteers from around the world trying to save lives, while across the border, men made a game of taking them. What the fuck was it about human beings anyway? What other animal systematically slaughtered its own kind?

Are you sure you want to look in that mirror?

Connor ate a snack bar from an MRE pack for lunch, rain still falling in sheets beyond the windows, battering the roof.

A small boy with bare feet rolled something along the floor. He must have been five or six years old, his yellow shirt dirty, his cutoff shorts worn. He stopped when he reached Connor and looked up at him through big brown eyes.

Connor held out his hand. "May I see?"

The boy trustingly dropped whatever it was onto Connor's palm.

It was a little car. The chassis was a small piece of bamboo. Plastic bottle caps had been nailed into it to serve as tires.

Connor nodded, met the boy's gaze, gave him back his toy. "That's a nice car. Did you make it?"

The boy smiled—and dashed back to his mother, who sat near the front entrance.

Connor found himself wishing he had his old box of Hot Wheels from home. There must be a hundred little cars in that box. His mother had saved them for the day when he had children of his own, but that wasn't going to happen.

Cruz's voice sounded in his ear. "O'Neal, this is Cruz. There's flooding out here. We might have trouble getting back to the vehicles."

Shit.

Connor put on his rain gear, making sure he still had

quick and easy access to his concealed Glocks. Then he checked in with Segal, who said the vehicles were high and dry. "Let's hope we're out of here before it gets much worse."

The helicopter was scheduled to arrive in less than an hour, which meant they needed to be back to the vehicles by then.

From inside the room, Connor heard the interpreter recounting new horrors.

"... slit her husband's throat and shot her children..."

Twenty minutes later, the door opened, and the last witness stepped out, veiled head to toe with only her eyes showing, her gaze on the floor.

Shanti appeared a few moments later, Noor behind her, both women's eyes filled with shadows, lines of grief on their faces. "Thank you, Noor. I couldn't have done this without you."

"I'm glad to be able to do something to help."

Shanti gave her a hug. "I'll see you here tomorrow morning."

Connor spoke into his mic. "Jones, meet us out front. We're moving."

"Copy that."

A crowd had gathered under the broad awning that stretched out above the hospital's front entrance, men, women, and children taking shelter from the downpour.

Without a word to Connor, Shanti opened her umbrella, stepped out from beneath the awning, and started down the hill. What had been a path was now an ankle-deep stream of muddy water.

"Be careful." Connor was glad that most people had gone inside. It gave him fewer potential threats to watch. "It's going to be slick."

They all slipped and slid down the path, cold water

filling his boots. From overhead, he heard the thrum of a helicopter's rotors.

"Right on time."

Shanti looked up, raindrops on her face.

No, not raindrops. She was under an umbrella. They were tears.

She was crying.

He couldn't blame her for that.

As they neared the bottom of the hill, the torrent rose until it reached her knees.

"Take my hand." Connor took her cold, wet fingers in his, steadying her as they made their way back to the camp's entrance, Cruz and Jones keeping a sharp eye out.

By the time they reached the vehicles, Shanti had gotten control of her tears, her emotions now cloaked. She closed her umbrella, shook it out, and climbed inside the Land Rover, handbag over her shoulder. Her jeans and boots were soaked.

Connor sat beside her, wet to the skin despite his rain gear. "Let's roll."

6

Shanti held it together on the drive back to the hotel, grateful that Connor hadn't asked her why she'd been crying or how she was doing. She would've had to say she was fine when, in truth, she felt sick to the depths of her soul.

You won't be any good to them as a prosecutor if you let your emotions take over.

He sat beside her, still in his rain gear, rifle in his hands, his gaze focused once more on the world outside. He'd taken her hand to keep her from falling, but the contact had been a lifeline, helping her to get control of her emotions again. She would never be able to tell him that, but it was true.

When they got back to the hotel, she went straight to her room, took off her muddy boots and socks, and went to work uploading the raw video and digital sound files via secured internet to the ICC's cloud site. She wanted the files safely in Bram's hands as soon as possible. That way, if anything happened to her or her equipment, Bram would already have the women's statements.

Each of the three women had identified Naing as being present and in charge when their villages were destroyed.

Take that, you murdering bastard.

While the first file uploaded, Shanti wrote her report and emailed it to Bram, highlighting for him the fact that some soldiers had recorded these atrocities on cell phones. Maybe there was footage out there somewhere that could prove Naing had ordered his soldiers to rape and kill.

She set the second file to upload and took a shower, tried to wash away mud and the lingering stench of cruelty. And still, the women's words, voiced by Noor, echoed through her mind.

A soldier slit her husband's throat and shot her children then raped and shot her. She pretended to be dead.

He took her baby and threw it into the fire. He and five other soldiers raped her while her baby burned.

I recognized my sister's voice. They were burning alive.

How could anyone be so vicious, so cruel?

Shanti turned off the water, leaned her forehead against the tile, helplessness and rage welling up inside her.

Don't do this.

She wasn't helpless. She was one of the few people in this world who could do something about these atrocities. She'd come to bring justice, to make sure that the man in charge of these crimes was punished.

She stepped out of the shower, toweled her hair dry, then put on a white top and a blue cotton sari, the one she wore on weekends at home.

The second file was still uploading, so Shanti sent a text to Connor asking for *cha*.

Do you want something to eat?

She couldn't even think about food right now.

```
No, thanks.
```

Ten minutes later, a knock came at her door.

She opened it to find Connor with a cart that held not only *cha* but a tray loaded with Bengali sweets—*sandesh*, *amriti*, and *chomchom*. Her mouth watered.

Maybe she was a little hungry after all.

He had changed out of his wet clothes and wore shorts, a black T-shirt, and flip flops, looking like a guy on his way to the beach if you ignored his shoulder holster and pistol. He pushed the cart into her room and closed the door behind him. "I ordered traditional tea, and they sent this up."

"I used to eat these as a child. I love *sandesh*."

"If you've got a few minutes, I have some news."

Shanti wasn't up for human contact tonight, but she remembered how reassuring it had felt to hold his hand. She willed herself to smile. "Join me."

She sat across from him and poured the tea, instinctively turning to light topics of conversation. "I hear more rain is forecast for tomorrow but not until late afternoon."

"Thanks." Connor accepted his cup of tea. "You don't have to play hostess for me, Shanti. I know you've had a hard day."

At those words, the mask she'd tried to hide behind slipped.

She raised her cup to drink, her hand stopping midair, her mind on the women's faces, the horror in their eyes. "What those women lived through—no one should have to suffer like that."

Dark brows drew together. "All of the things I've seen, all

of the things I've had to do—what happened to those women is some of the worst."

All the things I've had to do.

What did he mean by that?

"You were listening?" Shanti had promised these witnesses privacy.

"I didn't mean to overhear. The walls aren't very thick."

Their conversation last night came back to her. "Then you know what soldiers have accomplished in this part of the world recently—mass rape, burning babies..."

The moment the words were out, she regretted them.

His blue eyes went cold, his face hard. He set down his tea and stood. "I thought you would want to know that the two men who fired the RPG yesterday have been found dead. Their bodies washed up on the western bank of the Naf River."

Shanti had been about to apologize, but this news took her by surprise. She hadn't expected them to be found. "They drowned?"

"No, they'd been shot—a dozen rounds each. We're still gathering intel. We're going to try to identify them. If we can do that, maybe we can piece together the last days of their lives and figure out what they were doing in Nayapara with that RPG."

"Shot? But why would—"

"What's the first rule of assassination?" He turned and walked toward his room.

"I don't know."

He opened the door, looked back at her over his shoulder. "Kill the assassin."

"Connor I'm—"

With that, he shut the door behind him.

"—sorry."

CONNOR LEANED BACK against the closed door, rage and guilt churning in his gut. Could the woman not tell the difference between the good guys and the bad guys?

Maybe there's not as much of a difference as you'd like to believe.

He squeezed his eyes shut, tried to block the memory.

Frag out!

BAM!

He hadn't meant for it to happen. He wouldn't have thrown the damned grenade if he'd known. There hadn't been a goddamned thing he could do to take it back.

Fuck.

He drew a deep breath, stripped out of his clothes, headed for the shower. He washed away the sweat and the mud and then stood under the spray, his eyes closed, willing himself to let go, to forget. What was done couldn't be undone. He couldn't make it better by hating himself for the rest of his life.

He had no idea how much time had gone by—a minute, five minutes—when he opened his eyes again. He turned off the water, stepped out, and dried off.

The problem here was that he'd let himself get emotionally caught up in a client and her mission. He didn't give a damn what Ms. Lahiri thought about him. If she wanted to tell herself that he and the other Cobra operatives were no better than General Naing and his band of murderers, that was her bad judgment. He didn't need to deal with her bullshit while risking his life to keep her safe.

He sat at his desk, towel around his waist, and typed up a report for his bosses—Tower and Corbray—leaving out the personal conversations with Ms. Lahiri. He tacked on a request that someone in Denver drive up to Ault to get his box of Hot Wheels out of storage and ship it to Bangladesh as soon as possible. He knew that would raise eyebrows, so he explained that he wanted to donate it to the camp hospital. Then he shot his parents a quick email, telling them to expect someone.

He had just hit send when a light knock came at his door —not his main door, but the door to Ms. Lahiri's room. Figuring she wouldn't knock if it weren't important, he answered, still in his towel, shirtless, his hair uncombed and damp.

She stood there in that blue sari, the curve of her hips and her bare belly exposed, her mouth open as if she were about to say something. Her pupils dilated, her gaze sliding over him as if she'd never seen a man's bare chest before. "I ... uh..."

"Is it something important?"

"I just wanted to apologize." Her gaze was fixed on his abs now. "I shouldn't have said what I said. It was thoughtless of me."

All the signs of sexual arousal were there—the flush in her cheeks, her dark pupils, the way she was looking at him, the rapid pulse at her throat.

Connor's body responded, the rush of blood to his groin a warning that this was about to get extremely awkward. He willed his cock to knock it off, but it didn't want to listen, not with a beautiful woman staring at him as if he were dinner.

She seemed to catch herself, her gaze lifting to meet his. "Sorry to bother you. I just wanted to apologize."

"Thanks. I appreciate that." He truly did, but he couldn't stand here and chat about it. He started to close the door, afraid his dick was about to pitch a tent.

But she wasn't done. "I don't know why I said it. I was upset. I didn't think about how it might come across to you."

"Makes sense." He didn't want to shut the door in her face, but his dick wasn't obeying orders. "Don't worry about it."

"I know you're not like General Naing."

"Damned by faint praise." He closed the door enough to hide his groin, suppressing an insane impulse to drag her into his arms and shut her up with a kiss. "Maybe you should stop while you're ahead."

"Sorry." She was flustered now, her gaze again on his chest. "You've been hurt."

"Yeah. Shot. A few times." If she didn't move now, he was going to take her in his arms and kiss the hell out of her, his job be damned.

"I ... uh... should let you dress. Goodnight."

"Goodnight." Connor shut the door, leaned back against it, looked down.

Oh, for fuck's sake.

SHANTI UPLOADED the third and final video file, her mind filled with images of Connor. She'd known he was well-built. She'd been able to tell that from his biceps and the way his T-shirt stretched over his chest. But ... *wow.*

Smooth, tanned skin. Pecs sprinkled with dark curls. Flat, dark nipples. Ridges of muscle on his abdomen. A trail of dark curls disappearing behind that towel. A very respectable bulge.

Very respectable.

Shanti shivered.

She'd mostly dated other attorneys, men who spent

their days sitting at desks. Some of them liked to work out, but none of them looked like he did. She had never actually met a man with a six-pack or full pecs—or so many scars for that matter. The sight of him had made her blood run hot and turned her into a babbling idiot.

Her face burned at the memory of her own stupidity.

He probably didn't notice.

He'd stood there, staring down at her like an angry Greek god, all that strength, all that physical power right at eye level.

What would it feel like to run her hands over him? What would it be like to have sex with him and have all that man and muscle focused on her?

You'll never know.

She clenched her thighs together, tried to ease the ache there. She shouldn't be thinking like this. No, she shouldn't be, but who could blame her?

It had been more than a year since she'd slept with a man. Working sixty hours a week didn't leave much time for dating, and the last guy she'd dated had been so awful in bed that he'd made her want to swear off men. Finding a woman's clitoris couldn't be *that* difficult.

While the file loaded, she closed her eyes and let herself imagine what it would be like to be in bed with Connor. Soft skin and hard muscle beneath her palms. Those lips on her mouth, on her nipples. That muscular ass clenching as he thrust into her.

Heat flooded her belly, pooled between her thighs, the ache irresistible.

And then what?

Was she trying to torture herself?

She was working on the most important case of her life so far, perhaps the most important case she would ever have. Survivors were trusting her to do all she could to bring the monster who'd destroyed their lives and killed their loved ones to justice. She didn't need the distraction of a sexual liaison with the head of her security team.

No, really, she didn't.

She didn't.

She. Didn't.

He was probably lousy in bed. In Shanti's limited experience, most guys were.

Besides, the two of them were nothing alike. He lived in the US and worked for a private military company. She lived in The Hague and worked for the International Criminal Court. It's not like they could have any sort of future together. The last thing she wanted to do was to get involved with a man who spent his time in armed conflict—or who might go to work and not come home.

She thought of those scars. A round scar on his chest from a bullet that had to have come close to his heart. A deep gouge in his right shoulder. A scar on the left side of his abdomen that looked relatively recent.

All of the things I've seen, all of the things I've had to do— what happened to those women is some of the worst.

In his own way, *he* was a victim of violence, too.

Apart from child soldiers and others who were forced to fight at gunpoint, she'd never thought of professional soldiers being a victim of violence before. He had almost certainly killed, but he had also suffered as a result.

He'd shown empathy for the Rohingya people based on his own experience, and she'd thrown it in his face, following it up after her apology by telling him she knew he wasn't like General Naing.

Could she have been any more insensitive?

Her email alert told her that she had a new message.

Bram had written to say that he'd downloaded the three sound files and the first two video files and had saved them. He thanked her for her work and told her he was leaving the office for the evening and would download the third in the morning.

She glanced at her watch, saw that it was growing late. While the third video file finished uploading, she set her phone, camera battery, and her digital recorder to recharge and then got ready for bed. It was almost eleven when she finally crawled between the sheets, but it was much later before she finally fell asleep, her thoughts on Connor.

7

Connor rose early after a restless night, splashed water on his face, and dressed in jeans and a T-shirt. He'd been too horny to sleep and had finally given in and taken the problem in hand, jerking off to a fantasy of Shanti. Peeling off her sari. Exploring every inch of her sweet body. Fucking her on that king-sized bed.

Afterward, when he'd finally fallen asleep, Shanti had followed him. In his dreams, she'd been investigating him, asking him questions he didn't want to answer. It was a ridiculous dream. He'd already been exonerated, his combat record exemplary. He wasn't a war criminal.

This is what happens when you get too personal with a client.

That was then.

This was now.

Resolved to keep a professional distance, he left his room and walked to the ops room, where Shields was already at work on Pauline's list. "Anything?"

"Nada." She turned from her computer, picked up her

coffee, took a sip. "So far, everyone checks out. It's not a long list."

"Maybe she overlooked someone." Connor poured himself a cup of coffee.

"I'll keep digging."

"How about the two DBs? Has anyone identified them yet?"

"Nothing on that yet, either, but the Bangladesh Police seem fired up to resolve the case."

"Well, that's something."

Shields turned back to her computer. "What's this about a box of Hot Wheels? Are you bored?"

Connor didn't feel like explaining the whole story. "The kids at the camp have nothing. My old Hot Wheels were just sitting at home. I thought I'd give them to the hospital for sick kids to play with. They'd get more use that way."

"Aw!" Shields looked up at him, a smile on her face. "Under that Kevlar and that don't-give-a-shit exterior, you're a softie."

"Keep that secret, got it?"

"Sure."

Connor checked his messages and the weather forecast and then ate breakfast with the others. He had just finished his omelet when Shanti buzzed him on his cell phone. He placed her breakfast order with room service and sent Isaksen to take it to her room.

When Isaksen returned, Connor started their morning briefing. "Shields is still working on the list we got from the UN representative. We're still waiting for the Bangladesh Police to ID the two bodies. In the meantime, we should—"

Shanti flew through the doorway, wearing a fluffy bathrobe, a bright smile on her face, her phone in hand, her feet bare. "You've got it. They said 'yes.'"

"Got what?" Connor wasn't keeping up here.

"Permission to fly a drone. Doctor Khan just called."

"That's great news." Connor tried to ignore the way his pulse had picked up when she'd run in. "Thanks for letting us know."

Shields gestured toward a vacant chair. "Would you like to join us for the briefing?"

Shanti shook her head. "Thanks. I need to finish breakfast and get ready to go. I just wanted you to know as soon as possible."

Connor gave her a professional nod. "We appreciate that."

He waited until she'd gone. "Shields, get on the phone to Dhaka to confirm. Segal, get that drone ready. The rest of us can go over yesterday's exfil. Flooding made it difficult and downright dangerous. I had to hold onto the client to keep her from falling, which put my focus on her and not our surroundings. What are our options?"

"You mean besides Noah's ark?" Cruz asked.

The men laughed.

SHANTI SAT in the middle in the back seat of the Land Rover, Dylan on one side of her and Malik on the other, while Connor sat in the front passenger seat. Connor hadn't said a word to her since they'd left the hotel. She couldn't shake the feeling that he was still upset with her.

Can you blame him?

She had apologized. There was nothing else she could do. Besides, her job here was to collect evidence that could be used to support a warrant for General Naing's arrest, not to start a relationship with the very sexy head of her security team.

"Copy that." Connor turned to the driver. "We'll wait in the car until we find out what's happening."

Shanti wanted to know. "What is it?"

"The drone is showing a crowd of people not far from the hospital."

"I hope nothing bad happened." She knew from her experience yesterday how easily the camp could flood.

At least the rain had stopped—for now.

Pauline and Noor were waiting for them once again, but rather than getting out, Connor rolled down the window.

"What's going on?"

"It's awful," Pauline said. "A mudslide buried some shelters on the hillside just south of the hospital. We're trying to find survivors and bring them to the hospital, but so far, we've only recovered bodies."

Oh, God.

Connor talked it over with his team, trying to decide whether the situation warranted returning to the hotel.

Shanti wanted to tell him that she couldn't go back. She had four witness interviews today, four interviews she could not miss, but he already knew that. She had agreed to abide by his decisions, and she would honor that agreement. But she didn't have to like it. She let out a relieved breath when Connor told her they could go ahead with the day as planned.

"Jones, Cruz, you're with me. The rest of you stay with the vehicles and be ready to join us or to leave at a moment's notice."

"You got it."

Shanti turned to Isaksen. "What do you do all day while we're at the hospital?"

"Keep watch. Crack some jokes." He grinned, his Danish soft.

"That sounds awfully dull."

"You've never served in the military, have you?" Malik chuckled. "Most of the time, it's 'hurry up and wait.' We do a *lot* of waiting."

All of them laughed, except Connor.

He was all business. "Let's move."

Shanti pulled her headscarf over her hair, and they started off for the hospital, making their way along muddy paths, Connor ahead of her, Malik beside her, Dylan behind. She heard the crowd before she saw it—a murmur of voices mixed with shouts and raw wails of grief.

Her stomach knotted.

After all, they'd been through, these people didn't deserve this heartbreak.

As they drew close to the hospital, Connor stopped, making way for men who carried the dead and wounded on stretchers.

"One o'clock," Malik said.

"I see him," Connor said.

Shanti imagined standing in a clock and looked toward the one to see a man in a maroon T-shirt and gray *lungi*—a kind of sarong. He was staring straight at her, acting as if he wanted to talk to her. "He might be one of my appointments."

She would be speaking to a couple of male survivors today and might need Connor or one of the other men to be in the room with her so as not to violate Rohingya cultural norms.

"If he is, he can wait to talk with you until …" Connor's words trailed off.

Two men carried the body of a little boy on a blanket.

The child couldn't have been more than five years old, his yellow shirt muddy and torn. Resting on his lifeless chest was some kind of homemade toy—a little bamboo car.

Connor watched as they passed. *"No."*

It was only a whisper, but Shanti heard it.

She walked up beside Connor, saw recognition and shock on his face. "Connor?"

Did he somehow know this little boy?

A muscle clenched in Connor's jaw. "I spoke with him yesterday. He showed me his little car. I wanted to..."

Shanti waited for him to finish, but he said nothing more, obviously hit personally by the child's senseless death. "It's awful when children die."

"Let's get you inside."

As she entered the hospital, Shanti saw the man in the gray lungi watching her.

Connor took his turn standing out front amid the wails and weeping of those who'd lost loved ones in the mudslide. He'd sent Cruz to watch the back entrance, while Jones stood watch outside the interview room—part of Connor's attempt to put a professional distance between himself and Shanti. He also wanted to keep an eye on the guy who'd been watching her.

The man had noticed Connor and walked a short distance away, where he now stood, glancing over at Connor every now and then.

No, dude, that's not suspicious at all.

Connor drew out his cell phone, pretended he was looking at something on the screen while trying to snap a shot of the man's face.

Turn your head this way. A little more. Got it.

He sent the image to Shields. "Cobra, Team One. We've got a fighting-age male, maybe five-foot-four, wearing a maroon shirt and a gray sarong hanging out in front of the hospital. He had eyes on the asset when we arrived and moved off when I positioned myself at the entrance. I just sent you a shot. How copy?"

"Team One, this is Cobra. Good copy. We'll run it through the database."

Another body was brought in—an old man. His relatives walked beside the makeshift gurney, the women looking too worn down by grief to weep for him.

What a damned mess it all was.

His thoughts turned to the little boy. He'd been far too young to die.

About the same age as the boy in Syria.

Fuck.

Connor couldn't think about that. He had a job to do, and it didn't involve dwelling on shit he couldn't change.

The morning wore on, the clouds growing thicker and darker overhead.

They took turns making trips to the latrine. Connor dug into his pack for something to eat but ended up giving his trail mix and an energy bar to a couple of skinny kids. They needed the nutrition more than he did.

It was early afternoon when Jones' voice came over Connor's earpiece. "Her next appointment hasn't shown up, and she needs to hit the head."

"Copy that." Connor and Cruz met Jones at the back door and escorted Shanti to the bank of latrines set aside for hospital staff.

Shanti gave the three of them an awkward smile. "An armed escort to pee. I feel embarrassed."

Jones grinned. "You wouldn't last in the military, ma'am. Sometimes you just have to drop trou and squat down right next to..."

Jones caught Connor's expression and coughed, his oversharing at an end.

Shanti did her business while the three of them kept watch.

"There's our buddy." Cruz gave a nod toward the guy in the maroon shirt, who stood about twenty feet away. "He's trying mighty hard to act like he's not watching what's going on over here."

Connor hadn't yet heard back from Shields. "He was standing out front until we came back here. Anyone think that's a coincidence?"

"Hell, no," Jones said. "Want me to pull him aside and start asking questions?"

"Just keep an eye on him."

He shot them furtive glances, as if he knew they were talking about him.

Shanti stepped out of the latrine, washed her hands at a public sink. "I wonder what happened to my one o'clock. Maybe Pauline—"

The guy in the maroon shirt made a run for Shanti.

Jones thrust her behind him, covering her.

Connor dropped the suspect in a single move, pressed a knee to his lower back and a hand to the back of his neck. "Cuff him!"

The man cried out, struggled, pleading with them in a language Connor didn't understand. Cruz pulled a plastic zip-tie restraint from his belt and bound the bastard's wrists together.

Connor stood, dragged the man to his feet. "Search him."

Cruz patted him down. "There's nothing on him but this cell phone."

"You take! You take!" The man motioned for Shanti to take his phone.

Connor got into the man's face. "She doesn't want your phone."

"Take!" The man looked straight at Shanti. "Jafor Ahammed! Friend."

"Put the phone back in his pocket—if he has a pocket—and call camp security."

"Wait!" Shanti stepped closer. "Jafor Ahammed? *Tuáñr nam ki?*"

Connor had no idea what she was saying, but the suspect quit struggling.

He replied in his own language.

"He's trying to tell me something about Jafor Ahammed, my one o'clock appointment. I need Noor."

"You want me to bring him inside?"

A delicate eyebrow arched. "Unless you think you can't handle him..."

Jones chuckled. "I think we've just been insulted."

"Did you hear what she just said?" Cruz said, a big stupid grin on his face. "We can handle this skinny dude."

"Fine." Holding tightly to the suspect, Connor followed her back inside.

~

"HE SAYS HE IS RAFIQUE HALAD," Noor said. "He is a friend of Jafor Ahammed."

"Please thank Mr. Halad for coming to talk with me about his friend. Does he know where Mr. Ahammed is?" Shanti hoped Ahammed wasn't backing out.

But Rafique was speaking at the same time, words pouring out of him, an urgent and frightened expression on his face.

Noor held up her hands for silence, then spoke to Rafique again. "He says Jafor has gone missing and that the phone belongs to him."

"Missing?"

Shanti listened as Noor translated Rafique's story a little at a time.

"He lives in a shelter near Mr. Ahammed. The two came from a village near Maungdaw. They had to flee when the soldiers came. Rafique ran, but Jafor stayed and tried to save his wife and children."

Noor described a night of terror that began with a hail of bullets and ended with Jafor playing dead among the mutilated and burned bodies of neighbors and family.

"Jafor told Rafique one of the soldiers had dropped his phone, so Jafor took it."

Shanti's pulse skipped. "One of Naing's soldiers?"

Numerous survivors had described soldiers filming the violence. If Shanti could get her hands on that footage...

Noor nodded. "Yes, one of Naing's soldiers. He dropped the phone. Jafor saw it, and before they could bury the bodies, he climbed out of the pit, grabbed the phone, and ran for the mountains. It was dark, and they did not see him."

"This is the phone?" Shanti took it from him.

"He says that Jafor asked him to hide the phone somewhere because he was afraid men would come to take him away just like they took the British reporters."

"What?" Shanti stared at Rafique. "Jafor Ahammed spoke with the British journalists? Does Rafique know who abducted them? Did he see what happened?"

What was going on here?

Shanti listened while Noor and Rafique went back and forth, wishing she could speak the language herself.

Connor leaned down, spoke in a quiet voice. "Shanti, this isn't safe."

"He doesn't have any weapons."

"It's not him I'm worried about."

Finally, Noor turned to her. "He says Jafor told the British gentlemen about the phone. They asked the UN manager for help cracking the password, but she didn't know how. Two days later, the British men disappeared. Jafor asked Rafique to hide the phone because he feared those men would come for him, too. Rafique put it in a plastic bag and buried it under a rock near some latrines. Now Jafor is missing, and Rafique is afraid those same men will come after him. That's why he wants you to take it. He knew Jafor was going to meet with you."

Connor took the phone and turned to Noor, his expression grave. "Translate for me. Did this phone belong to one of the soldiers who attacked their village, and does it have video footage of the attack?"

Noor translated the question and Rafique's answer. "He says yes."

"Cobra, Team One, we're making our exfil now. Segal, Isaksen, request additional escort. Have the helicopter on standby. How copy?"

Connor's reaction sent Shanti's adrenaline soaring. "What? What's going on?"

"Cruz, pack her gear. Jones, make sure the hallway's clear."

"Roger that."

"What about my last appointment?"

"Reschedule it. Naing's men are looking for this phone. It's not hard to trace a cell phone if you have the tech."

That didn't make sense. "The phone isn't even turned on."

"It doesn't have to be on for them to locate it." Connor didn't explain further but turned to Noor once more. "You and Rafique should come with us. We can give you a safe place to stay while we sort through this. I'd like to ask Rafique a few more questions in a place where no one can hurt him."

Noor shook her head. "We can't go with you. Rohingya people must have permission to leave the camps."

Connor looked to Shanti as if to confirm this.

"It's true. I'll call Pauline."

Pauline answered on the first ring. Shanti told her that they had reason to believe Noor and Rafique were in danger, but she did not mention the cell phone.

Pauline told Shanti that only the Bangladesh government could grant permission for Noor and Rafique to go with them. "It could take weeks."

Shanti shared that news with Connor.

He shook his head. "Doesn't it figure? The best thing we can do is get that phone far away from here. If they're tracing it, they'll know it's gone and hopefully leave Rafique alone. Noor, can you tell him to stay away from his shelter and wherever he hid the phone? You shouldn't tell anyone about this, or it might put you in danger, too."

Noor's face was pale, but she nodded. "I understand."

Shanti hugged her. "I'll get in touch through Pauline. Thank you for your help. Please thank Rafique for his courage. I hope we haven't put you in any danger."

"The danger was here before you came. Go with God, Shanti."

"Segal and Isaksen are here. Noor, you and Rafique should go out the back door. If you see anything unusual, report it to camp security. We'll exit through the front entrance. Let's move!"

8

C onnor kept his mind focused on their surroundings, Shields giving them regular updates about what she saw in the drone feed. Shanti sat in the middle of the back seat, talking with Pauline. From the sound of things, Pauline wasn't responding the way she had hoped.

"So, you're telling me that no one looks for people who just disappear? I understand that the camp is large and that the job must be overwhelming, but Naing's men shouldn't be able to walk in and abduct people."

Connor didn't know how to tell Shanti this, but he'd bet cold, hard cash that Mr. Ahammed was already dead. Once Naing's men realized he no longer had the phone, he would have been worthless to them, a liability that needed to be eliminated.

"Also, one of the witnesses I spoke with today told me that human traffickers walk through the camp asking pregnant women to give them their babies. Apparently, she was raped by a soldier and became pregnant and freely gave her newborn to these criminals because her family had shunned her."

Shanti sounded surprised, proof that, despite her job and her family's history, she didn't understand how deeply fucked up this world was. Wherever there was chaos, slavers and traffickers showed up, looking for human property.

"But there has to be *something* the UN can do to shut the traffickers down and help end the stigma these women face. No, Pauline, but I ... Yes. Okay. Thanks."

Connor glanced over his shoulder to see anger and frustration on Shanti's face. "I take it that didn't go well."

"She knows about the traffickers. She says there's really nothing the UN can do about it. Can you believe that? They're the freaking UN."

Connor *could* believe it, but he didn't say so. "There are almost five hundred thousand people in Kutupalong. The UN's resources are stretched pretty thin."

"She says they don't have the personnel to protect Rafique or Noor or the witnesses and that only relatives can file a missing person's report with the Bangladesh Police for Mr. Ahammed. She said people go missing all the time."

Her concern for the others touched Connor, given that she was more likely to be a target now than any of them. "You might want to think about your own safety."

But his words didn't seem to register.

A moment later, she was speaking with her boss, bringing him up to speed. "I don't know what's on the phone yet. The battery is dead. I'll look when I get back to the hotel. We need to do something to protect the witnesses and my interpreter. Is there any way to bring them to The Hague and place them under protection?"

She spent the rest of the drive sounding very much like an attorney, discussing organizational bylaws, international agreements, legal precedents, and obstacles to bringing Noor and the others to the Netherlands.

Connor had to give Shanti credit. She didn't give up.

They reached the hotel without incident, he, Cruz, Jones, Segal, and Isaksen surrounding Shanti as they walked her to the elevators.

She let out a relieved breath when the doors closed and the elevator began to move, her gaze meeting Connor's. "Do you think they'll be safe?"

"I don't know, but you've done everything you can for them."

He could see in her eyes that she didn't think it was enough.

SHANTI WATCHED while Elizabeth plugged the smartphone into a charger, relieved when the start-up screen came on. Mr. Ahammed had most likely died to pass on this phone and the information on it. No one had told her this, but she wasn't naïve. She had to make sure his suffering hadn't been for nothing.

"We've got a heartbeat," Elizabeth said.

"Will you be able to crack the password?"

"This is a cheap Android knockoff, so that shouldn't be too hard. The Sayeret Maktal can crack even the latest iOS, so I'll get Segal in here."

Shanti watched while Lev and the guys everyone called "the geek team" worked together to hack into the phone. It didn't take long, Elizabeth, Lev, and the others trading high-fives and fist bumps.

"Now, let's see what secrets we can find. You say your witness took this from a Tatmadaw soldier?"

"Yes. He showed it to the British journalists, who asked

Pauline for help cracking the password. Now, he's missing, abducted like the journalists."

Elizabeth connected a data cable to the phone and plugged it into Shanti's computer, causing her photo application to open. "We've got lots of content."

There were hundreds of images, some showing a pretty Burmese woman and a little girl at home, in a park, in front of a spectacular golden pagoda. An elephant. A lounging Buddha. The same little girl smiling as she fed monkeys at the Yangon Zoo. The smiling faces of soldiers. Dozens of pics of noodles in bowls.

"I've never understood why people take pictures of their food," Elizabeth said. "Who sits around scrolling through photo albums of past meals?"

Connor entered, drew up a chair. "What have you found?"

"So far, it's all ordinary stuff," Shanti answered.

More food pics.

Elizabeth scrolled through them. "The guy likes his noodles."

When the files had finished uploading, Shanti sorted through the videos. Among those of the little girl and her mother were others that had clearly been filmed at night, each one showing up as a dark preview image.

Connor pressed his hand over hers, stopping her from clicking. "If it's what he said it is, it's going to be ugly. Prepare yourself."

Shanti tried not to let her annoyance show. "This is evidence. I'm a prosecutor."

They clicked on the video—and opened a door into hell.

Screams. Gunshots. Children crying. Mothers sobbing.

The camera wavered, moving quickly before focusing on

something—three men holding a woman down while a fourth raped her and the man holding the camera laughed.

Shanti's stomach rolled.

In the background, men with rifles beat an old man while bamboo huts burned, screams telling Shanti that the huts were not vacant.

And on it went, scene after scene and video after video of unspeakable violence and depravity. Rape. Beatings. Dismemberments. Lynching. Burnings.

No mercy. No compassion. No one spared.

Genocide.

Shanti tried to control her emotions and her body's response. She clicked on the third video, watched a soldier kick a decapitated head, laughing as it rolled.

Her stomach revolted.

She jumped up, ran to her bathroom, and threw up, her body shaking.

Someone came up behind her—Connor.

He knelt beside her, held back her hair. "It's okay, Shanti."

Mortified, she flushed the toilet, willed herself to breathe deeply, her stomach still in knots. "I'm sorry."

He drew her to her feet. "You've got no reason to apologize."

Still shaky, she made her way to the sink, rinsed her mouth, brushed her teeth, and splashed cold water on her face, while he stayed with her, his big body making the space seem smaller.

She dried her hands and face. "You must think I'm a wimp."

"No." His gaze was warm with concern. "You're having a normal reaction to some seriously fucked-up shit."

"You and Elizabeth aren't throwing up."

"We've been at this a little longer than you have."

Maybe it was his kindness, or maybe she was already at an emotional edge. Her eyes filled with tears, and she sank against him. "All of those people."

He drew her into his arms, held her, a big hand stroking her hair while she wept. "This is why we're here. This is why you're on this mission. You're a voice for every man, woman, and child these bastards hurt and killed. But being a badass prosecutor doesn't mean you're made out of granite."

His voice was deep, his body strong, the feel of his arms around her comforting.

She didn't know how long they stayed that way—a couple of minutes perhaps—but gradually she came back to herself.

She drew away, wiped the tears from her face. "Thanks."

"That soldier made these videos never thinking you would have them. He gave you the rope. Now, hang Naing with it."

She drew a deep breath, exhaled. Her stomach wasn't happy, and she still felt shaky, but she had a job to do. "Let's get back to work."

CONNOR STOOD in the doorway to Shanti's room, watching her work, unable to shake the thought of how *good* it had felt to hold her, as if she were precious, as if she belonged in his arms. He'd never felt that way with anyone, not even Mandy.

Dude, you're losing it.

He tried to tell himself it was just hormones, that he needed to get laid. But as he stood there watching her, he knew that wasn't true. He respected and admired her for her resilience and determination. This wasn't just a job for her. She truly cared about people.

In her own way, she was tough. She hadn't thrown up again. She hadn't shed another tear. She'd stepped out of that bathroom, chin raised, and had dived headlong into murder and chaos.

She'd begun uploading the videos to the ICC's cloud server and was now combing through the footage frame by frame with Shields' help to identify villages, army units, and individuals. In return for Shields' help and expertise, Shanti had agreed to share the footage with the CIA—provided they kept it top secret until an arrest warrant was issued for Naing.

"Oh, honey," Shields had said. "The Agency's job is keeping secrets. You could ask about the weather, and they would neither confirm nor deny that there *is* weather."

Jones came up beside Connor. "Why aren't we going after that fucker?"

Word about the videos and what they contained had spread quickly through the team, leaving the men grim-faced and angry.

"Remember what Tower said." Connor slapped him on the shoulder. "*She's* going after him, and we're helping her. So, we *are* going after him in a way."

"I think I'd rather light him up than help send him to prison."

Connor understood that. "You and me both."

He stepped into his own room for a quick video conference with Tower and Corbray. He brought them up to date on the situation, and both men expressed the same concern that Connor had.

"If it were up to me, she'd be on her way home tomorrow," Tower said.

Corbray agreed. "Until the bad guys know the videos are in ICC hands, they're going to be looking for that phone and trying to neutralize everyone who saw it."

But Corbray and Tower didn't know Shanti.

Connor tried to explain. "She missed an interview today thanks to our early exfil, and she's got three more days of interviews scheduled."

"Does she still need these interviews when she's got the videos?" Tower asked.

It was a reasonable question.

"She's here to get testimony from people who saw Naing at the massacres, not to prove that the massacres happened. There's a difference."

"Shit." Corbray rubbed his face with his hands. "Maybe someone else could come down to do those interviews while she heads back to the Netherlands."

"Or maybe she should wait until the situation cools down and come back later to complete that mission," Tower suggested. "One thing is sure—we can't lose her, and we don't want to lose any of you."

"I hear that."

"Does her boss, Mr. Meijer, know about this?" Tower asked.

"She called him on the way back from the camp, told him about the phone, tried to win his support for moving witnesses and her interpreter to the Netherlands. She's been uploading the videos to their cloud server and shooting him emails, so he must have some idea what's in them."

"I'll give him a call, see what he's thinking," Tower said. "Ultimately, it's up to him whether Ms. Lahiri stays or goes. Any word on the two guys who fired the RPG?"

"Not yet. We're waiting on the Bangladesh Police. Did you see Shields' report?"

While they'd been at the camp today, Shields had put together an analysis of the people on Pauline's list and had assessed that Naing had eyes and ears somewhere in Pauline's organization—a clerk or staff member with access to schedules and other information.

"What about the missing witness?" Corbray asked. "If Naing's men took him, it's possible they tortured information about Ms. Lahiri's arrival out of him."

Connor shook his head. "He wouldn't have known about the helicopter tour. Whoever ordered that attack knew right where she was going to be—and when."

"Right."

Connor asked what was on everyone's mind here tonight. "Any chance we can use these videos to talk Uncle Sam into letting us or DEVGRU hit this target?"

"And risk a war with China?" Tower laughed. "I doubt that would be their first choice. They are grateful for the intel, however. She should know that."

"I'll tell her."

"Keep us posted."

"Copy that." Connor ended the video conference and went back into Shanti's room to find her hard at work with Shields, some of the men standing or sitting on chairs around her, watching.

"Those are definitely army uniforms, not border patrol or militia," Shields said.

"Stop! Go back. A little more. Freeze it." Shanti pointed. "Can you blow up the background right there?"

"Let's give it a shot." Shields hit a few keys. "Well, hello, you son of a bitch."

"Oh, my God." Shanti stared, slowly got to her feet, her eyes wide. "It's him. It's Naing. We got him."

"THANKS, Elizabeth. I couldn't have done this so quickly without you." Shanti stood, rubbed the kink in her neck.

She still couldn't believe it. She had footage of Naing at a massacre.

"I just hope you can nail this bastard to the wall." Elizabeth stood, picked up her cup of coffee. "I heard about the mudslides today. That's the last thing these people needed. O'Neal was pretty shaken up. His Hot Wheels arrived this evening, but the little boy he had hoped to share them with is dead."

Okay, that made no sense.

"Hot Wheels?"

"He sent Cobra guys to his parents' farm in Colorado to get an old box of Hot Wheels out of the attic. He'd hoped to give one to that little boy and leave the rest for staff at the hospital to distribute to other children."

Shanti's heart melted. She remembered the stricken look on his face when he'd seen the child. Now she understood. "I had no idea."

Elizabeth gave her a knowing smile. "You're attracted to him. Oh, don't try to deny it. What red-blooded, hetero woman wouldn't be? Just be careful. There's no such thing as an uninjured soldier."

Before Shanti could ask her what she meant, Elizabeth was gone.

Attracted to him?

Okay, fine. Shanti could admit that. As Elizabeth had said, what heterosexual woman wouldn't be? But what had she meant by that last part?

Shanti turned off her computer and watched the screen go dark, wishing it were that easy to shut off her mind. She was drained, exhausted, but also strangely wired, as if she'd had too much coffee.

That's adrenaline.

She'd read lots of reports in her time with the ICC, and she had listened to witnesses describe terrible things. But *seeing* it, seeing the cruelty of it, hearing people's screams, watching soldiers laugh while they hurt, maimed, and killed in ways intended to inflict pain and humiliation—that was different.

She showered and then dug through her increasingly disorganized suitcase for her nightgown. She had uploaded all of the video footage and the stills to the cloud drive and sent Bram an email telling him she had video footage of Naing overseeing two of the massacres. Bram had congratulated her—and informed her that he wanted her home.

"It's not safe for you there," he'd said. "The men from Cobra tell me there's a leak somewhere in the camps, and that's why your helicopter almost got shot down. Now this phone with such important evidence... I don't want to lose you."

"What about the other witnesses I came to interview?"

"You can return later—or we'll send someone else when things calm down." He had assured her that the organization was having a conversation at the highest levels of the Dutch government about bringing Noor and the others to the Netherlands.

Shanti had felt relieved.

She'd sent Pauline a quick text message telling her that she might not be able to make it to the camp tomorrow and to cancel her appointments with her witnesses for the day. She couldn't help but feel that she was letting the other witnesses down, but she was in danger if she remained in Bangladesh. Besides, she wasn't going home empty-handed. She had several witness interviews. More than that, she had proof that Naing had commanded the massacres.

That was more than she'd hoped for when she'd come here.

She brushed her teeth and drew down her sheets, but hesitated when it came to turning off the light, images from the videos flashing through her mind.

Screams. Crying babies. Women stripped naked.

Think about something else. Think about ... Connor.

Well, that wasn't hard. Six foot plus of male perfection.

She turned off the light, lay back on her pillow, remembering how it had felt to be in his arms. She'd been too upset at the time to truly appreciate it, but she could remember how hard his body had felt, how he'd stroked her hair, how his voice had rumbled in his chest. She could get used to that.

Yeah, well, don't. You're leaving.

She was going back to The Hague. That meant she would be saying goodbye to him. She lived in The Hague, and he lived in Colorado. She wouldn't see him again—a sad thought.

She began to drift.

But it wasn't thoughts of Connor that followed her into sleep, but the screams of women and the laughter of soldiers.

Screams.

Gunshots.

Blood.

The houses were burning! She could see people inside— women and children. Where was Noor? Was she trapped inside, too?

Shanti ran toward Noor to set her free but stopped.

Heads. There were heads on the ground. She couldn't step on them.

One of them rolled and rolled, coming to rest near her feet.

And she saw.

It was her grandfather's face, his lifeless eyes staring up at her.

Shanti screamed.

9

Connor dried off from his shower and stepped into a clean pair of boxer briefs. He'd just pulled them over his ass when he heard a strangled cry in Shanti's room.

He grabbed his Glock, opened her door, and stepped inside, his weapon ready.

The room was dark—no movement, no sign of intruders —but he could hear Shanti weeping.

Her voice broke the silence. "Connor?"

She sounded afraid.

"Are you okay?"

She switched on her bedside lamp, looking defenseless and terrified, her hair in tangles, tears on her cheeks, her words coming in sobs. "There were soldiers... Noor was there... My grandfather..."

Her vulnerability and fear tugged at Connor, put a knot in his chest. He forgot that he was in his underwear and walked over to sit beside her, setting his firearm on her nightstand.

He'd already held her once today, so taking her into his arms again was easy. "Come here. It was just a dream."

She clung to him, her breasts pressing against his ribs, her head resting against his shoulder, her hair spilling like silk over his skin. "I was in one of the camps. Noor was trapped in a burning hut. I tried to reach her, but then I saw heads rolling on the ground. One rolled so I could see its face. It was my grandfather."

Connor knew what it was like to have nightmares like that. "Someone once told me that dreams are the mind's way of taking out the garbage. You saw some really awful shit today."

"I don't know how he did it."

Connor wasn't keeping up. "How who did what?"

"How can the soldier who filmed all of this *horror* kiss his wife and hold his daughter after what he's done? How can he rape and kill women and children one day and then go home to his wife and child the next?"

Her words struck that sore spot inside Connor, guilt sliding through him. "I guess he compartmentalizes it somehow."

That's what Connor tried to do.

It was an accident. It wasn't deliberate.

She drew away, looked up at him. "Last night, you said something about all the things you've seen and done. Do you have nightmares?"

"Yeah—sometimes." He wiped the tears off her cheeks with his thumbs, his gaze drawn to her lips. It would be so easy to lean down and taste them.

Not the right time and place for that, buddy.

Tower and Corbray would have his balls for breakfast if Connor touched her.

"Elizabeth told me about your Hot Wheels and how you wanted to give one to that little boy who died today. I'm so sorry he was killed. You'd made a connection with him. It was still incredibly sweet of you to try."

Connor brushed off her praise. He wasn't a hero. He'd likely been as motivated by guilt as anything else—as if giving one child a toy could make up for taking another child's life. "We aren't going back to the camps, so it doesn't matter."

You're pathetic.

"Maybe we can ship them to Pauline." That was Shanti —never giving up.

"Maybe."

Then Shanti grew quiet, her expression troubled. "How do you do it? How do you face down gunfire and make yourself fight, knowing you might die?"

"You have to make your peace with death. Then fear disappears."

"I can't imagine that."

"A man who isn't afraid of dying is dangerous." He didn't expect her to understand any of this, but that wasn't her fault.

How could she understand something she had never experienced?

"Does all of this ever become too much for you—the risk, the violence, the gore?"

That was a tough question to answer, especially when all he could think about was kissing her. "I have trouble going home."

Her brow bent in confusion. "Trouble going home?"

"I call it re-entry. It's like an action hangover. Best way to deal with it is more action—a little hair of the dog. Sometimes, it's easier to stay in the field."

What would she taste like? God, he wanted to know, the need to kiss her pulsing inside him like a heartbeat.

Don't do it.

He hadn't crossed a line with her yet. He was close right now, but he wasn't over. He hadn't yet done anything he couldn't put in a report to Tower and Corbray. He should leave her and go back to his room before he did something stupid. Besides, if she knew everything there was to know about him, she wouldn't want his hands on her.

He tried to remember what he'd been about to say. "It's hard to go from hitting a target to hitting the grocery store. One minute, you're hopped up on adrenaline, doing your best to achieve your objective and keep yourself and your fellow soldiers alive. The next, someone's asking if you want fries with that. When the adrenaline wears off, that's when the nightmares and the self-doubt set in."

SHANTI TRIED TO UNDERSTAND. "Why do you keep doing it? Why not leave and find a job that doesn't risk your life or place you in conflict with others?"

"This is the only thing I'm good at."

Shanti shook her head. "I don't believe that—not for a minute."

"I don't have a college education. I signed up straight out of high school. When I left the army, I didn't know what I was going to do. I was lucky to know one of the guys who works for Cobra. We served together. He got me this job."

Connor never used the term Delta Force and rarely mentioned the branch of the special forces in which he'd served. Technically speaking, the Unit didn't exist.

"Now you're out here risking your life again." She pressed her fingers to the bullet scar on his chest. "You've been hurt so many times. Where did you get this one?"

"Mosul."

She ran a thumb over the deep graze on his right shoulder. "This one?"

"Fallujah, I think."

How could he not remember?

She traced a finger over the scar on his belly, the muscles of his abdomen tightening at her touch. "This one looks new."

"I took a round to the gut last November. Some warlord tried to abduct a client and ambushed us at the airport in Mazar-e-Sharif. I think most of us got shot in that one. Jones took a round to the lung, came close to dying."

"That's awful. Is the client okay?"

"She's fine."

"Did you sit in her bed when she had nightmares, too?"

"Tower did." But Connor seemed distracted now, his gaze on her lips.

"Connor?"

"Yeah?"

"*Kiss me.*"

"God, yes." He drew her close and took her mouth with his.

Shanti's thoughts scattered, her breath catching as Connor brushed his lips over hers again and again, each caress making her pulse skip. He drew her closer, one big hand splayed across her back, the hard feel of his body sending shivers through her. But still, he took his time, teasing her mouth with his, nipping her lips, tracing their curves with his tongue until she trembled and burned.

He drew back, looked down at her, his brow furrowed, his eyes dark. "*Shanti.*"

For a moment, she was afraid it was over, that duty or conscience or some misplaced sense of gallantry had gotten the better of him. Before she could protest, he slid a hand into her hair, angled her head—and claimed her mouth in a slow, deep kiss.

Oh, yes!

She slid her hands up his bare chest and over his shoulders, arching against him, reveling in the feel of him, inhaling his male scent.

He groaned, his hand fisting in her hair, gentleness giving way to need. The intensity of his kiss left her breathless, his lips pressing hard and hot against hers, his tongue teasing hers with insistent strokes.

Arousal lanced through her, turning to liquid fire in her belly. Hungry for more, she kissed him back, challenging him for control, playing with him the way he'd played with her—nipping his lower lip, exploring his mouth, tasting his tongue.

He let her have her way—for a moment.

When he reclaimed control, she surrendered gladly, feeling delightfully overpowered and deliciously feminine in his arms.

He cupped one of her breasts through the thin cotton of her nightgown, ran his thumb over its puckered nipple, making her gasp. Then his lips came down on her pulse, pressing kisses against the sensitive skin of her neck.

All at once, he broke the kiss and withdrew his hand. "Shanti, I can't … I shouldn't… If we don't stop now…"

Shanti's body ached, her pulse thrumming for him. "But I don't want to stop—not yet. Don't you want this?"

He looked into her eyes, his gaze burning. "God, yes, but I'm breaking a half-dozen rules by being with you like this."

"I won't report you. Who's going to know?"

"I'll know." He ran a thumb over the curve of her lower

lip. "I don't want to do anything to jeopardize your safety or happiness."

She knew she was pouting, but she didn't care. She was wet and achy for him, and it had been so damned long. "Your refusal to continue kissing me is definitely injurious to my happiness."

He grinned, chuckled. "Now the attorney comes out. Can we negotiate? When we're back in The Hague, and I'm no longer assigned to your protection detail, I'll be more than happy to spend a night kissing you for as long as you want."

That was probably tomorrow.

She could live that long, couldn't she? "I'm going to hold you to that."

CONNOR WOKE up in a foul mood, edgy and frustrated. He hadn't slept much, but he wasn't tired, unspent sexual energy more potent than caffeine. He got up, dressed, and brushed his teeth, marveling at his stupidity, his lack of self-control.

He had gone into Shanti's room last night—and he'd kissed the hell out of her.

To be fair, he hadn't gone in there intending to kiss her. He'd heard her cry out and had thought at first that something had happened. When he'd realized she'd had a nightmare, he'd stayed to help her get past it.

That makes it worse, you idiot, not better.

He was in a position of trust. He was the head of her security team, for God's sake. She'd been vulnerable and afraid.

She wanted it. You know she did. She asked you to kiss her.

She'd kissed him back, pressing her body against his, arching into his hand when he'd touched her breast. Hell, she'd gotten pissed off when he'd finally stopped.

That doesn't change anything.

Fuck.

He couldn't think of the last time he'd wanted a woman like this. Every cell in his body ached for her. And now he was hard again.

Good job, dumbass.

He rinsed his toothbrush and packed his gear, doing his best to get his head out of his crotch and on the job. He was dressed, ready to go, and no longer erect in time for their morning strategy session, which he considered something of an achievement.

The others shuffled in, everyone making straight for the coffee.

Corbray and Tower joined them from DC and Denver, respectively.

Corbray started the meeting. "We're pulling you out. The ICC agrees that Bangladesh is just too hot for Ms. Lahiri right now. They want her and the phone back in The Hague as soon as we can make it happen."

Cruz raised his hand. "Why do they need the phone? They've got the videos and the stills. That ought to be enough to pull a warrant on this asshole."

Shields took this question. "There's a chance that they can use the IMEI number on the phone to trace it to a specific soldier. If they can prove the phone belonged to someone who serves under Naing, that's another piece of evidence."

"Then it's worth it," McManus said. "We need to put this whoreson away."

Tower took them through the plan. "Our helicopter will

be waiting at the airport. O'Neal, you and the asset and two others from your team will fly out on the bird to Dhaka. The rest of you will drive there in the vehicles. The jet, which is currently over the Pacific, will meet you in Dhaka and bring you to the Netherlands."

Corbray took over. "No one is to know she's leaving—not the hotel staff, not her UN contacts at the camps, not the witnesses, not even her interpreter."

They were just picking up and leaving.

It made sense.

"There's not much room on the helo, so our gear will need to go with the vehicles. The vehicles will leave first and drive toward the camps at the same time as yesterday. O'Neal, you, Cruz, and Jones will drive Ms. Lahiri and her bags to the airport when they're out of sight."

"What about the phone?" Connor asked. "If the asset keeps it with her and they're tracking it, they'll know she's not in the vehicles. Could we send it with our gear?"

"The ICC wants us to treat the phone like an additional asset."

Connor didn't like that. They were risking a living, breathing woman for the phone. Sadly, this wasn't his decision to make. If it were up to him, they would shred the damned thing. "Copy that."

SHANTI STARED AT CONNOR. "We're leaving right now?"

"We're not notifying anyone, not even the hotel staff."

"I sent Pauline an email last night telling her I didn't think I would be coming to the camp today because of the changing security situation and asking her to cancel today's appointments. Is that a problem?"

"Did you tell her you've been recalled and are leaving the country?"

"No."

Connor nodded. "I'll run this by Shields, but I think we're okay."

She glanced back at her suitcase. "What's going with me, and what's going with the rest of the team?"

"Your bags go on the helicopter."

"So, we'll be in The Hague tomorrow?" She hadn't forgotten the deal they'd made last night.

"Yeah, if we stay on schedule." His mind was clearly on security, so he didn't seem to catch her meaning.

"You haven't forgotten our ... arrangement?"

Lips that had kissed her senseless curved in a slow, sexy grin that made her shiver. "I haven't forgotten anything. Pack. We leave in forty-five minutes—and bring a headscarf."

"Forty-five minutes?" She stared after him as he left her room, heard him chuckle.

She moved as quickly as she could, folding her saris, gathering her toiletries, choosing what to wear. She packed her laptop in her suitcase and zipped the soldier's phone carefully in her handbag. She remembered what it had been like to climb into the helicopter the other day and skipped the skirt suit and heels for a pair of jeans, a T-shirt, and her boots. She tucked some bottled water into her handbag, along with her encrypted cell phone and some candied almonds. She managed to gulp down some *cha* and scrambled eggs, take her malaria pill, and brush her teeth before her time was up.

She stepped out of her room to find that Quinn McManus, Thor Isaksen, and Lev Segal had already gone in the Land Rovers. Elizabeth and two members of the computer team were staying behind to operate the drone that would see Shanti safely to the airport and to break down and pack up the computers.

"How are you getting home?" Shanti had come to like Elizabeth and to respect her skills. She didn't want to say goodbye.

"We'll catch a commercial flight back to the US tomorrow."

Shanti hugged her. "Thanks for all your help yesterday, and thanks for all you've done to keep me safe."

"You're welcome." Elizabeth hugged her back. "You just get that bastard, okay? The world doesn't need men like him."

"I'll do my best." Shanti stepped into the elevator with Connor, Dylan, and Malik, who carried her bags.

She wanted to make a joke about how she could get used to traveling like this—men to carry her luggage, helicopters waiting for her at the airport, private luxury jets—but they were all business now, just like they'd been on the trips to and from Kutupalong. At first glance, they looked like tourists—jeans, casual button-down shirts left unbuttoned and untucked over black T-shirts, baseball caps on their heads. But hidden beneath the button-down shirts were shoulder harnesses and weapons.

When the elevator doors opened again, she expected to see a shiny, black Land Rover. Instead, a green auto-rickshaw waited for them. She understood why they'd chosen this vehicle. It might not be bullet-proof, but it would blend in with the hundreds of others just like it on the roads.

"It's been a while since I've traveled in one of these."

Connor helped her in. "We'll need you to sit in the back and wear that headscarf. Cover your face if you can."

She did as he asked and found herself sandwiched once

again between Dylan and Malik. She supposed she ought to be nervous, but she wasn't.

Hadn't they kept her safe so far?

The gate went up, and they drove out onto the streets to be swallowed up instantly by traffic, auto-rickshaws, bicycles, pedestrians, vendor carts, and buses all vying for space on the crowded roadway.

Shanti inhaled the familiar scents, a sense of sadness settling over her at having to leave so quickly. When she'd first heard she'd be coming here, she had hoped to visit her father's cousins. She would just have to come again.

It didn't take long to reach the airport. They entered through a controlled gate and drove straight onto the tarmac, where Cobra's helicopter was waiting for them, its rotors running. It was smaller than the UN helicopter had been.

"Heads on a swivel," Connor said to his team.

He led Shanti straight to the helicopter and helped her climb in, the two of them taking their seats while Dylan and Malik got her bags out of the rickshaw. "Buckle up."

It all happened at once.

The helicopter starting to lift off without Dylan and Malik. Connor drawing his weapon. The co-pilot firing at Connor. Connor slumping to the side, blood spilling from his head. The co-pilot firing at Dylan and Malik below.

BAM! BAM! BAM!

Terror slid through her veins, her heart beating so hard it hurt.

She'd been abducted.

Connor was dead.

She was alone with his killers.

10

S hanti trembled in fear, her mouth dry, her pulse like thunder in her ears.

No! Connor! Oh, God.

But she didn't have time for grief because, at that moment, the co-pilot turned and pointed his pistol straight at her.

She shrank back into her seat, hands raised, sure she'd taken her last breath.

The man spoke to her in English. "You be a good girl. Don't make me kill you."

He climbed into the back, and for a moment, Shanti was sure he meant to open the door and dump Connor's body. Instead, he took Connor's radio and went back to his seat, listening via Connor's earpiece and laughing with the pilot about something. She couldn't hear what they were saying to each other. Maybe they were on a private channel.

"Bastards."

But they *could* hear her.

"Watch your mouth, Ms. Lahiri." The pilot turned just enough for her to catch a glimpse of his face.

"You?"

It was the Indian pilot who'd flown the UN helicopter.

He chuckled. "It's good to see you again."

"You flew the helicopter the day those two men fired that grenade at us. Did you know they were going to do that?"

"Of course, but they never planned to hit us. It was supposed to frighten you away. No one wanted to hurt you. Sadly, you're stupid and chose to stay."

"But why? You work for—"

"I work for money. The pilots who were going to fly you today developed fatal headaches, so I took the job."

Shanti stared in horror as the two men laughed. "You *killed* them?"

"They were in the way."

Whoever the poor people were, they had worked for Cobra and had been sent here to protect her. Now, they were dead.

Shanti sat there, shaking, adrenaline making it hard to think. The helicopter had almost reached the Naf River now. They were flying her to Myanmar.

Of course, they are. Think!

They were going to take the phone. They were going to take the phone and kill her just like they'd killed Connor and the pilots and...

Connor's words from last night came back to her.

You have to make your peace with death. Then the fear disappears.

A man who isn't afraid of dying is dangerous.

Make your peace with death. Make your peace with death.

How the *hell* did a person do that?

She didn't want to die.

Neither did the Rohingya men, women, and children in those villages.

They'd wanted to live as desperately as she did. They'd had hopes and dreams. All of that had been stolen from them. Life didn't matter to Naing and his men. It didn't matter to the two men in front. Killing her would be easy for them.

A man who isn't afraid of dying is dangerous.

A man who isn't afraid of dying ... can think and fight.

Shanti's pulse slowed, and her fear began to lessen, replaced by a strange sense of power. Connor had died fighting to protect her. Now, she would fight to defend herself—and to bring his body home.

She glanced over at Connor, pain splitting her breastbone to know he was...

She stared.

His chest moved slowly up and down.

He was breathing!

Thank God!

Relief flooded her, warm and sweet.

But how?

He'd been shot in the head. No one survived that. Unless...

Maybe it wasn't as bad as it seemed. Still, the bastards in front clearly believed he was dead. They hadn't searched him for weapons or tried to restrain him. If he moaned in pain or regained consciousness, they would kill him.

Oh, no, they won't!

She reached over, took his hand, gave his fingers a squeeze—and she saw.

His gun.

It had fallen to the floor of the helicopter behind his left foot. They must not have noticed it, or they would have taken it away.

Or maybe they think you're too afraid to do anything with it.

Quietly, carefully, she reached over with her leg, caught the weapon with her heel, and slowly pushed it toward herself. With the earphones on and the thrum of the rotors, not even she could hear the quiet sound of the firearm sliding along the floor.

The two men pointed toward something in the sky just ahead of them.

Cobra's drone.

Shanti saw her chance.

She bent down, grabbed the pistol, tucked it beneath her.

The gun was heavier than she'd imagined it would be, but she had it now. If they tried to shoot Connor again...

Could you do it? Could you kill a man?

To save Connor's life, yes, she could.

CONNOR'S HEAD felt like it had been split in two, pain throbbing inside his skull. He opened his eyes, saw red.

Blood.

Where the *hell* was he?

He was about to raise a hand to wipe his eyes when someone squeezed his fingers.

He blinked.

Shanti?

She shook her head, pressed a finger to her lips, then pointed.

Two men sat in the front of the helicopter, but he didn't recognize them.

The helicopter.

They had arrived at the airport, and he'd escorted Shanti on board. Then one of the bastards had drawn a weapon and... *nothing*.

He'd been shot, and the helicopter had been hijacked.

He didn't have to wonder where the bullet had struck him. He seemed to have all of his bodily functions, so the round must not have penetrated. It had grazed his temple, knocking him clean out and making him bleed like a stuck pig.

Shanti mouthed words to him. *They think you're dead.*

They were in for a nasty surprise.

How long?

She held up one finger. *About an hour.*

Where are we?

She pointed down. *Myanmar.*

Fuck.

Then Shanti showed him something he hadn't expected to see. She was sitting on his Glock.

His heart gave a thud.

Damn. He was in love now.

How had she managed that? How had the woman who was afraid of firearms found the courage to recover and hide one under the noses of two armed assholes?

He pointed to his right side. *I have another one.*

Amber eyes went wide, her lips forming a surprised "Oh!"

She pointed up. *Drone.*

So, the drone was following them. Had Cruz and Jones been hit?

Connor had no way of knowing. His radio was gone.

They killed the pilots.

Ah, shit.

Connor hadn't known John Hatch or Robert Davis well, but Hatch had come from the Coast Guard with the reputation of being a kickass chopper pilot. Corbray and Tower would take this hard. Cobra had never suffered a fatality before.

He closed his eyes, took stock of his situation. He was flying over Myanmar with two unknown assailants who had just killed two operators, stolen Cobra's helicopter, and kidnapped him and his client. He had two pistols, limited flying skills, no backup, and no idea how his body would react if he got to his feet and needed to fight.

It sucks to be you.

He had only two things going for him—he was armed, and their captors thought he was dead.

He willed his aching head to think. He could neutralize the co-pilot now, put a gun to the pilot's head, and order him to turn it back to Bangladesh. The fact that the Myanmar Air Force hadn't shot them out of the sky meant that the pilot was probably in touch with someone on the ground. If the hostiles on the ground lost contact with the pilot, they might scramble and shoot the bird out of the sky.

If the pilot didn't cooperate, Connor would have no choice but to get rid of him and try to fly this chopper himself.

The other option—waiting until they landed to make a break—wasn't viable. He'd bet his ass they were headed to some kind of military facility. Then he'd be facing dozens if not hundreds more armed hostiles. It had taken one shot to knock him out. It would take one to kill him—or Shanti.

And if they got ahold of Shanti...

Women's screams from those videos echoed through his mind.

He wouldn't let them touch her.

How the hell had this happened?

That's not your problem.

His problem was getting Shanti—and that damned phone—to safety.

There was only one survivable course of action. They were getting farther away from Bangladesh and safety with every passing second and closer to wherever that bastard Naing wanted Shanti to be.

He opened his eyes, slipped a hand inside his shirt, slowly withdrew the second Glock. He carried anti-personnel rounds in his handguns, rounds designed not to over-penetrate, so there was little chance of damaging the flight controls or having a round ricochet and hit Shanti.

She watched him, wide-eyed, as he pressed the pistol into the back of the co-pilot's seat—and fired.

BAM! BAM!

Shanti flinched and covered her ears at the blast, saw the co-pilot slump forward.

In a heartbeat, Connor threw off his safety belt, pressed his gun against the side of the pilot's face, and yanked something out of the control console—the interface cable to the pilot's helmet. "Turn this bird around and fly us back to Bangladesh—*now*."

The rage on his bloodied face made her pulse skip. This was the military part of him, the part that had fought and killed, the part that risked his life in war but had trouble coming home.

The pilot laughed and kept flying deeper into Myanmar.

"Turn it around, fucker, or I'll blow your brains out!"

"Who will fly the helicopter if I'm dead? You? That girl?"

"I'll fly it. I'm a former special forces operator and spent years flying these things. If you want me to blow your head off, fine. I was giving you a chance to live."

This time the pilot did as Connor asked, turning the helicopter around.

Shanti exhaled the breath she hadn't realized she'd been holding.

"How did they flip you?" Connor sat back but kept the gun pointed at the pilot's head. "Money? It's always money."

"Fuck you!"

"No, thanks. Traitors aren't my type." Connor sagged against the back of the co-pilot's seat but kept the gun still pointed at the pilot's head.

He must have been in pain or dizzy or both.

Had the pilot noticed?

Connor gritted his teeth, sat up straight again.

She needed to help him somehow. "Do you want some water? An Advil?"

He shook his head, his gaze fixed on the pilot. "How far to the river?"

"About two hundred fifty kilometers—if we don't run out of fuel."

Shanti's heart gave a hard knock. "Run out of fuel?"

Connor grinned. "Nice try, asshole. I can see the fuel gauge from here. They filled the tank in Cox's Bazar."

Oh, thank God.

Shanti looked out her window on an undulating sea of green below—hilly monsoon forest dotted with little villages. It seemed so peaceful, and yet—

BAM! BAM!

Shattered glass.

The pilot slumped forward, and helicopter lunged

downward and rolled onto its side, leaving Shanti's stomach behind.

"He drew a pistol. I didn't have a choice." Connor somehow managed to climb into the front and unbuckled the pilot. "Help me move him!"

But Shanti couldn't seem to find her feet, the helicopter spinning beneath her, disorienting her, making her dizzy. She unbuckled her safety belt and grabbed the pilot by his arm, pulling with all her might until he fell onto the floor near her feet, a hole in the side of his head, lifeless eyes staring up at her.

"*Oh, God.*"

An alarm beeped.

Connor sat in the pilot's seat. "Buckle in! This might get a little rough."

She did as he said, reminding herself that he'd spent years flying helicopters. He knew how to handle this.

Everything will be okay. Everything will be okay.

"Hang on!"

The forest rushed up at them, what she'd thought were rolling hills looking more like mountains now and looming right in front of them.

The skids hit treetops, and then the world spun out of control.

"We're going down!"

"*What?*"

"Hold onto something!"

They hit the ground hard, the force of impact knocking the breath from Shanti's lungs. Stunned, she sat there, one thought going through her mind.

She was alive.

"Are you okay?"

She sucked in a painful breath. "Yes."

"They probably saw where we went down. We'll strip what we need from this bird and get out of here." He climbed into the back seat, unbuckled her safety belt.

Stunned, she sat there for a moment.

"Come on, Shanti. On your feet." He opened the door on her side, climbed over her, and stepped down.

She picked up his pistol from the floor of the helicopter where it had fallen during the chaos and handed it to him.

"Thanks." He helped her to the ground, blood on his right cheek and temple and in his hair. "Are you sure you're okay?"

Her legs felt like jelly. "Just shaken up, I think. How about you?"

He stepped back, looked at the chopper. "I'm good, but this bird is beat. I hope they don't take it out of my paycheck."

The helicopter's skids were bent, its tail rotors crumpled, its boom buckled. She didn't have to be an expert on helicopters to know it wouldn't fly again.

He climbed back inside, searched the corpses, then hopped to the ground, the dead men's weapons in his hands. "That's my first helicopter crash as a pilot, and, as chopper crashes go, it wasn't bad."

"Your first crash?"

He tucked the pistols inside his waistband. "I've only spent about three hours flying helicopters and never on my own."

"What?" Shanti gaped at him. "You told him you'd flown helicopters for years."

"That's called 'bluffing.'"

Shanti's legs gave out, landing her flat on her butt.

≈

CONNOR SAW Shanti drop to the grass. "Hey, you okay?"

"You said you knew how to fly one of these! That whole time, I kept telling myself it would be okay because you knew what you were doing."

Head throbbing, he walked over to her, took her hands, pulled her to her feet. "I got us safely down, didn't I?"

She laughed, a manic kind of laughter.

He couldn't blame her for being upset.

He kept hold of her hands, looked into her eyes. "This is about survival now, Shanti. I know this must have been terrifying but—

"Terrifying?" Her expression turned to rage. "I thought you were dead! I thought they had killed you! There was so much blood and…"

Warmth blossomed behind Connor's breastbone, some part of him touched to think she'd been afraid for his sake.

He drew her into his arms. "I'm okay, Shanti, thanks in part to you. I'm sorry you went through that. This should never have happened."

But Shanti wasn't finished, words burbling out of her. "I kept remembering what you'd said about making peace with death. I didn't know how to do that. But when I saw you were alive, I thought you might moan or move and then they'd shoot you again. I squeezed your hand, tried to wake you, to warn you."

"It worked." He stepped back, hands on her shoulders. "Thank you."

"I saw you'd dropped your gun, so I pulled it across the floor with my foot and waited until they were distracted to pick it up. I told myself that I would pull the trigger to save your life if I had to. I was going to kill them."

That was a huge step for a woman who'd grown up terrified of firearms and who had committed herself to nonviolence.

"That was incredibly brave."

"I don't feel brave."

He released her, tucked a finger under her chin, lifted her gaze to his. "Being brave just means doing what you have to do, even when you're afraid."

"Have you ever been afraid?"

"More times than I can count." That seemed to surprise her. "You are strong, Shanti. I know you are. You need that strength now. There are two hundred fifty kilometers between us and the border. Soldiers will be trying to find us. They'll have helicopters, vehicles, and maybe even dogs—and we'll be on foot."

"Won't Cobra or the US government send a rescue team?"

"They'd have to get permission from the Pentagon for an op like that. Myanmar won't allow it. Your abduction will already be an international incident."

"They'll say I was spying."

That wasn't out of the realm of possibility.

"Shields and the others know right where we are, and I've got an encrypted satellite phone in my backpack. But for now, it's up to us to save ourselves. I'll call them once we're away from here. Our priorities at this moment are survival, evasion, and escape. Do you understand?"

She nodded, but he was pretty sure she didn't get the big picture. How could she? She had no military training. Nothing in her life as an attorney and the daughter of wealthy academics could have prepared her for this.

He'd gotten them out of one hot mess and landed them straight in another.

"We need to get away from this crash site as soon as

possible. There are probably choppers on the way to our position right now. Turn off the encrypted cell phone we gave you. We don't want Naing getting a ping on our location."

"I thought you said you could still track a phone even when it's off."

"That's using the IEMI number. No one outside of Cobra has that information for these phones. But any cell tower or stinger set-up can get a ping off a phone that's turned on. Shields will still be able to follow us. We take what we need from the helicopter and get moving."

She seemed to get ahold of herself, fishing the phone out of her handbag and shutting it down. "What can I do?"

He climbed up on the crumpled boom, opened the baggage compartment, and tossed down a first aid kit and Hatch and Davis' luggage. "Search their bags. Put anything that might help us survive in your handbag, but remember, you'll be carrying it all the way to the border."

With that to keep her busy, he climbed back into the bird, opened the rear storage compartment, and took out what they needed. A backpack with a first aid kit and a jungle survival kit. Emergency rations and water. A K-Bar knife rig for his ankle. An M4 rifle with a BE Meyers MAWL infrared laser scope and six loaded thirty-round magazines. Extra ammo for the rifle and for his Glocks.

After that, he checked the corpses again. One had a lighter in his pocket that might come in handy. Both had water and energy bars. He stripped both men of their IDs so that Shields could have a go at them. He located his radio near the co-pilot's feet, but it was smashed, useless. Well, they were out of range anyway.

He jumped down, found Shanti sorting through the

contents of Hatch and Davis' bags, tears on her face. He should have known that would be a hard job for her.

"This one had a photo of his wife and kids." She slid it into her handbag. "His malaria pills are here, too. Mine were in my luggage, which never made it on board. I hope there's enough for us both."

"Good call. If he's got rain gear, bring that, too. Can I have one of those Advil?"

She dug around in her massive handbag, opened a small bottle, put a yellow pill in his hand. "Your head hurts, doesn't it?"

"Yeah." He popped the pill, took a drink. "When Naing's men come down on us, and they will, they're going to try to kill me to get to you. They'll try to take you alive. He wants to know what you know and—"

From behind him came a strange, low grunt.

Crunch!

The helicopter shuddered.

He turned, dropped to one knee, weapon raised, to see a massive black bull with curved horns. The animal was pissed off, its body rippling with muscle.

"It's a wild gaur," Shanti said softly. "He must think the helicopter is an intruder. My father told me they're not usually aggressive toward people."

The enormous animal didn't seem to notice them but rammed the nose of the chopper once more.

Crunch!

"Shit." Connor lowered his weapon, shouldered the backpack, and checked the M4. "Let's get out of here. Leave the phone."

11

S hanti repeated what he'd said, sure she'd misunderstood. "Leave the phone?"

"As long as we've got it, they're going to be able to find us. Keep the encrypted cell you got from Cobra. Shields can use it to ping your location."

She unzipped an inner pocket in her bulging handbag, drew out the soldier's phone. "Bram told me to hold onto this."

"Bram didn't know you were going to be abducted and crash in the jungle. This is about our survival now. Better an angry boss than ending up dead."

Shanti dropped the phone. "I'm ready."

Behind them, the guar bellowed again.

Crunch!

Connor checked the compass from the survival kit and pointed northwest. "The pilot took us about a hundred fifty miles inland, heading southeast. Bangladesh is roughly a seven-day walk in that direction."

Seven *days*?

Shanti followed him, glad she'd worn pants and boots

and not a skirt and heels. Then she remembered all the things her father had told her about the monsoon forests. Her gaze jerked to the forest floor, looking for any sign of snakes.

Connor looked back at her. "You walking on eggshells? We need to go faster."

"There are so many poisonous snakes here—cobras, kraits, vipers on the ground, vipers in the trees. There are tarantulas, too."

"I would worry about the creepy things that carry guns, not the ones with fangs. Just watch where you step. We need to put a lot of miles between us and the crash site before nightfall. This area will be crawling with soldiers soon."

Rifle in his hands, he set a brisk pace, leading Shanti uphill and down, through muddy gullies and over streams. She did her best not to slow him, sweat pouring down her face, gibbons and other monkeys chattering in the trees around them, the air thick, humid, and buzzing with insects. She was grateful for the bug repellent she'd brought with her—and for every hour she'd spent on the elliptical trainer at the gym. Still, her thighs burned, her lungs hurting for breath as they made their way through underbrush and up a steep hillside.

Connor stopped, cocked his head as if listening. "Hear that?"

"Monkeys?" She tried to catch her breath.

"Choppers, flying in from the south, heading to the crash site. Keep moving."

"Won't they know where we're going?"

"They'll know we're headed generally toward Bangladesh, but that's it. The farther we get from the crash site, the tougher it is for them to find us."

Onward they went, Connor leading the way, reminding

her to go easy on the water, helping her up steep pitches thick with vines, his gaze always searching their surroundings, his confidence keeping her panic at bay. The handbag on her shoulder seemed to grow heavier with every step, the strap pinching her skin.

The sky was thick with clouds when he stopped. "Let's take a quick break."

She sat on a rock—and shot to her feet again, remembering she needed to check for snakes and spiders. Seeing nothing, she sat, took out her water, and drank. How the small amount of water they had was supposed to last seven days, she didn't know.

He unzipped a pocket on his backpack and drew out a phone with a small antenna. "It's O'Neal. Did you find Hatch and Davis? God, I'm sorry to hear it. Nah, I'm fine. Got creased on the temple. It knocked me out cold for an hour. She's unhurt, just shaken up. They're dead. We've got five MREs plus the water we can carry. I've got the M4 from the bird, two Glocks, a Hi-Power, and a Norinco."

He listened now, saying, "copy that" or "good copy" every so often.

"I'll check in after we make camp," he said at last.

He ended the call. "Cruz and Jones are uninjured. Shields got drone footage of the abduction. They found Hatch and Davis dead in a hangar at the airport. Right now, the ICC, UN, and US government are putting pressure on Myanmar to allow a search-and-rescue operation. So far, the government of Myanmar has not responded."

"If there's footage, they can't say I'm here as a spy."

"They can say whatever they want, but the world can prove them wrong." He helped her to her feet again. "We're going to keep pushing till dusk and take cover. Shields is using our GPS coordinates and drone footage to guide us. She wants us to veer a little more to the north."

"The drone is still following us?"

Connor shook his head. "They had to recall it before the Myanmar military discovered it had entered their air space, but she saved the footage of the landscape beneath our flight path. They've been following our cell signals since we left the crash site. They're also monitoring Myanmar's air space and military coms. Hopefully, they'll be able to warn us if search helicopters head our way."

Shanti asked him the question plaguing her since they set out. "Do we truly stand any chance of making it back alive?"

He brushed a strand of hair off her cheek, his gaze going soft. "I'll get you home, princess. I promise."

IT WAS GETTING close to dusk with a light rain falling when Connor came across a footpath. Because it headed generally in their direction—and because the terrain would be easier for Shanti—he followed it, Shanti a few steps behind.

He had to give her credit. She hadn't complained about the pace or the insects or being thirsty or hungry, though he could see she was uncomfortable. He didn't think she'd spent much time in her life roughing it, and this was about as rough as it got.

He wished to hell he had a drone overhead and Shields' voice in his ear telling him what lay ahead. He'd gotten used to that and felt blind without it. A good pair of infrared goggles would have come in handy, too. He'd suggest that to Corbray and Tower at the debriefing—if he made it back.

He glanced back, saw that Shanti was breathing hard

and sagging under the weight of her handbag. "I'll take that for a while."

"I can carry it."

"I know you can, but let me give you a break. I've been trained to do this sort of forced march. You haven't."

She lifted it over her head, her T-shirt shifting to reveal a red mark on her shoulder. "Thanks."

The damned thing probably weighed thirty pounds.

He put the strap over his shoulder. "Look for a good campsite, someplace with good tree cover but not too much undergrowth. I don't want to be walking in the dark, not with predators on the prowl."

"Sounds good." She smiled, clearly trying not to laugh. It was the first smile he'd seen on her face in hours—a sign that she was bouncing back. "I'm not sure that handbag goes with the rest of your look."

He glanced down at himself. "Are you kidding? This is what all the operatives are wearing this season."

Shanti laughed. "Trendsetter."

They set off again.

She seemed to have an easier time keeping up now. "How far do you think we've come today?"

"I doubt we managed more than twenty miles, but it was hilly terrain."

They kept moving, the sun getting lower on the horizon, the forest thick and dark on both sides of the path. More than once, he'd been sure he heard helicopters, but they seemed to be far to the south. Then up ahead, he saw it— the roof of what appeared to be a tree house or a lookout tower.

He took Shanti's hand, pulled her off the path and into the cover of the forest. "There's something up ahead—a tower of some kind. I'm going to do a little recon. I don't want to make camp too near a village. If anyone sees us..."

She nodded.

"Stay here, no matter what." He handed her the sat phone. "If you hear gunfire and I don't return, use this to contact Cobra. You'll need to be clear of tree cover and other obstacles. They'll guide you. Head northwest."

"Please be careful." She stared at him through wide eyes, the thought of facing this alone clearly frightening for her.

It scared him, too, the idea of her being out here by herself putting a knot in his chest. He couldn't let that happen. She was strong, but she wasn't prepared for this.

"I will." He ducked down, kissed her, startling them both. "Stay hidden."

He made his way carefully through the darkening forest, rifle at the ready, rain lashing his skin as he moved toward the tree house. There was no sign of people—no chickens clucking, no smell of wood smoke or food, no voices.

Up ahead, the forest opened into a clearing, and he saw a half dozen of them—structures built high in large trees. He waited, looked through the infrared scope, but saw no one. Moving closer, he spotted a wooden sign. Some of the writing looked like it was in Burmese, but there was also English.

Welcome to Adventure Trek Camp

A camp? Seriously?

In the center of the camp was a well with an old-fashioned iron pump. He didn't know how clean the water was, but he could deal with that.

He moved to the nearest tree house and climbed the ladder. There was no lock on the door, so he looked inside, the place empty apart from several tarantulas. There was a mattress in the middle of the bamboo floor, mosquito netting around it.

Hell, yeah.

He climbed down again, cleared the next one and the next. The place was deserted, probably because it was monsoon season.

Who wanted to hike through Myanmar in mud and pouring rain?

Feeling like he had stumbled on a Hilton Hotel, he made his way back to Shanti, who sat huddled in the shelter of a large tree looking entirely out of place, exhausted and miserable. "What if I told you that you could sleep in a bed tonight and give yourself a sponge bath?"

"Really?"

"There's a deserted camp ahead. What I thought was some kind of lookout tower is a tree house used by hikers. No one's there now, probably because it's the off-season. There's shelter, and there's a well. We'll have to treat the water to be safe, but we can refill our empty bottles."

Shanti's face lit up like it was Christmas.

SHANTI FOLLOWED Connor into a little village of empty tree houses, found herself smiling. "I would have loved one of these as a kid."

"I've been in all of them. This one is in the best shape with no leaks in the roof." He turned back to her. "You stay down here while I clear it out."

"Clear it out?"

"Some ... wildlife has moved in."

"I don't think I want to know what you mean by that."

He grinned. "You don't."

He climbed the ladder, pack on his back, opened the door, and disappeared inside. One of the windows opened, and something fell to the ground with a *plop*.

She didn't look to see what it was.

Another *plop* and another and another.

A few minutes went by, followed by yet another *plop*.

He opened the door. "Come on up."

She climbed the bamboo ladder, feeling creeped out but also desperate for rest. It was a tall ladder but very sturdy, rising maybe forty feet above the forest floor, taking her to a landing or balcony of sorts.

She walked through the door—and almost sighed. The room was dark, but dry and clean, four shuttered openings in the walls letting in what was left of the daylight. A low, wooden table sat along one wall, a kerosene lamp at its center, while a full-sized mattress sat on a low platform against the other wall, surrounded by a canopy of mosquito netting. Compared to sleeping on the forest floor...

Well, there was no comparison.

Connor was busy cutting a space blanket with a knife. "I'm going to cover the windows to block light and keep out mosquitoes. We'll be able to use my flashlight and that lantern. There's a little kerosene left."

He pulled a roll of duct tape out of his pack and taped a generous square of silver fabric, the dark side facing outward, to each window. Then he took some matches and lighted the lamp.

A warm glow filled the space.

Shanti's stomach growled.

Connor turned to face her. "Our priorities are water, treating any injuries or blisters, food, and sleep. We need to be out of here by daybreak. I'm going to draw water from the well and filter it so we can refill our bottles and wash up."

"What should I do?"

"Check yourself for blisters, cuts, and scrapes. Try to get your feet dry. You don't want an infection."

Shanti took off her shoes and checked her feet. They were sore, but there were no blisters. She had a scratch on her right shin. Her handbag had rubbed a spot raw on her right shoulder, but the skin wasn't broken or blistered.

Connor returned carrying a tin bucket full of water. "It looks clean, but I'm not taking any chances."

He took a filter out of his backpack, and Shanti helped him run the water through it and pour it into their water bottles, then treated each with a Steripen to kill anything the filter missed. "You did well today. I know you weren't ready for this, but you didn't give up, and you didn't complain."

Sitting close to him like that, she could smell the salt and sweat of his skin—an appealing masculine smell. "You saved my life."

"You might well have saved mine." He stood. "I'm going for more water."

"For washing?"

"I need to clean this damned graze on my head."

CONNOR SAT STILL and tried not to swear while Shanti cleaned his wound with sterilized water and antiseptic, her hands in sterile gloves. "Don't worry about hurting me. It's going to hurt no matter what. The important thing is to make sure it's clean."

"If this had been even a millimeter more to the left..."

"Don't think about what didn't happen." Connor watched her face as she worked, her concern warming him. Most of his relationships with women had been about sex and nothing more. It felt good to have a woman *care* about him.

She's your client, and this isn't a relationship.

Right.

He gritted his teeth against the burn of the antiseptic. He had already looked at it with the signal mirror from the jungle survival kit. "You'll need to suture it."

Her eyes went wide. "I don't know how to do that."

"I'll talk you through it."

He got out the suture kit, handed her the instructions, and explained how it worked. "Just do your best. It doesn't have to be pretty. The main thing is to close the skin to prevent infection."

"I don't want to hurt you."

"There's no way around that, princess."

She seemed to steel herself, a look of hard determination coming over her face as she took hold of his skin with the forceps and ran the needle through it.

Connor sucked in a breath.

"I'm so sorry."

"Don't be. You're doing what needs to be done. I appreciate that."

She ran the needle through to the skin on the other side, pulled the skin tight, then knotted the thread several times before snipping it. "That's one."

"Good work."

As injuries went, this wasn't the worst wound he'd received or the most painful. Sitting close to Shanti like this, having her take care of him, almost made it worthwhile.

You're an idiot.

God, she was beautiful—beautiful, smart, brave. He'd worked with hundreds of Cobra clients over the past few years, and few of them could have handled what happened today the way she had.

The fact that she'd been willing to kill to save his life...

It didn't matter to him that she probably wouldn't have been able to do it. The fact that she'd resolved to try moved him.

"Two," she said. "Why do you call me that?"

"Call you what?" Endorphins and pheromones were making it hard to think.

"Princess."

"I don't know. It just fits." It was then that his mouth took off and started saying things without his brain's permission. "The first time I saw you in a sari, I thought you looked like a princess. You were so beautiful. You blew me away."

She stopped stitching, her eyes looking into his. "Really?"

"Yeah." If she hadn't had a needle in his scalp, he might have kissed her. "When you met with Dr. Khan, you had all the dignity of royalty."

She went back to work. "I was nervous."

"It didn't show."

"Three." She started the fourth suture. "So, you like women in saris?"

"I don't know about women, but I sure as hell like *you* in a sari."

Her lips curved in a smile. "I'll remember that if we make it back to The Hague."

He caught her wrist. "Not if, Shanti. *When*."

It took a dozen stitches before Shanti had finished. She bandaged the wound and sat back, looking relieved. "I hope I never have to do that again."

He felt the stitches through the bandage. "You did a good job."

After that, he gathered together all of their food supplies —the emergency rations in his backpack, the stuff he'd taken off the pilots, the snack bars, and the almonds Shanti had in her handbag. "It's going to be a hungry seven days."

Each MRE had 1,250 calories. That meant they'd be getting about six hundred calories each per day—barely enough to keep going.

He split the spaghetti and beef sauce entree from one of the five MREs with her but saved the rest of the meal—chocolate chip toaster pastry, peanut butter, breadsticks, raisins, grape jelly, and Accessory Packet B, which turned out to be Skittles—for later.

"This is what you eat when you're deployed?"

"Only when I have no choice."

She licked her plastic spork. "It's not too bad."

He couldn't help but laugh. "You must be very hungry."

After they'd finished their meal, he went down for another bucket of water, which he treated and then set aside to cool while he reorganized his gear.

"Use this for a quick sponge bath. Save some for me if you can. I'm going out to walk the perimeter. I'll be back in ten."

He checked his weapons, put on his rain gear, and went out in the downpour, leaving her to her bath.

12

S hanti undressed, laid her clothes across the mattress, and went to work cleaning the cut on her shin. It was a little deeper than she'd thought and needed antiseptic and a bandage from the first aid kit. When that was done, she knelt naked by the bucket of cold water, took a bar of soap and a large gauze pad, also from the first aid kit, and dipped both into the water. She washed her face first and then her throat and nape, working her way down her body, washing away sweat and stress.

Oh, the water felt good, bringing her back to herself after a day so terrifying and strange that it didn't seem real. She'd been abducted, watched Connor get shot, held a gun, seen Connor kill two men, lived through a helicopter crash, seen an angry wild gaur, and walked twenty miles through the monsoon forest. And now, she was sleeping in a tree house—as one apparently did in these situations.

You'd be in General Naing's hands—or dead—if not for Connor.

She remembered the fury on his face when he'd forced the pilot to turn around, a kind of feral anger she'd never seen. Before today, that kind of rage might have terrified her, but today it had made her feel safer. He'd done what he'd done to save her life and his. He had killed two men—and she was grateful.

She abhorred violence. And yet...

Did that make her a hypocrite?

For good people like you to build a better world, Shanti, there have to be people like me willing to back you up with force. Otherwise, the bad guys win.

What if he was right? What if justice and freedom and all the things she loved depended on some level of violence to secure them?

She poured a little of the water into an empty water bottle to rinse her skin and wash between her thighs, letting the water spill to the floor. Thank God she wasn't on her period. *That* would be a drag to manage in the jungle.

She filled the bottle again, this time pouring it over her head, working the water through her hair. She didn't have shampoo, so that would have to do. She found her comb, crawled inside the mosquito netting, and sat on the bed. She had just started combing the tangles from her hair, when the door opened and Connor stepped inside.

She dropped the comb, covered her bare breasts. "Is it ten minutes already?"

He said nothing but barred the door behind him, his gaze sliding over her, water dripping off his camo-pattern rain gear and onto the wooden floor.

Embarrassed to have gone over her time, she tried to explain. "I cleaned a cut on my leg. I guess I took too long. Sorry. I was just combing my hair. I'll get dressed and—"

"Let me help."

Her pulse quickened.

He took off his rain gear and his boots and socks

and slipped inside the mosquito netting to sit behind her, his weight making the mattress shift. "Give me your comb."

His voice was deep and soft like it had been the night he'd kissed her.

Had that been just last night?

How her life had changed in twenty-four hours.

She handed him the comb, one arm still covering her breasts, her nipples drawing tight at the memory of what it had felt like to kiss him.

He caught the damp mass of her hair, drew it over her shoulder so that it hung down her back, his fingers grazing her nape, the accidental touch sending shivers down her spine. "I love your hair."

"I didn't have shampoo." *That was a stupid thing to say!*

"Doesn't matter. It's still beautiful—like black silk." He took the comb and slowly worked from the ends, taking care not to pull her hair.

He sat so close that she could feel his body heat, so close that she could smell the salt of his skin and the scent of rain that clung to him.

He set the comb on the mattress beside her, his big hands sliding up her arms to cup her shoulders, his touch making her shiver. "God, you're beautiful."

Other men had said that, but it hadn't affected her the way it did now.

She tilted her head to the side in invitation, hoping against hope that he would forget the rules for just a moment and kiss her. Yes, he was still her bodyguard, but the situation was different now, wasn't it?

The first tentative touch of his lips against her skin made her gasp, her heart racing, tingles spreading along her nape. "*Yes.*"

His hands moved to cup her breasts, felt their weight, gave them a gentle squeeze.

She leaned back against the hard wall of his chest, arched to press herself deeper into his hands, heat flooding her belly as he circled her already puckered nipples with his thumbs. He took his time, rubbing the aching tips with callused palms, rolling them between his finger and thumb, plucking them with his fingertips, lavishing them with attention until she was wet and aching.

She decided to take a chance. "I want you, Connor."

"I haven't cleaned up yet."

"I'll help."

"Are you sure?"

She took one of his hands, pressed it against her racing heart. "I know you said you'd kiss me again when we got to The Hague and this was over, but I don't know that we're going to make it. I don't want to wait. I want you *now*."

SHANTI'S WORDS washed over Connor, desire punching him in the solar plexus. In terms of excuses to fuck, fear of imminent death was a pretty good one. He knew he was treading on thin ice, knew it could cost him his job, but he couldn't seem to care. He'd promised to get her back home alive, and he intended to keep that promise. Still, he'd spent his entire adult life in conflict zones and watched more than a few good men die. Not every story had a happy ending. If he was going to die out here, he would take something of Shanti with him.

Carpe fucking Diem.

He moved outside of the mosquito netting and made quick work of getting naked, unable to take his gaze off her

—those perfect breasts with their dark brown nipples, her rounded hips, her smooth brown skin, the gentle curve of her belly. His cock was already hard, impatient for her, but he was not going to rush this.

She looked him over, and he could tell that she liked what she saw, her gaze lingering on his erection in a way that made him harder. She reached for the bucket, a clean square of gauze, and a little bar of soap, and got on her knees.

He ducked beneath the mosquito netting, knelt before her, offering himself to her. She dipped the cloth in the water and then washed his face, careful not to hurt the wound on his temple. She moved onto his neck, then his shoulders and his arms, squeezing his biceps as if testing his strength. When she reached his chest, she seemed to forget what she was doing, her hands exploring his pecs, her fingers threading through his chest hair, her thumbs teasing his nipples, making his abs jerk tight.

It was the sexiest sponge bath he'd ever had—if not the most efficient.

"You having fun?"

"I've never met a man like you."

"You've got that right." He took the gauze from her, let her play with his body while he finished washing.

When he had finished, he drew her down to the bed, his mouth claiming hers. The two of them rolled together, locked in a scorching kiss, their legs tangling, her breasts pressing against his ribs, her hands sliding down his back to squeeze his ass. She felt so good in his arms, all fire and silk.

He broke the kiss, tasted the skin of her throat, her scent intoxicating, her pulse beating hard and fast against his lips. But he needed more of her.

He pressed kisses to her collarbone, the divot at the base

of her throat, her breastbone, her heartbeat frantic against his lips. Then he cupped one lush breast, took its pebbled nipple into his mouth, and sucked.

She drew in a quick breath and moaned, her back arching, her fingers sliding into his hair. "Oh, *yes*."

He went from one sweet nipple to the other and back again, sucking them to tight, swollen peaks, unable to get enough, Shanti twisting beneath him, her hips sending a message his body couldn't ignore.

He slid one hand down the soft skin of her belly, nudged her thighs apart with his knee, then cupped her, dark curls beneath his palm, her clit already swollen.

He explored her, moaned. "You are so wet."

She bent her knees, let them fall open. "I want you inside me."

That's when it hit Connor—he didn't have a condom.

Maybe she had it covered. "Are you on the pill?"

She shook her head, looking adorably miserable. "I don't suppose that fancy survival kit comes with condoms?"

He shook his head. "*Shit.*"

Need for her burned in him.

"Can you just pull out? I know it's not the safest way, but..."

His heart gave a hard thud, some part of him stunned that she trusted him so completely. "Are you sure? I'll do my best, but it's risky."

"After today, I'm willing to take a few risks."

Hell, he couldn't blame her for that.

But Connor hadn't had unprotected sex since he was a teenager. It went against his personal code. If Shanti had been any other woman, there's no way he would even have considered it. But she wasn't like any of them.

He slid a finger inside her, got it good and wet, then stroked her clit. "Tell me what feels good."

She reached down, adjusting the pressure, showing him just how she liked it, her nails biting into his skin when he got it right. "Just ... like ... *that*."

God, she was a wet dream, a fantasy come to life—beautiful, responsive, sexy as fuck. He wanted to make her come. He wanted to make her scream. He wanted to give her all the pleasure she could take.

Her eyes were closed now, her brow furrowed, her lips parted, every exhale a little whimper. One of her hands had come to rest on his shoulder, her nails digging into his skin. "Inside ... me ... *please*."

He slid two fingers into her and went for her G-spot, fucking her with his fingers, his thumb now busy with her clit. Shanti moaned, her head rolling on her pillow, dark hair spilling across her face. He could tell she was close, so close, her whimpers spurring him on. He lowered his mouth to a dusky nipple once again and suckled.

She came with a cry, bliss shining on her face, her inner muscles clenching hard around his fingers, making him ache to have his cock inside her.

He kept up the rhythm, waited until her orgasm had passed, then settled himself between her parted thighs, holding himself above her so he could see her face.

She opened her eyes, gave him a sexy smile that he felt all the way to his balls.

His gaze locked with hers. "Are you sure you want this?"

She slid her hands up his chest. "God, yes."

∾

STILL FLOATING from one of the most intense orgasms of her

life, Shanti watched Connor's face as he entered her with a single, slow thrust, his expression one of pleasure mingled with sexual need. She couldn't help but moan as he filled her, stretched her, buried himself inside her, his cock thick and hard.

"God, you're tight." He held himself still inside her, kissed her, gave her a moment to get used to him, his blue eyes dark. "It's been a long time since I've done this without a condom. I forgot how incredible it feels."

She let her hands explore him, some feminine part of her thrilled by the rock-hard feel of him. "Your body is so different from mine."

He chuckled. "Thank God for that."

He began to move, slowly at first, taking his time.

Oh, it felt good—that slow stroke, that deep stretch. Then again, just watching him as he rocked into her turned her on, the muscles of his belly contracting, his biceps and shoulders tense from holding himself above her.

He picked up the pace, thrusting harder, faster.

Excitement shimmered through her to see the effect she had on him. In the short time she'd known him, he'd always been in control of himself, even on the helicopter, his rage just a tool. But she could see his control fraying a little more with each thrust.

His breathing was faster now, his lips parted, his muscles tight, sweat beading on his chest. Then he stopped, opened his eyes, an expression like pain on his face. "God, Shanti, you feel *so* good."

Then he drew a deep, slow breath, as if willing his body to relax, his control returning. He adjusted his hips, levering himself upward. When he thrust again, the base of his cock grazed her clit, the sweet shock of it making her gasp.

"Oh, what are you ...?"

"I want this to be good for you, too."

She'd never had multiple orgasms before, but she didn't tell him that, mostly because she couldn't think. She held onto his shoulders, the tension inside her building once more, thrust upon thrust, until *she* was the one about to lose control, her body hovering on the shimmering crest of a second climax. "*Connor.*"

Pleasure washed through her, pure and golden. He stayed with her, keeping up the rhythm until the last ripples of bliss had passed. Then he shifted his hips once again and thrust himself into her, driving deep and hard and fast, his body drawing tight.

He pulled out with a groan, Shanti reaching down to finish him, his cock jerking in her hand as he came on her belly. He collapsed onto one elbow beside her, breathing hard, his chest glistening with sweat. "Holy fuck."

He wiped her clean with the gauze she'd use for her bath, then stretched out on the bed beside her and took her into his arms, the way he looked at her making her feel like the only woman in the world.

"I've never done that before," she managed to say, exhaustion overtaking her.

"Neither have I." He had to be insane to try the withdrawal method.

"No, I mean I've never come twice like that."

He raised his head, looked down at her. "Seriously?"

"Seriously."

"Then it's about damned time." He kissed her hair. "I hate to ruin the mood, but we should get dressed. We do *not* want to get caught with our pants off."

She moaned in protest, snuggled closer to him. "I like you naked."

"I like you..." His head came up, his expression grim. "Did you hear that?"

"Hear what?" The rain had stopped, but she didn't hear anything.

In a blink, he was on his feet, weapon in hand.

Adrenaline brought her wide awake.

He walked over to the table and put out the lamp, leaving her to grope in the darkness for her clothes.

Had Naing's men caught up with them? If they had, how were she and Connor going to get down from the tree house without being seen?

"I'd give my left nut right now for night vision goggles," Connor said softly, his voice coming from near the door. "Stay down."

And then she heard it—a strange guttural sound, deep and sonorous.

That wasn't soldiers.

Connor opened the door, a sliver of moonlight spilling over him to show that he had his weapon raised. He glanced outside—and grinned. "Holy shit."

"What?"

"Elephants."

Shanti hurried over to him. "Wow!"

There were seven elephants. They strolled through the camp, not seeming to notice Connor and Shanti.

"It's a group of males."

"How can you tell?"

Connor pointed, a grin on his face.

"Oh! Good grief."

"I've always wanted to see elephants in the wild."

"All you had to do was sign up for the Jungle Abduction Tour. Don't you wish you'd brought your camera?"

13

Connor woke early the next morning, Shanti in his arms. For a moment, he watched her sleep, a strange tenderness filling his chest. He could still smell her on his skin, still taste her on his tongue, still hear the cry she'd made when she'd come.

He ought to be angry with himself. He'd had unprotected sex with a client, who was depending on him for her survival. He'd broken all the rules, done things he'd never imagined he'd do. Still, he couldn't bring himself to regret it.

Since Mandy, sex had been little more than a transaction. Buy a pretty woman a few drinks, go back to her place, trade orgasms, toss the condom in the trash, drive home, take a shower. No drama. No strings. No risk.

But last night had been different. Was it because he'd gotten to know her a little before getting naked with her? Was it because he respected her? Was it because he hadn't worn a condom?

Maybe there was something about her—her sense of justice, her mind, the way she made him feel bigger than life when she looked at him, trust in those beautiful eyes.

Hell, he didn't know.

He'd come in from the rain to find her naked, and nothing in the world could have dragged him away from her. She'd been responsive, soft, passionate. Even as he told himself he shouldn't risk having sex with her again, he knew he would.

He hated to wake her. She looked so at peace in her sleep, dark lashes on her cheeks, lips slightly parted, face relaxed. The world she would wake to wasn't peaceful at all, but the sun would be up soon.

He rolled onto his side, kissed her. "Wake up, princess."

She moaned, snuggled against him—then sat bolt upright. "Are they here?"

"No, it's okay. But it's time to get up and get moving."

They were already dressed apart from footwear, so he went straight to breakfast, taking out what remained of last night's MRE and mixing up some cold cocoa to go with their chocolate chip toaster pastry and Skittles.

She braided her hair and put on her socks and boots. "Everything is still wet."

"That's monsoon season in the jungle."

She sat beside him, sipped her cold cocoa, and ate her half of the pastry and Skittles. "This would have been my dream breakfast—back when I was in kindergarten."

Connor tried to imagine a little version of Shanti and found himself smiling. "I wanted chocolate chip pancakes."

"Chocolate chip pancakes?"

"That's what my mom made us for birthdays and on holidays—Christmas, Easter morning, the Fourth of July."

"My dad always made us waffles for Christmas morning. He thinks they're cool—all those little syrup pockets."

This surprised Connor. "He celebrates Christmas?"

"My father is a secular Hindu. He and my mother taught

me to respect all religions as expressions of culture and the human struggle to find meaning in life. We went to Hindu festivals, ate a mix of Bengali and American food, celebrated Christmas and Halloween and Easter."

"For us, it was church every Sunday. It never made sense to me, and I've seen too much shit since then to change my mind."

"I'm sorry."

"Don't be. I'm where I'm meant to be. I'm able to do a job most people can't."

It wasn't an exaggeration. Only about ten percent of the soldiers who tried out made it through the training and selection process to become an operator.

Finished with her breakfast, she took out the bottle of malaria pills she'd taken from Hatch's luggage, handed Connor one, and took one for herself. "There's enough for the two of us for nine days."

"We won't be here that long." Not if he had anything to say about it.

While she packed their gear, Connor went down the ladder for a quick recon and to check in with HQ.

It was Tower who answered. "I need a sitrep."

"We're good. Clear skies this morning, which means we need to keep under cover and move fast."

"They mobilized troops from an army base about sixty klicks east of you, so they'll be on the ground and in the air today. It looks like they've set up a perimeter forty miles west and northwest of the crash site. You're going to have to get through that. Also, the area you're heading into was the site of the Arakan Campaign in the last world war. You'll need to watch for unexploded ordinance and other hazards."

"Copy that."

"You should know that Myanmar has accused the US of sending operatives into the country to interfere with their government. They're not going to cooperate. Everyone you meet will think you're the enemy, so avoid locals. You've got a major river coming up. They're going to use that as a choke point. There are only three bridges that cross it, and you can expect those to be under guard."

Shit.

"Is the river swimmable?"

"You'll have to judge that for yourself. You've got rain forecast for the afternoon. We're working on some possibilities for an exfil, but nothing has come together yet."

In other words, they were still on their own.

"Stay sharp, O'Neal. I don't want to lose anyone else."

"Roger that."

Connor climbed back up the ladder, found her ready to go. He shared what Tower had told him and knew the news must be overwhelming for her. "If you feel like you're getting a blister or you start feeling sick or dehydrated, I need to know. Otherwise, we stick to the tree cover and move fast."

There was fear on her face but also determination. "Got it."

He drew her into his arms. "I'm sorry, Shanti. I'll do my best to get you home."

"I know you will." There was that trust again—pure and complete. "Just don't do anything stupid and heroic."

"Okay." He grinned, ran a thumb over her cheek.

And because he couldn't stop himself, he kissed her. "Let's go."

SHANTI FOLLOWED Connor through a dense forest of teak

and bamboo, the terrain getting steeper, the air stifling. Helicopters flew in a grid pattern to the south, their rotors buzzing like giant insects, the ghostly howls of gibbons, manic chatter of macaques, and the calls of birds filling the air.

Connor set a punishing pace, moving quickly up the mountainside, his gaze searching the landscape around them for danger. While he was clearly in his element, she struggled along behind him, sweaty, hungry, and thirsty. She didn't want to hold him back—or be the reason they didn't make it back alive.

Six more days.

The thought overwhelmed her—until she reminded herself how lucky she was to be alive and free right now.

She could do this. She had no choice but to do this.

Her stomach growled, her junk-food breakfast long since digested. She'd heard him say he had five of those MREs. Spread over seven days, that meant one half of an MRE each per day. Those extra ten pounds she never seemed to lose were history.

It's the Run-for-Your-Life Diet.

Gnarled tree roots, liana vines, and ferns tried to trip her, while mosquitoes buzzed in the shadows. If she hadn't been wearing mosquito repellent and the long-sleeved jacket Connor had loaned her, they would probably have eaten her alive by now.

Something slithered past her foot, making her jump.

A lizard.

Connor glanced back, stopped. "You okay?"

She nodded, kept going until she reached him, then stopped and tried to catch her breath. "A lizard. I thought it was a snake."

"Let's take a quick break."

Shanti wanted to sink to the ground but thought the better of it. She took her water bottle out of her handbag—the damned thing weighed a ton—and took a few sips, mindful of the need to make it last.

"Stay here for a minute and rest. I'm going to hike up to the top of this ridge and see what's on the other side."

She wouldn't argue with that. "Okay."

He moved up the mountainside with long strides, rifle in his hands, disappearing from view among the trees.

It was the first real break she'd gotten since they'd left the camp this morning and it gave her time to think—about last night, about the way he'd made her feel and how he'd held her afterward. He was her fantasy lover come to life, the first man to make her come twice. She couldn't help but feel connected to him.

Even so, she knew this wouldn't last. Once they got back to The Hague, he would have his job, and she would have hers. They didn't live in the same hemisphere, let alone the same country. That's why she would gladly take whatever he gave her now and sort the rest of it out later. Of course, they had to survive first.

She glanced around, spotted a little creature that looked like a cross between a squirrel and a mouse darting through the underbrush. Above her head, orchids bloomed, somehow growing on the bamboo, the air full of the unearthly howls of gibbons. Then one of the branches on the bamboo moved, raised its head.

A green snake.

Shanti stepped back.

Was it a tree viper?

Connor appeared, moving toward her, silent and fast. "There's a village just across a creek—a farming village with just a few houses and fields. There are soldiers. I couldn't see how many. We're going to have to veer to the west to avoid it. Remember that everyone here believes that we're the enemy. We can't be seen. Do you understand?"

Chills skittered down Shanti's spine. "Yes."

"Are you rested?"

"As rested as I'm going to get."

"I know you're hungry. Try to put it out of your mind. When we're past that village, we can each have an energy bar."

An energy bar. It sounded like a feast.

"The helicopters are going to be on top of us soon."

They set out again, making their way to the top of the ridge. Because the trees were thinner there, they moved quickly over and down into dense tree cover again. Going downhill was easier than going up, though rain had left the ground muddy and slick, forcing Shanti to hold onto bamboo stalks and tree branches.

"Careful." Connor took her hand and helped her down a particularly steep and muddy section.

They hadn't yet reached the creek when the sound of a helicopter drew near.

"Time to disappear." Connor took her hand again and drew her deeper into the concealment of the trees and sat. "Get down."

She sat beside him, looking up, the helicopter beating down on them.

He got out his camo-colored rain poncho and threw it over the two of them, then pulled her close. "Relax."

Heart pounding, Shanti closed her eyes, rested her head against his chest, the helicopter almost there.

～

"BREATHE, Shanti. They can't see us."

She exhaled, her face pressed against his chest, and he could feel her fear.

If Connor had been alone, this would be a different situation. He'd been trained to control his fear, to push himself to the limits of his endurance, to go without food for extended periods, to hunt and live off the land if necessary. This wasn't the first time he'd had to put those skills to the test.

But it wasn't just his life on the line now. Shanti had none of his training or experience. She depended entirely on him to get her safely home again. That made him vulnerable in a way he'd never been before.

He didn't blame Shanti. She'd done nothing to put herself in this position. She was doing everything he asked of her, giving it all she had. No, he blamed whatever had gone wrong at the airport and left Hatch and Davis dead.

Now it was up to him to make sure she made it out of here alive.

The helicopter sounded like it was directly overhead now.

"What happens if he *does* see us?"

"He won't." Connor knew she wouldn't be satisfied with that answer. "If he did, he'd relay our location to ground forces, and they would converge here, possibly with dogs, and try to chase us down."

"How will we know?"

"If he thought he saw something, he would hover, stay right on top of us. See? He's already moving off."

She seemed to relax. "What did Tower mean when he said they had created a perimeter?"

"They've tried to guess which direction we went and how far we might have gotten and have saturated the area with soldiers and helicopters in hopes that we'll run into their net." He pressed his lips to her hair. "I'm not going to let that happen."

When the helicopter had gone, they pressed on, soon coming to the little creek. It was maybe ten feet across and less than a foot deep.

Connor was going to help Shanti walk across a fallen log, but she stomped into the flowing water and over to the other side.

"My boots and socks are already wet, and they'll get wetter when it rains. Why waste time crossing the log?"

He found himself grinning. "Now you're thinking like an operator."

They pushed west to avoid the village, twice more taking cover to evade search helicopters. When he was certain they'd made their way safely around the village, they stopped for a quick lunch of energy bars and water and then veered to the northwest.

Clouds were moving in now, settling over the mountains like a blanket, sending the helicopters back to the safety of their landing pads.

"Time to break out the rain gear. It's going to pour."

They hadn't gone another ten minutes when the rain began to fall. The dense tree cover kept some of it off them, but the forest floor beneath their feet grew more slippery, especially on steep terrain. It was a hard slog up one slope and down the next, even for Connor, and it slowed them down.

After an hour of this, he stopped for a break, splitting what was left of last night's MRE—raisins, breadsticks, peanut butter, and grape jelly. "We'll go for a couple more hours until sunset and find a place to camp."

They pressed on, one step after another, uphill and

down. Eventually, the rain let up, and the cloud cover lifted. With the change in weather, the cries of monkeys and the whirring of the helicopters returned.

Shanti glared up at the sky. "Can't they give up and go home?"

"Is General Naing the sort of man who throws in the towel?"

She didn't answer, but it had been a rhetorical question anyway.

They pushed on, twilight settling over the forest.

Connor stopped. "It's time to make camp."

"We should just keep going."

"You're exhausted, Shanti. You need to rest. The jungle's a different world at night. Lots of those things you don't like come out to hunt when the sun goes down."

From somewhere to their north came the well-timed howl of some angry cat—and not the kitty kind.

Shanti's eyes went wide. "Right."

"I'll scout a good site if you want to—"

"No! No. I'll come with you."

After a moment, they came to an area where the forest was pockmarked, small round craters in every direction.

"Shell holes."

"What?"

Connor pointed. "This region of Myanmar was part of the Arakan Campaign in World War Two. The British took on the Japanese here and won."

Shanti reached down and picked something up—a piece of worked stone. "This looks like part of a building."

"Keep your eyes open."

Then, ahead and to his right, he saw a strange vertical tangle of vines.

Rifle still in hand, he approached carefully. "I think I found the building."

The bombed remains of a larger structure stood there, reclaimed by the forest, stairs crumbling, but paint still visible.

Shanti came up behind him. "I think this used to be a *mandir*."

"A what?"

"A Hindu temple."

14

Shanti watched as Connor walked up the stairs with rifle raised, moving with a predator's grace and confidence.

"Clear." He walked back down. "It's definitely a porch, part of what was an entrance. It's not as nice as the tree house, but we're not going to find anyplace better tonight. At least it's dry and off the ground."

She followed Connor up the crumbling stairs. There were stone carvings on the three columns and the wall, but in the dark, they were hard to see.

"Same routine as last night, but we can't spare water for a bath." Connor propped his rifle against one of the surviving columns, the stone pockmarked and weathered. "Check your feet. We're going to have to sleep with our boots on, but try to get your feet dry first. Then we eat."

Shanti sat with her back against what would have been the temple wall, took off her soaking socks and boots, and wiggled her toes. "No blisters—not on my feet anyway. I think the strap from my handbag has rubbed my shoulders raw."

She had switched sides when her right shoulder had become too painful, so now both sides hurt.

Connor took off his boots and socks. "Let me see."

He pulled her shirt aside. "No blisters yet. Let's get something on those."

He pulled out the first aid kit, took squares of moleskin, and fixed them over the raw spots. "I've got room for some of the stuff you're carrying in my backpack. You can use the handbag for water and personal stuff."

"Won't your pack be heavier?"

"It won't be the heaviest pack I've carried—that's for damned sure."

While the first aid kit was out, she checked the wound on his head and replaced the bandage. "It doesn't look infected, but what do I know?"

"Thanks." Connor put the first aid kit away and took out another MRE. "Let's see what's for dinner. Chili with beans and cornbread."

He tore open one of the bags, poured in a little water, and propped it up against his rifle. Then he opened the outer packaging for the chili and stuck the inner packet into the bag with the water. He saw her watching. "It's a chemical reaction. It enables us to cook without fire."

Almost immediately, the spicy scent of chili filled the air, making Shanti's stomach growl and her mouth water. A few minutes later, their dinner was done.

He took out the square of cornbread and handed half of the bread and chili to Shanti, along with another plastic spork. "Try to eat slowly."

Shanti did her best, but she was so hungry. The cornbread was dry, but she didn't care, the small meal taking the edge off her hunger, leaving her so tired she thought she might be able to sleep sitting right where she was.

While she finished, Connor took something out of his pack. It had a green camo pattern like everything else. He shook it out, revealing it to be a … weird sleeping bag?

"It's a bivy sack. You unzip the top, which has a tight fabric mesh, and you sleep inside away from rain and insects. Do whatever you need to do, and then it's bedtime."

Reluctantly, she put on her wet socks and boots again. "If we get through this, I'm going to take the longest bubble bath in the history of the world."

He grinned. "Can I watch?"

"You can get in the tub with me." She walked down the stairs, looking for a little privacy, but the night was dark and full of strange noises.

Connor must have seen her hesitate. "You're fine where you are. I'll take a leak off the edge over here. I promise I won't watch. Tell me when you're done."

"I trust you." When she was finished, she was all but stumbling from exhaustion. She washed her hands with a towelette then scooted, wet boots first, into the bivy sack. "There's room enough for two in here."

She hated the thought of him sleeping exposed.

"We're outside tonight, so I need to be free to move. I'll wake you if I hear anything. Don't worry. I've got a space blanket. This isn't the first time I've spent a night out in the jungle. Bugs don't like the way I taste anyway."

She heard herself say something, the words barely registering with her mind. "Then bugs are stupid."

Connor chuckled, zipped the bag around her head. "Sweet dreams, princess."

Before she could respond, she was sound asleep.

❧

Connor left their shelter, looking for a break in the forest canopy. This was the trouble with trying to hide. Dense vegetation interfered with the satellite signal.

He found a spot about fifty meters away, where he could see stars overhead. "Hey, Tower. She's fine. She's asleep. We found some kind of ruin—part of a temple destroyed in the war. The sky was full of birds searching for us. We had to veer west to get around a small farming village. The rain made it slow going."

"It looks like you put thirty-two miles behind you today. How are the food and water holding up?"

"Not ideal. We need to find another water source soon, and we're splitting one MRE a day. We've got three more."

"The sooner you get out of there, the better. We're working with the Pentagon on some plans to speed this up, but the situation is volatile. Sunrise is at oh-five-twenty-two, so get some rest."

"Copy that."

Connor walked back to their shelter, wrapped himself in a space blanket, and leaned back against one of the columns with his rifle. He quickly fell into a doze, a part of him listening to the sounds around him for anything that could be a threat.

A rustling of leaves brought him awake. He raised the rifle, looked through the infrared scope, and saw what looked like a large, gangly house cat with spots. It saw him —and vanished.

Nearby, Shanti lay in the bivy sack, sound asleep.

Just the thought of her put a hitch in his chest, some nameless longing sliding through him. He wanted ... what?

A lover? Someone waiting at home? Someone to share his life with?

He'd tried that, and he knew how that story ended.

Shanti is nothing like Mandy.

Shanti.

God, he wanted her. He wanted her to be safe. He wanted her to pardon him, to tell him that the boy's death hadn't been his fault.

What the hell is wrong with you?

He needed sleep. That's all.

Or maybe it was the circumstances, being alone with a beautiful woman who was utterly dependent on him to stay alive. Survival situations had a way of making people bond —or so he'd heard. After years of fighting, the Unit had become his family. He was closer to those guys than he was to his brother.

And how many times did you sit in the dark watching your Unit buddies sleep?

That would be never.

He closed his eyes and dozed again, his mind filling with erotic dreams of Shanti, her breasts, her delicious ass, her mouth on his cock.

This time when he woke, his boner was to blame.

He ignored it, eventually drifting into a dreamless sleep.

The pitter-patter of little feet woke him.

For fuck's sake.

An enormous tarantula walked by him, earning a free flight into the forest thanks to the butt of his rifle.

He checked on Shanti. She was still asleep, her breathing deep and even. Then he glanced at his watch.

Roughly an hour till dawn.

He'd gotten a solid three hours of sleep since his dick had woken him.

He raised the rifle, glanced around them, checking for other intruders. Seeing nothing—no movement, no unreasonably huge arachnids, nothing that might find them tasty —he closed his eyes again.

Ratatatat!

Heavy AK fire poured out of a hut at the far end of the destroyed Syrian village, making it impossible for his team to make their exfil. Connor had thought they'd neutralized all of the hostiles when they'd arrived. Then again, fighting ISIS was like a game of asshole whack-a-mole.

"How many hostiles?"

"I'm guessing at least five."

"I've got this, chief," Connor said. "I'll work my way south. Keep them distracted. I'll take them out, clear the house."

"Keep your head down, O'Neal."

"You got it."

Connor crept along the ground, rifle in hand, wind blowing sand into his mouth. It wasn't far—half a city block by US standards—and his buddies were laying down some serious cover fire. Hell, he might not even have to toss a grenade if they kept that up. They might take these guys out before he got there.

He reached the end of the village, took cover behind a low stone wall.

Ratatatat! Ratatatat!

Some bastard was still alive in there, keeping the men pinned down.

Connor pulled a grenade off his belt, checked his aim, pulled the pin—and threw it. "Frag out!"

A small child, a boy of maybe five years old, stepped out of the house, big brown eyes taking in what was left of his village.

God, no!

Why the hell hadn't they known there were children inside?

There was nothing Connor could do.

But then the boy was gone, and Shanti stood in his place.

How the hell had she gotten here?

She smiled at him.

"Run, Shanti!" he shouted for her, motioned frantically, knowing it was too late.

BAM!

The grenade detonated, shrapnel tearing Shanti apart, her blood spilling—

"Connor!"

SHANTI TRIED to wake him from what was obviously a nightmare. "Connor!"

His eyes flew open, anguish on his face. "Shanti?"

He reached for her, searching her as if checking to make sure she was okay.

"I heard you call my name. I thought Naing's men were here, but you were having a bad dream."

"Shit." He nodded. "Sorry."

"Last time, it was me who brought *you* running. I won't keep count if you don't."

He closed his eyes, the nightmare clearly still dragging at him.

"I'm fine, see?" She took his hand, pressed it to her cheek.

He drew a breath, exhaled, glanced at his watch. "It's time to get up anyway—just a few minutes to sunrise."

Shanti stepped away from the *mandir*, needing privacy. When she returned, he had breakfast, such as it was, waiting for her.

"Vegetable crackers, freaky cheese spread, and more Skittles." He handed her a packet labeled *Lemon Lime Beverage Powder, Carb Fortified*. "Mix half of that in one of your bottles of water, give the rest to me. It will help keep you going."

While Shanti ate her breakfast, the monsoon forest came alive around them, birds erupting into song at first light, macaques screeching like drunk soccer fans. She could tell Connor was still upset about the nightmare, the line of his jaw hard. "Did I do something wrong? In your dream, I mean."

He took a bite of cracker, shook his head. "It wasn't really about you."

Elizabeth's words came back to her.

There's no such thing as an uninjured soldier.

"Do you want to talk about it?"

"No."

Well, that was final.

He popped his last cracker in his mouth, walked down the stairs and a short distance away, satellite phone in his hand. "I need to check in."

It was then that a slender ray of light played over one of the columns, revealing the stonework she hadn't been able to see last night.

She laughed, traced her fingers over small sculpted figures of men and women having sex in pretty much every way conceivable. She looked from one to the next, moving from column to column.

She was still looking at the little figures when Connor returned.

"What is it?"

She pointed to an image of two women holding another woman's legs apart while a man penetrated her. "Erotic art."

A dark brow arched. "On a temple?"

"In the Hindu tradition, sex isn't viewed as something

dirty or sinful. It's sacred, like other parts of life. It was Hindus who wrote the Kamasutra, remember?"

"Kamasutra. Right." He leaned in, looked at the carving of a man entering a woman from behind while she took another man's cock into her mouth. "I can't imagine what my folks would say if you put stone porn on their church."

That made Shanti laugh. "It's not porn. It's sacred."

"Okay. Sex is good. I'll buy that."

Shanti leaned in to examine another. A woman stood, one leg around her lover's waist, while he penetrated her. "You'd have to be close to the same height to do that."

"Not necessarily." He gave her a slow, sexy smile. "Want to try?"

A jolt of lust shot through her. "Aren't we running from the bad guys?"

"We can be quick."

That meant no orgasm for her. Still, she'd be lying if she'd said looking at all this erotic art hadn't made her want him.

Take what you can while you're with him. You could end up dead today.

He moved in on her, backed her up against the column, the hard ridge of his erection pressing against her belly, making her womb clench. "The first dream I had last night was about fucking you. I woke up with a hard-on. You were sound asleep."

"I'm wide awake now."

"Is that a 'yes'?"

"Yes."

He unzipped her jeans, slipped a hand inside her panties, moaned. "God, you're already wet."

She might have said something, but he found her clit. Oh, he hadn't forgotten anything he'd learned about her body the other night, sweet strokes making her ache. Soon, she was grinding against his hand, the first glow of orgasm building inside her.

Un-freaking-believable.

Abruptly, he stepped back, jerked off her jeans and panties, and unzipped his fly, letting his erection spring free. Then he grabbed her ass with both hands and lifted her off her feet. "Wrap your leg around my waist."

His voice was gruff, his eyes dark.

She tried to do what she'd seen in the sculpture, wrapping one leg around him while standing on the other, but he was too tall, her left leg dangling. "To hell with it."

She wrapped both legs around him, moaning with pleasure when he thrust himself into her. It felt so good, *so* good, his deep thrusts striking that sensitive place inside her.

She came hard and fast, her cry lost in the noise of the jungle.

Jaw tight, he withdrew, set her on her feet. Shanti knelt before him, finished him with her hand, his head falling back on a moan as he came.

He rocked on his feet, reached out with one arm to steady himself, palm against the column. He leaned in, pressed a kiss to her nose. "You are too much."

"Are you telling me you've never had hot jungle sex before?"

"Apart from you? No. I've only ever been in the jungle with sweaty men, and they're not my type."

"Well, I've never come that fast before."

"Really?" He frowned. "We need to talk about the kind of men you date."

"There haven't been many."

"Good."

"Are you jealous?"

"Why should I be jealous of losers who couldn't make you come?"

Shanti's knees turned to jelly.

He got out the towelettes, helped her clean up and dress. "Time to go. Today is going to be a long day. I'll fill you in along the way."

15

Invigorated by sex, Connor led Shanti northwest, sharing what Shields had told him but leaving out the plans for a possible emergency exfil. He didn't want to get her hopes up only to dash them if the plans fell through.

"How are we going to cross the river if all the bridges are under guard?"

"That's what I have to figure out. If I take out the soldiers on and around the bridge, they'll know pretty quickly where we are and bring everything they have down on us. I need to find another way."

"I can swim."

"Good to know." He wasn't sure anyone could swim this, but he didn't say so.

Shields had said that the river, which cut through a deep gorge, was flowing high and fast now because of the monsoon. Naing was concentrating his army there, using the river as a choke point, knowing that, sooner or later, they would have to cross it if they wanted to make it back to Bangladesh.

Connor set a tough pace, and soon Shanti was breathing

hard. He tried to offer her some encouragement. "We came thirty-two miles yesterday. I want to do the same today, river or no river."

That sounded less like encouragement and more like a command, so he tried again. "You're doing great, Shanti."

They'd been moving at a good clip for about an hour when he once again heard the distant whir of helicopter rotors, this time to the east. "They're far away—for now."

But that didn't last. By the time they stopped to rest just after noon, they'd had to take cover from helicopters twice.

"I thought ... yesterday was hard." Shanti tried to catch her breath, strands of dark hair that had escaped her braid sticking to her sweaty cheeks.

"You know what Navy SEALs say."

She shook her head. "What?"

"'The only easy day was yesterday.' SEALs do like to whine."

That made her smile.

They ate one energy bar each, washed it down with water.

Connor kept his poncho tucked into his belt, as they were likely to need to camouflage themselves again at a moment's notice. "Shields says Naing's army is concentrated along this side of the river. The closer we get, the greater the chance of running into his troops. Keep quiet and pay close attention."

"I understand."

They pushed on, heading northwest, afternoon clouds moving in. They crossed another creek and were headed uphill when Connor heard the sound of rushing water. He followed it west through vines and bamboo canes, hoping it might be a spring or a cleaner source of water than the creek, which was muddy enough to put his filter out of commission.

A little waterfall. It spilled from a height of about twenty feet, joining the creek below, flowers blooming in vines on both sides. The water was cold and clear.

"Perfect."

Shanti caught up with him. "It looks like a postcard."

"We'll stop here, refill our water bottles."

Drinkable water was the first rule of survival.

He took out his filter and collected their empty bottles.

"If this is going to take a while, can I undress and take a shower?"

"If you're quick. It's going to be cold."

She took out the soap, stripped out of her clothes, which she laid out on a rock, and walked, naked and beautiful, past flowering vines to the waterfall.

Something stirred inside Connor at the sight of her, something beyond sexual desire, something more primal.

Shanti was Eve. She was a goddess. She was life itself.

She ought to have been carved in stone and put on a temple—those lush breasts, her slender waist, the flare of her hips. He would have worshipped at that altar.

She stepped into the water, gasping as it spilled over her, her nipples instantly drawing tight. "Oh!"

Connor couldn't take his gaze off her any more than he could quit grinning, the sight both arousing and funny. He'd never seen anyone take such a fast or fumbling shower. It lasted a minute tops, Shanti rubbing the soap over her skin and even in her hair and then letting the waterfall rinse her clean.

She stepped out of the water, arms crossed over her chest to warm her. "I can't believe how cold that was, but, oh, it felt good. You should try it. I dare you."

"You *dare* me?" Okay, he was dumb and male enough to take her up on that. "You take over filtering water when you're dressed again."

He showed her what to do. Then he stripped, grabbed the soap, and walked to the waterfall to show her how he handled a cold shower.

The moment the water hit his skin, he sucked in a breath, stunned, his balls retreating into his abdominal cavity. "Son of a ...!"

Shanti laughed. "Told you so."

CONNOR LED SHANTI THROUGH A RAVINE, climbing over fallen bamboo canes and half-rotted teak logs, careful with every step. He'd already seen a few snakes.

The ground began to rise again, the forest canopy thinning. From somewhere ahead, he heard it—men's voices.

He motioned for Shanti to get down. "Stay here."

She nodded, eyes wide.

He moved silently uphill, dropping to his belly and inching forward as he neared the edge of the forest.

Fuck.

He counted thirty soldiers, some milling around, others manning a roadblock on what must have been a highway. All were heavily armed, mostly with Chinese weapons— Norinco QBZ-95s with bayonets attached.

These bastards weren't fucking around.

A farmer rode up to the roadblock with a hay wagon only to be stopped while soldiers stabbed at the hay with bayonets.

Then, out of the corner of his eye, Connor saw something moving in the grass toward him. A cobra. It was probably attracted to his scent.

Ah, shit.

It was time to get out of here.

He began to scoot backward, froze. One of the soldiers was headed his way.

Connor hoped Shanti was paying attention and had the sense to get down and hide. He drew out his pistol, knowing that if he fired, he would give himself and Shanti away and bring the rest of those soldiers rushing into the ravine.

The soldier stopped at the edge of the forest about twenty feet to his left, unzipped his fly, and pissed in the grass.

Great.

Connor didn't feel like dying because some fucker needed to take a leak. He looked from the soldier to the snake and back again.

The soldier froze, slowly drew his sidearm.

Connor tensed, sure the bastard had seen him.

No, the muzzle wasn't pointed at him. It was aimed at the snake.

If the soldier missed and came closer, he would see Connor. He might even be able to make out Shanti.

BAM!

The snake jerked and lay still.

Connor held his breath as the soldier walked over to his kill, picked it up, and turned to show it to his friends, somehow not seeing Connor, who lay in the grass a mere three feet away. The soldier walked back to the others, showing off his prize.

Holy shit!

Connor exhaled, backed away from the road and down

into the ravine, making his way slowly and silently toward Shanti.

She lay in the undergrowth, a look of terror on her face. She threw herself into his arms when he reached her, holding onto him as if their lives depended on it. "I thought he'd seen you. I thought he was going to kill you. And then the snake..."

Warmth blossomed behind his breastbone to know she cared. "For a minute there, I wasn't sure which one of them would have the honors—him or the cobra."

But they didn't have time for this.

"The forest ends up ahead at a highway. Troops have set up a roadblock—about thirty hostiles with rifles and bayonets."

"Bayonets?"

"We need to backtrack." He saw the fear on her face, touched a hand to her cheek. "Hey, it's okay. They don't know we're here."

He led her back the way they'd come then pushed more to the west. Once again, they reached the highway—it was nothing more than a two-lane dirt road—but this time there were no soldiers.

They crouched near the roadside, Connor listening for helicopters or approaching vehicles. "Go!"

Shanti ran, heading for the cover of the forest on the other side, Connor beside her, rifle at the ready.

"That's one obstacle down. The bigger one lies ahead."

It was late afternoon when they reached the river.

Shanti stared. "How can we cross that?"

A torrent of muddy water rushed through a rocky gorge a hundred feet deep, tossing up foam, swirling in rocky eddies.

Yeah, no way were they swimming that.

Connor locked down his own emotional response. "Let's work the problem."

He reached into his pack for his binoculars. "There are three suspension bridges—two to our north and one farther south. The bridges are under guard, so we need to find a safe place to downclimb, cross the river, and climb out again without being seen."

Hope seemed to fade from Shanti's face. "What we need is wings—or a miracle."

"Don't give up on me now, princess. We'll make a miracle if we have to." He kissed her, shouldered his rifle. "I'm going to do a little recon. Stay here. Keep low, and stay quiet. I won't go far."

Exhaustion and despair on her face, Shanti plopped down on a rock.

Connor walked along the rim of the gorge, looking for a good place to downclimb. The rock was solid with lots of holds. For a serious climber, it would be a piece of cake. He could probably manage it. But Shanti...

Then he saw it just ahead—a cairn.

He walked over to it, saw that it marked a stairway cut into the stone. The stairs went down about ten feet and seemed to stop at the edge of the cliff. He walked down the stairway, wondering who had carved it and why it was here —and then he saw.

A rope ladder spilled down the side of the cliff to the river, connecting with a bridge made of rope and planks of wood. A rope ladder on the other side led back to the top again. It had likely been used by the people who lived in this area prior to the construction of the suspension bridges.

With any luck, it was still intact.

He made his way back to Shanti, grabbed his pack. "Come on. I want to show you something."

"What is it?"

"It's our miracle."

~

"THAT'S NOT A MIRACLE. That's crazy." Shanti stared through the binoculars at the rope bridge below, almost dizzy. "Whole planks are missing."

She was done with this running-through-the-jungle thing.

"Do you have a better idea?" Connor took back his binoculars, tucked them in his pack. "I'll test it first."

He walked to the edge where the stairs ended, grabbed the rope guides, and gave them each a good, hard yank. "Here goes."

Shanti could barely breathe as Connor turned to face her—and stepped over the edge and onto the ladder.

He put his full weight on the first rung, gave a little hop, and then stepped down to the next. The wood creaked, but it held. If it could support his weight, it would support Shanti's. Or so she told herself.

He climbed back up. "It's good. There are some missing rungs, and it rocks a little when you move. But I think it will hold."

"What if it doesn't?"

"That's why it's good to have a backup plan." He reached for his pack, drew out a coil of orange and yellow rope. "We'll wait until dusk when thermal crossover makes it harder for spotters on the suspension bridge to see us with their infrared scopes. Then I'll make you a harness and set up an anchor. If you fall, I'll stop you."

Shanti didn't know what thermal crossover was, but she

was more afraid of falling than she was of guns. "Won't I just pull you over the edge?"

"Not a chance. You'll see."

They ate their dinner—chicken and noodles with vegetables—and watched as the sun sank behind a horizon of clouds, turning them pink. If she'd been a tourist and not running from an army, she would have loved this.

"When it's not trying to kill us, this is a beautiful place."

Connor looked into the sunset, pink-gold rays making his face seem impossibly handsome. "I suppose it is. It's been years since I've been able to look at a jungle and see anything other than a job site."

After they'd eaten supper, Connor got out a pair of leather gloves and set about building the anchor, securing one end of the rope around the trunk of a sturdy teak tree. Then he wrapped the rope around his waist, knelt before her, and began to tie the free end around her hips and between her legs.

"Let me adjust this. It won't be comfortable, but it will hold you."

She stood still, her pulse already racing.

He got to his feet, cupped her face between his palms. "You can do this, Shanti. If you slip, trust that I'll catch you —and *don't* scream."

"Right."

They got into position—Connor on the stairs, Shanti on the edge facing inward.

"Don't look down if it scares you. Remember to give me three tugs on the rope when you're down. If I fall, you keep going.

"Don't you dare."

He gave her a lopsided grin. "Good copy."

Shanti hesitated, her heart thudding.

This is the way home, the way to safety.

Her gaze on Connor's, she took hold of the guide ropes and stepped over the edge and onto the first rung. The ladder swung a little, but the step held.

Connor fed her a little rope at a time as she climbed carefully down. "You're doing great. One step at a—"

A rotten plank broke beneath her feet, the pieces falling to the water below.

She gasped, a scream trapped in her chest, her hands clinging tightly to the swaying ladder, her pulse pounding in her ears. Then she realized that she hadn't fallen at all, not an inch. Connor had caught her, just like he'd said he would.

"You're okay," she said to herself. "You're okay. Keep going."

She moved faster now, confident that Connor would keep her safe. Another rung broke, but she kept going.

The river was so loud at this point that she wouldn't have been able to hear Connor if he were to call for her.

Just a little farther.

Another step and another and another.

Relieved to be almost down, she looked up—and saw a man falling headlong toward the ground.

Connor? God, no!

He flew past her, landing on stone with a sickening thud.

Not Connor, but a soldier, his throat slit.

Panic hit her veins with a rush of adrenaline.

The soldiers had found him. They'd found Connor.

He was fighting for his life, and there was nothing she could do to help him.

B lade in hand, Connor jumped back, the bayonet missing him by inches. He grabbed the second soldier's rifle, used it to yank him down the stairs. The soldier fell with a grunt, landing at Connor's feet. Connor wrested the firearm from his grasp, bayoneted the soldier through the chest, then knelt, waiting.

Three tugs.

Shanti was safely down.

Whoever they were, these two hadn't expected to find him. They'd come up behind, looking surprised to see him. Maybe they were off duty and just taking a stroll. Damned bad luck for them.

When he didn't hear anyone else, he looked over the edge.

Shanti stood near the base of the ladder, looking up. He didn't need to see her face to know she was probably scared to death.

He motioned for her to step back, pushed the second soldier's body over the edge, and then hurled the men's rifles out over the water, where they landed one at a time with an inaudible splash. He ran up the stairs, untied the rope from the tree, and let it fall. Then he put on his pack, slipped his rifle strap over his shoulder, grabbed onto the ladder—and did his best rendition of a fast-rope down to the river.

Shanti stared at him, eyes wide, clearly stunned. "Are ... are you okay?"

"I'm fine." He knew this was hard for her, but he couldn't do anything about that. He would have asked her to help him search the dead bodies but figured she wasn't up for that. "Gather the rope. Get it coiled up again."

That seemed to draw her out of her shock, and she went to work.

Connor dropped to his knees, searched each man's knapsack and pockets, and retrieved 9 mm ammo, two full canteens, and two pouches of snacks. He packed the goods away, rolled one body into the river and then the next, letting the water take them.

He found Shanti watching him. "If soldiers discover their bodies, Naing will know exactly where we crossed. It will narrow his search and make getting home a hell of a lot tougher."

"I understand." She handed him a tight coil of rope.

He shoved it into his pack. "These two probably have friends who will notice when they don't come back. They have infrared scopes like I do. We need to cross this river and climb up the other side before they come looking. The rocks retain heat, and sunset will confuse their scopes for a few minutes. But if they find us while we're climbing, we'll make easy targets. Speed is survival. I'll cross the bridge first. Stay a few feet behind me, and hold on tight to the side ropes. If I fall through, you keep going. When we reach the other side, I'll climb up first, and belay you like I did before."

He glanced up at the rim to see whether any soldiers

were up there, then made straight for the bridge. It swayed more than the ladder, but it held. Several planks were missing, and some were broken or barely hanging on, but he made good time, Shanti keeping up behind him.

He heard her gasp, looked back to see that her left leg had slipped between two rotted planks, and reached out to help her up. "Easy, Shanti. You've got this."

He kept going, glancing back at the rim every few minutes, knowing that he and Shanti would be easy to hit.

So far, so good.

The first shot came just as they reached the other side, the bullet whining past his ear before he heard the crack of the rifle.

"Take cover! Get down!" He dove behind a jumble of boulders and aimed his rifle, searching through the scope for his target.

There on the rim above stood four uniformed soldiers, one of them aiming a rifle directly at him. If he tried to take them out one at a time, the others could hide or run. They had a better view of him than he had of them.

Shanti crouched behind him now, breathing hard. "What do we do?"

A round hit nearby, a fragment of bullet or rock creasing his shoulder.

Fuck.

"Stay down!" Connor switched his rifle into three-round burst mode, raised it, and opened fire, gunfire echoing through the gorge. Two men dropped, then the third.

The fourth ran.

Connor fired again, and he fell. "We need to get the hell out of here. This area will be crawling with hostiles soon."

He stood, rifle in hand. "On your feet, Shanti."

Those soldiers had radios, and it was a good bet they

had called this in. It was also possible that a company was encamped nearby that had heard the gunfire. Either way, Naing would soon know precisely where Connor and Shanti had crossed the river.

SHANTI HURRIED over rounded river rocks and boulders to the other ladder, her heart still in her throat. More afraid of bullets than falling now, she started climbing as fast as she could, not waiting for Connor or the rope.

Don't look down. Don't look down.

Some hideous multi-colored spider had made its web between two of the rungs, but Shanti gritted her teeth and moved past it.

Up and up and up.

She came to a place with several missing rungs, the gap too wide for her. "I can't reach! It's too far!"

"I'm going to boost you." Connor came up beneath her, nudged his head between her thighs from behind, as if to give her a ride on his shoulders. "Hold on tightly to the ropes and climb with me."

He rose up the ladder, lifting her with him while she held on for dear life. "Can you reach the next rung now?"

"I'll try." She raised one foot, just managing to catch it with her heel. She slid her leg through and then another, as if she were climbing onto a swing. Then she pulled herself up, making the mistake of looking behind her.

It was so far to the ground.

Don't look down.

"Beautiful. Keep going."

She was almost there. If she fell now, if Connor fell, they

would hit the ground like those two soldiers had. They would die.

Don't think about it.

She climbed and climbed.

Relief flooded her as she pulled herself over the top and onto the carved stone stairs on the other side and crawled to safety, Connor right behind her.

He checked his rifle. "The only way to evade these bastards now is to put a lot of miles between us and the river. I know you're hungry and tired—"

"I can handle it." She would *not* be the reason they died out here.

Connor's lips curved in an approving smile, sweat beading on his temples. "Listen to you—Princess Shanti of the Jungle."

He led the way, sticking to rocky ground, moving at a pace that left her almost running behind him. She welcomed it, knowing that every step led her farther away from Naing and his troops and closer to freedom. Up a steep slope, down a rocky ravine, across a creek, and up again. Through dense undergrowth. Across a grassy field where macaques sat eating…

"Mangoes!"

Connor walked over to the tree, sending the macaques into a screeching fit, most of the troop running away or disappearing into the trees. "Take just a few."

They picked fruit, Shanti dropping it into her handbag. Then Connor took advantage of the lack of tree cover to check in with his boss, giving him a quick update, while Shanti devoured a mango, the fruit taking the edge off her hunger, sweet juices spilling down her chin.

"Strong copy, Cobra. We'll head north and keep to the mountains." Connor tucked his cell phone away, picked another mango, and ate. "We've made thirty-six miles today. They want us to stick to the mountains and head straight north for now. The cover is better, and there are fewer roads."

The last of the light began to fade, leaving them in the dark, the birds going silent.

Connor stopped, took out his flashlight, aimed it low. "I don't see any way to keep going if we don't have some light. Stay close."

Shanti focused on the circle of yellow light in front of Connor's feet, doing her best to step where it was safe.

On and on they went, hour after hour, Shanti hollow with hunger and weighed down by exhaustion. She thought for a moment of asking Connor to let her take a nap, just a few minutes of sleep right here on the ground. But she couldn't fail him. Then it came to her that this is how so many Rohingya survivors had come to Bangladesh—fleeing on foot through the mountains at night. She couldn't fail them either.

Shanti kept going, step after weary step, a light rain falling.

It must have been close to midnight when Connor stopped, turned the flashlight toward an unusually long and high mound of vines to their right.

Shanti fought to catch her breath. "Are we there yet?"

"I think we might be." He stepped closer to the vines, moved the light over it, and chuckled. "Well, hello."

Shanti saw something white poking out of the green leaves, stepped closer—and realized she was looking at the top of a human skull. She clapped a hand to her mouth, choked back a scream.

"Don't worry about him. He's a friend."

"What do you mean?"

Connor pushed the vines carefully aside, revealed a red circle surrounded by white and blue. "It's a British Blenheim bomber from the war. Our buddy here was shot down, and he's been here ever since. Let's see if the fuselage is intact."

Shanti stayed where she was while Connor walked around the plane, stepping through deep undergrowth.

"It looks like he lost a wing, but the fuselage is mostly unbroken. There's a hole here big enough for us to enter and shelter for the night."

"You want to *sleep* in there?" Shanti would rather keep walking.

"Don't worry." Connor's teeth flashed white in the darkness, a note of amusement in his voice. "I'll make sure no one else is home before we move in."

Connor left Shanti to heat their MRE—Beef Tacos with Santa Fe Style Rice and Beans—and went about making their extremely cramped shelter safe, the interior of the plane lit by his flashlight, rain falling hard outside. He had already cleared the plane of anything that might bite, including a young Burmese python. To keep predators out, he taped old webbing from inside the plane over the hole in the fuselage and covered that with one of the squares of space blanket he'd brought from the tree house. It wasn't a serious obstacle, but it would keep out mosquitoes and snakes—and give him enough warning to respond should anything bigger and meaner come for them.

That meant he could truly sleep tonight.

When that was done, he took out the first aid kit, put on a glove, and treated the shrapnel wound on his shoulder. It wasn't deep and hadn't bled much.

"You're hurt."

"It's just a nick." He finished with that, then replaced the bandage on his temple with a clean one and put the first aid kit away.

"I think dinner is ready."

He got the towelettes out so they could wash their hands, and then it was time to eat. "Today was hard, but you handled it."

"The only easy day was yesterday, right?"

"You got it."

"What happens tomorrow?" There was apprehension in her eyes.

"I wish I knew." He took another bite, ravenous for real food. "They'll send all of their resources to this side of the river. There will be helicopters and soldiers on foot. They might bring dogs. The best way to defeat them is to keep moving. Just do what you did today, and with any luck, you'll be in The Hague in two days."

She didn't look as relieved by this news as he'd imagined she would. "I thought you said it would take seven days."

"That was back when I didn't know what a hard charger you were. It would have taken us seven days if you'd been able to go only twenty miles a day. But I think we gained a good forty-five miles today. That leaves about fifty miles ahead of us."

They would be the fifty most dangerous miles of their journey, but she didn't need to hear that now.

She nodded and said nothing, probably beyond exhaustion.

He finished eating, pulled out the food he'd taken off the soldiers he'd killed. "Do you know what this stuff is?"

Shanti took a packet of what looked like crumbly tamales without the corn husks. "These are peanut rolls."

Connor took one, ate it. "They taste like Butterfingers without the chocolate."

"These are tamarind flakes—like fruit chews made of tamarind. These little dark nuggets are called jaggery. It's made with cane sugar and date tree sap."

Connor took a piece of jaggery, popped it in his mouth, sugar melting on his tongue. "I like it. This isn't a lot, but together with the mangoes, it will give us some extra calories."

Shanti nodded, but didn't eat, sitting there, looking at nothing, a distant expression on her face. He'd seen that look on young soldiers' faces after a day of fighting. He's seen it on the faces of civilians who'd fled their homes to survive.

Say something.

"How are you feeling?"

Can't you do better than that?

She shook her head. "I'm alive. That's all that matters, right?"

He reached over, took her hand. "I can see that something's bothering you."

She seemed to hesitate. "Those men you killed today—I was relieved and happy that they died. You saved our lives. They were strangers who weren't there by choice. They were ordered to come after us. They have families and friends, maybe wives and children. But I was *relieved* when they died. What kind of hypocrite am I if I talk about nonviolence and then feel good about it when someone else gets killed?"

Her question stung. He had made a career out of killing. Dealing out death—very selectively and with perfect precision—was part of his job description.

This isn't about you, dumbass.

He ran his thumb over her knuckles. "You're not a hypocrite. Every living thing wants to survive, Shanti. What you're feeling—the relief that they're dead and you're not—is normal."

"Do you really think so?"

"I know so." He'd felt that emotion more times than he could count. "It's normal, too, to feel some conflict. No one wants to kill. But you're not responsible for those men's deaths. I am. Or Naing is—with my help. Naing arranged to have our guys, Hatch and Davis, murdered and you abducted. He mobilized his army. He gave the orders, and they earned their paychecks by following those orders. They wouldn't have hesitated for a moment to kill either of us. In fact, they came close to doing just that."

She lifted her gaze to his. "I wouldn't be alive right now if not for you, Connor. I don't even know how to thank you. What you've done for me, risking your life and killing to keep me safe... It must be hard to carry the weight of their deaths, of killing. I think now maybe I understand what you mean by re-entry."

What was she trying to say? Did she believe he'd made some heavy personal sacrifice killing those men today? Was she implying he should feel *bad* about what he'd done? He didn't. It had come as naturally to him as breathing.

She didn't understand anything about his life.

"Don't worry about me. I don't feel bad about killing someone who's trying to kill me or one of my clients. That's my job. I kill when I have no other choice, and I get paid to do it." Done with this conversation, he reached for his back-pack and pulled out the bivy sack. "It's time to get some shut-eye."

17

S hanti woke from the oblivion of sleep to find herself using Connor's lap for a pillow. She didn't even remember falling asleep.

He rested a hand on her shoulder. "It's time to get moving."

"Good morning." She sat up. "Did you sleep?"

"Yeah."

"I would give anything for tea."

"Looks like we've got 'Orange Beverage Powder, Carb-Fortified.'"

"Lovely."

He set out their breakfast of peanut rolls, M&Ms, and fresh mangoes without speaking, a cheerless expression on his face, his jaw dark with stubble.

At first, Shanti was too groggy to think much of it, but when he began to pack up without a word, she began to wonder if he was okay.

"Is something wrong?"

"You mean apart from being chased through Myanmar by the Tatmadaw?"

Okay, that was a more sarcastic answer than she'd expected.

She wiped her face and hands on a towelette, got her handbag ready to go while he took down one of the squares of space blanket and crawled to the front of the plane. He seemed to be searching for something, even moving bones.

"Sorry to disturb you, guys."

"What are you doing?"

"Looking for dog tags. Three families back in the UK never found out what happened to their loved ones. I might be able to bring them closure."

Shanti's heart melted. "That's wonderful."

"These guys gave their lives for us. The least we can do is let their families know where they are. The British government might be able to repatriate their remains."

Ten minutes later, they'd left the crashed plane behind. The sun was just rising, the forest still quiet and dark.

"I need to find a break in the canopy to check in."

They came to a rocky rise, a valley of dark treetops stretching to the horizon, clouds sitting thick and low. In the distance, Shanti saw what looked like water.

"Is that the Bay of Bengal?" They were getting closer.

But Connor had taken out his sat phone. "Cobra, O'Neal here. Do you have the GPS coordinates of the location where we camped for the night? Tag that spot. Pass the coordinates to British intelligence along with this flight number."

He gave them a number he'd memorized. "It's a Blenheim. Yeah, seriously. There were three men on board when it went down. I've got two sets of dog tags. I couldn't find the third. The names are ... McWilliams and ... Leighton."

From her end, the conversation after that was just a lot of "copy that" and "good copy" and "strong copy, Cobra."

Then the sun's first rays stretched out from the east, spilling out over the clouds to reveal a landscape that took Shanti's breath away. Golden pagodas rose above the forest canopy. There were dozens of them, gilded finials pointing to the heavens.

Connor ended the call. "Naing's army is about to saturate this area. We need to move—and fast. Last night's deluge will have destroyed our scent track, so they won't use dogs unless they have some idea where we are. Cobra has a fishing boat sitting in the river just across the border, waiting for us. The goal is to reach them by tomorrow night."

"Look." Shanti pointed. "Isn't it beautiful?"

Connor glanced at the scenery. "Let's move."

She knew their situation was serious, but he didn't have to be cold. "Are you upset about something?"

"Why do you think I'm upset?"

If he thought he was going to derail Shanti's line of questioning with that trick, he was sadly mistaken. "That is *not* a denial."

"Lawyers." He stopped, turned to face her. "This is going to be the most dangerous part of our journey. The monsoon forest will eventually turn into fields, and we'll lose our cover. Speed is survival, so there's no time for pointless talk."

There was a hard edge to his voice, his blue eyes cold like slate.

Shanti stared at him, stung by what felt like a rebuke. "Pointless talk? I asked because I care about you."

"Care about getting home alive." He turned and walked away.

She fell in behind him. "I do!"

Then their conversation last night came back to her.

I don't feel bad about killing someone who's trying to kill me or one of my clients. That's my job. I kill when I have no choice, and I get paid to do it.

She'd noticed the change in his demeanor then, but she'd been too exhausted to make anything of it.

"I'm sorry if something I said last night hurt or upset you."

He said nothing but kept moving.

"So, now you're just going to clam up? Fine."

Don't worry about it now.

Fifty miles.

Only fifty miles to the border, and then...

She would fly back to The Hague, and he would head off to some other part of the world on another assignment. Life would return to normal.

But it wouldn't.

After this—after Connor—nothing would be normal again.

CONNOR PUSHED AHEAD, trying to decide what made him hate himself more—the fact that he'd crossed a line and had sex with a client or the fact that he'd hurt her just now. She had reacted to his words as if he'd slapped her, staring up at him through wide amber eyes.

Son of a bitch!

If he'd kept his hands to himself and his dick in his pants, they wouldn't be in this situation. Having sex with her had opened them both to emotions that had no place in the here and now. They were in a survival situation, for God's sake.

I wouldn't be alive right now if not for you, Connor. I don't even know how to thank you. What you've done for me, risking your life and killing to keep me safe... It must be hard to carry the weight of their deaths, of killing.

Did she think he could have served in the Unit for a decade if he felt guilty about pulling the trigger? Why should he feel guilty for doing his job?

You do feel guilty—about the boy.

Connor thrust that thought aside. This was about Shanti, not Syria. It was about boundaries, doing his job, maintaining a professional distance from a client.

Even as he told himself this, he knew it wasn't true. Some part of him had felt judged by her last night, and yet, she hadn't meant it that way at all. She hadn't said anything negative. She'd been trying to thank him and work through her feelings about what she'd seen. Instead of trying to understand, he'd shut her down.

You've been a dick.

He stopped, exhaled, turned to face her. "I'm not upset with you. You didn't do or say anything wrong. You've done everything I've asked you to do. Got that?"

Apparently, he'd gone out of his mind because, in the next instant, he slid his hand into her hair, ducked down, and kissed her. It was just a brief touching of lips, but it centered him again, smoothed his rough edges. He found himself looking into her eyes, saw that she was confused by this.

So was he.

What the fuck? "Okay, then."

Yeah, you set her straight, man.

"O-okay." She was fighting not to smile.

He moved on, leaving her to follow.

The buzz of helicopters began as soon as the sun was up,

the birds moving over the forest about twenty klicks south of them. Connor could only hope that he and Shanti had covered enough ground last night to stay ahead of Naing's men.

If not...

He pushed Shanti as hard as he could, heading down into a forested valley full of golden pagodas and Buddha statues, each statue sitting serenely on a stone plinth surrounded by bamboo and teak trees.

"I wonder who put these here," Shanti said, breathing hard.

"Maybe they had a sale on Buddhas—buy one, get fifty free."

He stopped just after noon to eat and rest, giving them both more calories than he usually did, hoping to help Shanti keep her energy up. Starvation diets didn't mix well with extreme exertion.

Shanti looked up. "The helicopters are getting closer."

"They'll be on top of us soon." Connor had already taken out his rain poncho to use for concealment. "But you're a pro at this now."

She shook her head, lines of worry on her face. "Hardly."

"You're handling the stress and deprivation better than most people would."

How could she be sweaty and exhausted and still look beautiful to him?

She wiped mango juice off her fingers with a towelette and changed the subject. "Why don't you have a girlfriend?"

"That's out of the blue." When people asked questions like that, they usually had a reason. He answered her, addressing both her question and what he assumed was her motivation for asking. "The work I do isn't compatible with relationships. Most guys in special forces are divorced, some of them more than once."

"But not you."

"I lived with a woman once. I thought it was the real thing. My unit had a tough deployment, lost a couple of men. I came home pretty messed up by it. Mandy threw me out three weeks later—and, no, I didn't hit her or hurt her. I just couldn't get back into the swing of normal life and drank too much."

"I'm sorry. It doesn't sound like she was very sympathetic. You were grieving."

"Yeah."

"So, because of her, you avoid women?"

"Unless I'm stuck in the jungle with them." He couldn't help but grin at Shanti's surprised reaction. "I don't avoid women. I love women. I avoid anything ... serious. That way, no one gets hurt."

"You just keep it casual." Was that a note of disapproval in her voice?

"That's right." He supposed it was a good thing to get out in the open, given that they'd had sex. He didn't want to hurt her or mislead her. "These guys you date, the ones who don't make you come—have you ever gotten serious with one of them?"

"No, not really." She tucked a strand of hair behind her ear. "I just didn't feel it."

"Feel what?"

She looked away as if searching for the right words, then met his gaze. "Fireworks. Passion. Excitement."

Connor felt a punch of lust. Was she saying she felt those things with *him*?

That revelation ought to have rung his alarm bells. But all he could think about was how much he would love to give her some fireworks right now, maybe bend her over and fuck her from behind.

Not here. Not now.

Not with enemy helicopters and an army beating down on them.

He shouldered his pack, stood, drew her to her feet. "Like I said, you've been dating the wrong guys."

A rustling behind him brought him around, rifle raised. "Shanti, get down!"

Standing not thirty feet away from them was a bald man in maroon robes.

The man smiled. "How good for you that I have found you."

SHANTI LOOKED UP, expecting to see Connor talking to a soldier. But the man who stood there was no soldier. "I think he's a monk."

The man pressed his palms together in a gesture of greeting. "Welcome. I am Ashin Dempo, and I am, as you say, a monk. But I fear you are in danger. I offer you shelter and a place to hide. I have no weapons."

Connor didn't lower the rifle, but that didn't seem to bother Dempo. "How do you know soldiers are looking for us?"

"They are looking for two people, two Americans—one a male who is armed and very dangerous and the other a young female. But we must be quick."

Shanti shook her head. "A lot of Buddhist monks are in league with the military. Some have even fueled the genocide here."

Dempo's smile faded. "This is sadly true, but I am not

among them. I spent four years at hard labor in a government prison after the Saffron Revolution and then lived in exile in Thailand before returning under an amnesty. I stand for peace."

"Where did you come from? You weren't here a moment ago."

"Long before these troubled times, the monks at our monastery used caves to build a system of tunnels. Many empires have ruled over us, and there have been many wars. These tunnels have kept us safe. I can hide you, give you clean water, food, and a place to rest while this storm passes."

Overhead, the beating of helicopter rotors drew nearer.

"Why would you help us?" Connor still hadn't lowered his rifle. "Wouldn't that put you and your monastery at risk?"

"If we are discovered, yes, but doing the right thing in such hateful times is never without risk. You know this, Ms. Lahiri."

Alarm shot through Shanti to hear a stranger speak her name, but before she could say a word, Connor stepped forward, rifle still raised, fury on his face. "How do you know who she is?"

"Even we monks watch the news. I listen to the BBC. It is widely reported by your news media that she was abducted and crashed in my country. But come. Let us take shelter in the tunnels. Otherwise, I fear you will be found by men more menacing than I."

Shanti's pulse pounded in her ears, the helicopter almost on top of them now.

She could tell Connor didn't trust Dempo, his expression unyielding. She didn't trust him either. What was to stop him from taking them prisoner himself and turning them over to Naing for favors or a reward for the monastery?

"Go." Connor glanced upward. "We'll follow."

Dempo turned and hurried through the trees to a rock outcropping, Shanti and Connor behind him, Connor still holding his rifle at the ready.

Then Dempo disappeared.

Connor glanced back. "Hurry, Shanti!"

He ducked between two rocks, Shanti close behind him just as the helicopter flew overhead. She found herself in the mouth of a narrow cave, a gate of iron bars propped open with a rock.

"They cannot see you here." Dempo gestured around him. "These tunnels are unknown to all but the most trusted monks. We rarely use them."

He bent down, moved the rock, and started to close the gate, an old, rusty padlock hanging from one of the iron bars.

"Whoa, wait a minute. You are *not* locking us in." Connor still hadn't lowered his rifle. "Shanti, take the padlock."

"Yes, of course. Please, take it—and the key." Dempo held it out to her, seeming unruffled by their mistrust. "This door is kept locked to keep out predators. No one wants a leopard joining us for meditation."

Connor lowered the rifle at last. "How many entrances do these tunnels have?"

"Five." Dempo reached into his robes, pulled out a smartphone. "All but this one are locked, and all are well hidden."

He turned on the phone's flashlight. "There's no signal down here, but the light comes in very handy."

Off he walked, chuckling to himself.

Shanti looked over at Connor. "Do you trust him?"

"Hell, no."

"Why did you follow him then? We could have taken cover out there."

"And risk being blind under my rain poncho while he waves the helicopter down with those red robes of his? No, thanks. He knows who you are. I need to know why. If he's telling the truth, he could really help us out. If he isn't... Stay close to me."

"You think I'm going to run off on my own in here?"

Connor grinned. "You've got a smart mouth, princess."

18

S hanti followed Connor and the monk through the cave, its jagged, rocky walls eventually giving way to smooth surfaces. "This must be the part the monks built."

"Yes, yes." Dempo stopped, raised his phone so they could see paintings, colors of ochre and saffron and royal blue swirling together to depict fanged supernatural creatures, scenes of skulls and destruction, and images of Buddha attaining enlightenment. "These were painted by monks in the light of butter lamps hundreds of years ago."

Shanti took it all in. "Amazing. They've painted a different world."

"Or a metaphor for the brutality of our world." He moved on. "I was a soldier once. The army came to my family's village, and I was conscripted as a child. I've held a rifle in my hand, and I have killed those I was told were my enemies."

Shanti knew colleagues who'd prosecuted warlords over the conscription of children. "Why did you become a monk?"

"Killing sickened me. When you take a life, you are wounded, too. No soldier comes home without injuries."

Shanti was stunned to hear him echo the words Elizabeth had said to her just days ago. She glanced up at Connor, wondering if he would say something, but his expression was closed, his jaw tight.

"What about killing in self-defense?" she asked.

"That may be different, though as a monk I am forbidden to kill, even in that circumstance. I find peace in that."

"I'm an agent of karma," Connor said at last. "I find peace in that."

Dempo chuckled. "And very well you might be."

The tunnel seemed to go on forever, the entire length covered with paintings. Gradually, Shanti began to relax. It was a relief not to be listening for helicopters, not to be scrambling to get beneath Connor's rain poncho, not to wonder whether someone was pointing a rifle at them and about to shoot them in the back.

And snakes—it was *so* nice not to worry about snakes.

"You must be very important if Naing has sent his army after you, Ms. Lahiri. The BBC says you work for the International Criminal Court."

Shanti thought through her response, careful not to reveal anything. "I'm also an agent of karma."

Dempo chuckled again. "Then I must do all I can to ensure that you succeed. Who am I to stand in the way of ripening karmic fruit?"

At last, they came to some stairs. Up and up they climbed—Shanti lost count somewhere after one hundred twenty—until they came to a small, underground room with five doors in its walls, one dark set of stairs winding upward.

"From here, one can use any of these tunnels. This area

is off-limits to all but the most trusted monks." Dempo pointed. "Should you need to leave quickly, this tunnel will take you west out beyond this valley and toward the river. It is marked with a fish."

Shanti could just make out the little fish painted above the door.

"Good to know." Connor glanced around. "How far are we from the border?"

"Only thirty miles."

Thirty miles.

It was both a thrill and a little scary to be so close—and still so far away.

"I'll take you up the back stairs to my private quarters so that no one will see you. Being an abbot has its advantages."

Connor started to speak, but Dempo cut him off. "There is no need for you to surrender or conceal your weapons. No one will see us."

Connor nodded. "Good."

More stairs led them to a simple wooden door.

"I need to clear the room," Connor told Dempo, raising his rifle, standing to the side of the door. "Shanti, stay here. If there's any trouble, run down and get the hell out of here."

"I assure you there will be no trouble." Dempo pushed the door open and let Connor move past him.

Connor pivoted through the doorway, only to return a moment later. "Clear."

Dempo gestured for Shanti to enter. "Please, be my guest."

Shanti stepped into a small room that held a bed, a low table, a shelf with prayer beads, books, a little shrine with a seated Buddha, and a meditation cushion. There were three doors—the one they'd just come through, another that must lead to a hallway, and another that led to ... "A bathroom!"

"As I said, being abbot comes with privileges. I apologize that I cannot provide you each with your own room."

"We've been on the run for four days through the jungle together. We'll manage." Connor walked over to the only window, careful to stand off to the side, still very much in military mode, his jaw tense.

"There are soldiers out there. Do not let them see you," Dempo warned him. "No offense, but you two do not look like one of us."

"No offense taken," Connor said.

"Now, you can rest. There is a nun here whom I trust with my life. She is my daughter, though no one knows that. She will come with food, drink, and clean robes for you to wear while you're here. You may stay until you feel it is safe to move on again. Lock the door if you must. There is no lock on the outside." He pressed his palms together again and left them.

Shanti went to stand beside Connor, saw helicopters in the sky and below, a road with soldiers and army vehicles. They would have been out in that right now if not for Dempo. "Do you trust him now?"

Connor's expression hadn't changed. "We'll see."

"God, I want a shower." Shanti walked into the bathroom.

"Don't get naked yet." It wasn't in Connor's nature to feel secure in unfamiliar places, especially ones he didn't control.

"You think this is a trap? He helped us escape the helicopters, let you keep your weapons, showed us how to get out of here in an emergency, and left the gate and this door unlocked."

"That's all well and good, but I had a rifle pointed at him." It wasn't impossible to imagine that Dempo had lured them here, promising them everything they needed—water, food, shelter, safety—so that he could sell them out to Naing's soldiers.

Hadn't he admitted to being one of them in the past?

"Can I at least take off my boots and socks?"

"Sure." Connor stayed by the window, watching troops drive up and down the road leading into the forest.

The monastery seemed to stand on the edge of a small town, simple homes squatting along the banks of a small river, the mountains rising behind them.

A light knock.

Connor drew one of his Glocks, stepped out of the line of sight. "Open the door, but stay behind it."

Shanti did as he asked, her pulse spiking.

A young woman wearing pink robes, her head shaven, walked into the room carrying a tray with a teapot and cups. She showed no fear at the sight of Connor's gun. "I am Mya, Ashin Dempo's daughter. I have brought you tea."

"Tea!" Shanti's elation almost made Connor smile.

He lowered his weapon, watched as Mya carried the tray to the low table, knelt, and arranged the pot and the cups.

"You must be weary. Soon, I will bring you food and robes. Please refresh yourselves." She stood, pressed her hands together in front of her chest like her father had done, and left them.

Shanti sat beside the table, poured tea into both cups. "Would you relax?"

"Does it have caffeine?" He left the window, walked over to where she sat.

Shanti raised her cup, sniffed it. "It's green tea, so, yes, it does."

He sat, set his rifle down beside him, took the cup she offered.

"Mmm." She closed her eyes, sighed.

He took a sip, the warm, earthy taste preferable to even one more sip of the orange-flavored beverage. He tossed it back.

"It's not whiskey." She poured him another cup.

"I'm thirsty."

"You know, apart from being abducted, and the helicopter crash, and having to hide every five minutes from soldiers, and scary rope ladders, being shot at by the river, and seeing snakes and disgusting spiders and bugs, this has been a big adventure."

"If I subtract all of that, what's left? Sleeping in a tree house? The stone porn temple? Eating MREs?"

She smiled over the rim of her teacup. "You."

Connor's heart gave a sharp thud, what she'd said yesterday coming back to him.

Fireworks. Passion. Excitement.

Yeah, there were red flags all over this. Was she getting attached to him? She shouldn't. She deserved better than to get mixed up with a man like him. Still, he'd be lying if he said a part of him wasn't gratified.

A knock.

Mya came in with a tray laden with food, the scents making Connor's mouth water. She knelt beside them and set each dish on the table between them. "Rice. Fish and rice noodle soup. Vegetables and herbs. Chicken in curry."

"Thank you, Mya." Shanti gave the woman a warm smile. "After the past few days, this is a feast."

Mya lifted a strap from her shoulder, setting a large cloth bag on the floor. "Here are robes to wear while I launder your clothes. You will also find all you need for the cleansing of the body."

"You and your father are very kind."

"If you would put your garments in this bag and set it outside the door, I will launder them and return them to you tonight. And don't worry—if anyone sees your clothes, I'll tell them they belong to tourists here for a retreat."

But Connor had other concerns. "Where is your father going to sleep? Won't the other monks wonder if he doesn't return to his room tonight?"

"My father has told us all that he plans to chant and meditate through the night for the healing of this world. They know he will be in the Great Hall, and some plan to join him. I will tend to you. No one misses an insignificant nun."

There was no deception in Mya's brown eyes, no hint of a lie.

"What's below us? If Dempo is in the Great Hall and someone hears us moving around up here…"

"My room is below yours. No one will know you are here."

Connor was starting to believe this was real—a sanctuary in the middle of hostile territory. "Thank you, Mya."

She stood, pressed her palms together, then left them to eat.

Connor and Shanti washed their hands in the bathroom and went straight for the spoons, neither of them up for figuring out how to make rice balls with their fingers.

Shanti moaned at her first bite of the chicken curry. "It's so good."

"Don't eat too fast, princess. You'll make yourself sick." Connor took a bite, the mingled flavors of chicken, garlic, ginger, and turmeric exploding on his tongue.

The soup was good, too, and the fresh vegetables and herbs—cucumber, carrot, cilantro leaves, and sugar snap peas—helped to make up for days of MREs.

"Do you trust him now?"

Connor knew what she was truly asking. She wanted to know whether he believed the two of them were safe. "We need to be on our guard. All it takes is one slip, one mistake, one person seeing or overhearing something they shouldn't. But, yes, I think we can trust Dempo and Mya."

When she had finished eating, Shanti stood, drew down her zipper, peeled off her jeans and panties, and left them on the floor. "I'm getting naked and taking a shower."

Connor let his gaze travel over her slender legs to the dark curls at the apex of her thighs, hunger replaced by an altogether different appetite. "Mind if I watch?"

∽

SHANTI DREW her T-shirt over her head. "I'd rather have you join me."

She dropped her shirt on the floor then unclipped the front clasp of her bra, the heat of Connor's gaze making her nipples tighten. She dropped her bra, too, then reached for the bag that Mya had left them, taking out the robes—maroon for Connor and pink for her—and setting them on the bed. Then she carried the bag into the bathroom. She took out the toiletries, calling back to Connor. "There are toothbrushes, toothpaste, soap, shampoo, a comb, a towel, and—"

Warm skin pressed against her from behind, Connor's naked erection hard against her lower back, his hands on her hips. "And?"

Her thoughts scattered, her breath catching. "A... a razor."

"They thought of everything, didn't they?"

"Yeah, except for condoms."

Connor chuckled.

There was no shower stall, just a drain in the floor, but compared to bathing out of a bucket and under a freezing waterfall, it seemed a luxury.

Connor reached over, turned on the water, adjusted the temperature. They stepped under the spray together.

He peeled off the strips of moleskin he'd stuck to her shoulders where her handbag strap had rubbed her skin raw. "You're bruised and scratched up."

"That's nothing. You've been shot." Shanti carefully removed the bandages from his temple and his shoulder.

"What can I say? It's been a rough week at the office."

It hit Shanti again how close Connor had come to being killed—first on the helicopter and then near the river. "You'll have scars because of me."

"It's not your fault, Shanti."

Desire turned to tenderness, Shanti overwhelmed by all this big, beautiful man had done to keep her alive, standing between her and Naing's army, putting his body and life on the line for her. Yes, it was his job, but that didn't make what he'd done less dangerous—or less heroic.

While he washed his hair, she smoothed soap over his body from his shoulders to his toes, aroused by the feel of him—the strong beating of his heart, ridges of muscle, soft skin, the rasp of his body hair against her palms, the weight of his testicles, the hard length of his erection.

He rinsed away both shampoo and soap and then quickly shaved, his face ruggedly handsome. "That's a relief. The damned stuff itches. Your turn."

He took the soap from her, big hands moving gently over her breasts, her shoulders, her back, her bottom, her belly, her thighs, her calves, as if to smooth away the fear of the past few days, the concern on his face making her heart melt. "What have you done to me, Shanti? I can't get enough of you."

Excitement trilled through her.

He massaged shampoo into her hair, his fingers caressing her scalp, her nape, her temples, his touch both sensual and soothing.

She ducked her head under the spray to rinse the shampoo away, feeling truly clean for the first time since the morning she'd been abducted.

He turned off the water, and they stood for a moment, wet skin to wet skin, his muscles against her softness, the nearness making Shanti deliciously aware of the differences between them.

They dried each other with the towel. Then Shanti took his hand, led him to the small bed, and drew him down onto the mattress beside her.

Connor cupped her jaw with one hand, his gaze searching her face, the intensity in his eyes making her pulse skip. "Shanti."

She was about to ask him what he was thinking when he claimed her mouth in a deep, demanding kiss.

Yes.

She slid her fingers into his damp hair and surrendered to him, long days of deprivation and worry melting away as his mouth plundered hers. She'd never met a man who kissed like this, tongue and lips and teeth a coordinated assault on her senses, the excitement stealing her breath, making her heart race.

He dragged his mouth from hers, his lips coming down

on the sensitive skin of her throat, one big hand moving to cup her breast, his fingers finding her nipple.

She was already aroused from her shower, little darts of heat shivering through her, making her ache. "*Oh, yes.*"

He raised his head, looked down at her, the knowing smile on his wet lips and the lust in his eyes telling her he knew *exactly* what he was doing to her. "Remember, stay quiet. I don't think monks are used to hearing women scream."

"I don't scream when I come."

A dark eyebrow arched. "Is that a challenge?"

Another dart of heat.

Then he lowered his mouth to her breast, flicking her aching nipple with his tongue and nipping it with his teeth before sucking it into the heat of his mouth.

Her exhale became a moan, her fingers fisting in his hair, the sweet ache between her thighs making her hips shift, her body already seeking release.

He shifted to the other breast, licking, nipping, suckling her, the fingers of his free hand making circles over the skin of her belly, caressing the curve of her hip, tickling its way up her inner thighs. Where his hands went, his mouth soon followed, his lips spreading fire over her skin, making her burn, covering her with goosebumps.

He rose up onto his knees, moved down to the foot of the bed, catching her ankles and lifting her legs. "I want to taste you."

She sucked in a breath, her pulse skittering as he parted her with his fingers, lowered his mouth to her, and tasted her with a long, slow lick, two fingers sliding deep inside her. "Oh!"

He played with her for a while, licking and teasing her, his fingers driving her crazy, then he drew her into his mouth, suckling her clit like he had her nipples, his fingers stroking that special place inside her.

She moaned, the combined sensations staggering. Her fingers found their way to his hair again, digging in, holding on, pleasure coiling so tightly inside her that she thought she might break. "*Connor.*"

She shattered, biting back a cry as climax took her, bliss shaking her apart.

He stayed with her, maintaining the rhythm until her orgasm had passed. Then he settled himself between her thighs and buried himself inside her with a slow thrust, his cock wonderfully hard. He drove himself into her, his gaze locked with hers as he pushed her over that bright edge once more, catching her cry with a kiss.

But this time he was right there with her. He pulled out, spilled himself on her belly, breath hissing from between clenched teeth. For a moment, he sat between her thighs, the two of them breathing hard. Then he wiped her clean with the damp towel, put it in Mya's bag, and set the bag outside the door.

Shanti was almost asleep by the time he crawled into bed beside her. He drew her close, and she snuggled against him. Soon, they were both asleep.

19

C onnor woke from a dreamless sleep, Shanti curled against him, her dark hair covering them both. The world outside the window was dark, the sound of chanting coming from somewhere below. Not wanting to wake her, he lay there, just watching her, overwhelmed by an unfamiliar sense of tenderness.

He ought to be angry with himself. He'd broken Cobra's rules. He'd broken his own rules about unprotected sex. He'd gotten himself in over his head with a woman who deserved someone far better than him. Instead, he felt ... peace.

Where had she come from? What was it about her that did this to him? He had kissed every inch of her, tasted her, drowned himself in her—and still it wasn't enough.

You love her.

Adrenaline punched through him.

Oh, no. Hell, no. He didn't do love. He did sex. Good sex. But just sex.

Keep telling yourself that.

He listed all the reasons he couldn't love her, all the

reasons he shouldn't love her. She was out of his league, a beautiful Harvard-educated attorney from a wealthy family. He was a farm boy who'd gone into the military and now worked as hired muscle. They lived half a world apart. There were things about him she didn't know, reasons for her to hate him. Hell, he struggled to hold it together in the real world.

He ran all of this through his mind, hoping it would clear his head, take away this emotion, set his head straight. But it didn't.

He loved her.

Unable to resist, he kissed her awake. "Hey."

"Hey." She glanced around. "What time is it?"

"No idea." He ducked down, kissed a dark nipple.

She smiled, stretched, raised her arms above her head, offering herself to him. "I'm all yours."

God, he wanted her, but he couldn't touch her again. If she knew what he'd done, she wouldn't want his hands on her. She thought he was a hero. He wasn't.

He sat up. "Shanti, I can't. I…"

Great time to have a pang of conscience, idiot.

Fuck.

Was he truly going to tell her? She would hate him. It would drive a wedge between them. Then again, maybe that's what they both needed.

She sat up, concern on her face, her dark hair covering her breasts. "What is it?"

He shook his head. "I'm not who you think I am. I'm not a hero. I've done things that you would…"

She rested a hand on his arm. "I'm listening."

God, how was he going to do this? He'd only ever talked about this with his CO during the after-action review. The army had absolved him of any wrong-doing, so he'd tried to forget it. But the guilt had never gone away.

"I fought with 1st Special Forces Operational Detachment-Delta, what you all call Delta Force." He'd never told a woman which unit he'd served with, not even Mandy. "Before I joined Cobra, I spent a decade carrying out secret operations on behalf of Uncle Sam, moving in and out of war zones—Afghanistan, Iraq, Syria. I was good at it. I enjoyed it. Most of the time, anyway."

"I've seen you in action. I have no trouble believing that."

He drew a breath, tried to steel himself. "We did some work in Syria, took out some high-value ISIS targets, broke up their communications, took out their explosives and weapons caches. That sort of thing."

Why the fuck was he doing this? The two of them could never be together, so why expose himself? Why not just enjoy the moment?

Too late to back out now.

"We hit a bombed-out village, blew up a cache of explosives. Intel said the village was deserted, apart from fighting-age males, probably all ISIS." Connor's stomach knotted. "We came under fire during our exfil and got pinned down —at least five fighters firing AKs at us from the cover of a bombed-out house on the edge of town. I ..."

His body started to shake.

Did you think this would be easy?

"Someone had to do something."

She laced her fingers through his—an anchor. "Naturally, that was you."

Connor's heart began to hammer. "I volunteered to make my way around to the other side to take out the hostiles with a grenade or two. The Unit guys kept up a steady fire on the house while I worked my way toward the place. I took cover behind a rock wall, a pile of rubble, really, then tossed a grenade."

Frag out!

Connor saw the boy clear as day in his mind as he stepped out, looked around.

"I'm here, Connor. You can tell me."

Connor let out a breath. "In the next moment, a little boy stepped out of the house. He couldn't have been more than four or five years old, just a little guy. He looked around at the world we adults had broken with big brown eyes and then—"

Shanti waited. "And then?"

Connor's throat went tight. "I couldn't call the grenade back. I couldn't do anything but watch him die. I've killed children, Shanti. I've killed children, too."

It took all his courage to meet her gaze.

There were tears in her eyes. "Oh, Connor. It was an accident. You didn't target that boy. You didn't walk into that house, point a gun at his head, and pull the trigger. I have no doubt that if you could have saved him, you would have."

Connor shook off the absolution that she offered him, self-loathing seething inside him. "He died because I—"

"He died because terrorists who wanted to kill you and your fellow soldiers hid in his house and used him and his family as human shields. That's a violation of Protocol One of the Geneva Convention."

Her words brought him up short. "Is that … is that true?"

She smiled, tears on her cheeks. "I'm a human-rights attorney. I specialize in war crimes and crimes against humanity. I do know something about it."

~

SHANTI'S HEART broke for Connor. It hurt to see him in so much pain, rage and despair on his face, his body tense and trembling. Now Shanti understood what Elizabeth had meant. Connor's military service had left him wounded on the inside, where no one could see it, where the world could conveniently ignore it, even as it asked him to risk his life again and again.

Fighting back her tears, she raised his hand to her lips, kissed it. "You are not a monster, Connor. I'm so sorry that happened. I can't imagine how awful that must have been. But it's not your fault."

His jaw was tight, his lips a grim line, and she could feel the war he waged inside himself. "If I had waited just a moment, if I hadn't been so quick with the grenade..."

She leaned in, cupped his jaw. "Don't do that to yourself. Don't beat yourself up. You don't deserve it. You threw the grenade, yes, but the ISIS fighters put that boy in danger."

Then it came to her.

"Why did you tell me this now?"

"It felt wrong to kiss you, to have sex with you, when you probably wouldn't want me to touch you if you knew."

The ache in her heart grew stronger. "You told me so that I would know I was sleeping with the enemy. Is that it? You wanted to give me a chance to tell you to go to hell."

He nodded, his jaw still tight. "I know the ICC ran background checks on all of us before they hired Cobra. I know they researched our military records. The army absolved me, so there's nothing about it in my file. There was no way for you to know."

She wanted to tell him that he was almost certainly suffering from post-traumatic stress, that his grief over the boy only proved how big his heart was, that she loved him.

What?!?

Oh, God! She loved him!

She was in love with Connor.

She felt a moment of panic but pushed it away. Connor didn't need to deal with her emotions right now. He sat there, naked, both physically and emotionally, his heart torn from his chest and lying at her feet. He'd thrown it there so she could have a chance to reject him like his former girl-friend had.

She scooted closer to him, ran her hands up his arms. "It didn't work. I'm not going to push you away, Connor. You are still a hero in my eyes."

It wasn't enough to tell him.

She would have to show him.

She got up on her knees, pushed him back onto the mattress, and straddled him, stretching out on top of him. She claimed his mouth, kissed him the way he had kissed her, slowly at first, letting it build as he came alive in her arms.

His hands grasped her hips, but he let her set the pace.

She kissed her way down his throat to his sternum, her hands exploring him, soft skin and coarse curls beneath her palms. He smelled of soap and sex and salt, the scent of his skin stirring something inside her. She wanted him.

She licked a nipple, felt his belly jerk tight, licked it again, then the other one, lavishing the same attention on him as he'd given her. It turned her on to feel his body's response—his hard cock, his quick inhale when she nipped a sensitive tip, the tremors that passed through him with each flick of her tongue.

But she wanted more.

She kissed her way down his ribs, over the ridges of muscle on his belly, and along those obliques just above his hips. Every inch of him was precious to her. The little mole next to his navel. The scar on his abdomen. That tempting trail of dark curls that led to his erection.

She looked up, saw him watching her with blue eyes that had gone dark. Without breaking eye contact, she sat up, took his cock in hand, and began to stroke him. "Show me what you like."

His brow furrowed, he reached down with one hand to guide her, increasing the pressure. "Oh, yeah."

His eyes drifted shut, one hand fisting in the sheets, his hips thrusting into her hand. But she wanted more for him. She let him savor this for a while—then bent down and licked the head of his cock.

His eyes flew open. "Shanti."

She smiled, did it again. "You taste like me."

He shivered.

She repositioned herself between his thighs and took him into her mouth, stroking the length of him with her fist and her lips, swirling her tongue around the swollen head, doing her best to get the pressure and the rhythm right.

He caught her hair, moved it aside so that he could watch. "You are so hot."

She kept it up, taking cues from his hips when he wanted her to go faster, harder. She could tell he was near the brink, all those amazing muscles going tight.

He raised her head off him. "If you don't stop—"

"You don't have to pull out this time."

His belly jerked at those words. "Shanti."

She went down on him again, his fingers fisted in her hair now, his breathing ragged, his eyes closed again.

He arched off the bed, biting back a groan, his cock jerking in her mouth as he came, his body shaking with pleasure.

She took all of him, keeping her mouth on him until his

climax had passed. Then kissed her way back up his body again, her heart full. "You're still my hero."

"YOU ARE way too good at that." Connor felt lighter than he had in years.

Shanti's reaction had blown him away, lifting a heavy weight off his shoulders, stripping away years of guilt and rage. She hadn't condemned him. She hadn't blamed him. She hadn't withdrawn from him. Instead, she'd supported him, offered him understanding and compassion. She'd also given him the best head of his life.

God, he loved her.

Admitting that to himself made his heart soar—and scared the shit out of him.

They lay in bed for a time, her head on his shoulder, his fingers tracing the curve of her spine, their conversation drifting from the joy of indoor plumbing to the fact that coriander and cilantro were the same plant to what it had felt like for Shanti to grow up being a part of two different worlds—always being asked where she was from, having people assume she was Latina, being viewed as a foreigner when she was in Bangladesh despite her citizenship.

"I always had the feeling that my grandmother was disappointed I wasn't somehow more Bengali. She called me her American granddaughter. She spent the rest of her life grieving for the grandchildren she'd lost."

"I'm sure she loved you, but that's one hell of a loss to overcome." Connor kissed her hair. "We should get dressed before Mya shows up with supper. I'm not sure how she'd feel about *this*. We're in a monastery, after all."

Connor needed help with his robes, while Shanti managed just fine on her own.

Connor looked down at himself. "I feel ridiculous."

"You make a very sexy monk. Look at those biceps."

A short time later, Mya brought their supper—tea, potato curry with peas, fresh vegetables, sliced guava, fish soup.

"Two meals on the same day." Shanti took Mya's hand. "Thank you, Mya. You and your father have been so kind."

Connor and Shanti took turns feeding each other, some part of Connor amazed by the simple joy of sharing a meal with her. They had just finished when he heard it.

Engines. Men's laughter. Loud voices.

He stood, went for his rifle and handguns, and checked them. If anyone came through the door, he wanted to be ready. He moved over to the window, careful to stay out of sight, using his infrared scope to see in the dark.

Son of a bitch!

"General Naing. He's down in the courtyard."

That bastard Dempo had betrayed them. He'd given them everything they needed—food, shelter, a place to rest, even laundry service—just to keep them here until Naing could arrive.

"*What?*"

"Get your boots on, grab your gear, and let's go."

A knock.

Connor stepped back, raised his rifle, finger on the trigger. "Go down the back stairs, and don't stop for anything."

Shanti hurried toward the secret stairway when Mya spoke.

"Please, I've come to help."

Connor shook his head. "Shanti, go!"

Shanti darted past him, hurried over to the door, and unlocked it.

"Damn it! You're supposed to obey my orders!"

"Sorry, not this time."

Mya stepped inside, fear naked on her face, the bag that held their clothes hanging from her shoulder.

Connor glanced out into the hallway, shut the door, locked it. "What the hell is going on? I saw Naing out there."

"The general and some of his men have come unexpectedly, seeking my father's blessing to help him find you. My father does not believe they will search the monastery. You may remain if you choose. I have brought you food for your journey and robes to hide your hair and faces if you choose to leave us. Your clothes are here, too. They're clean and dry. Wear them beneath your robes. I will take you to the tunnel and down to the river where a small boat awaits."

"Thanks, but I think I'd rather head out on our own."

It had been a mistake to bring Shanti here.

"And if you run into anyone, do you speak our tongue? A monk and two nuns traveling will not draw the attention of soldiers, but a man and a woman..."

Okay, she had a point there.

"Give us a minute to pack up and change."

Mya stepped out the back door, while Connor and Shanti finished gathering their belongings, dressed, and put on their robes once more. When they joined Mya, she adjusted their robes and handed them each a saffron-colored robe made of thicker fabric. "Cover your hair and draw this close around you."

Connor wasn't easily able to reach his Glocks dressed in all of this, but it did hide his rifle. He took his flashlight out of his pack, handed it to Shanti. "Let's go."

Down the stairs they went, back down to the large room

with the five doors, and into the tunnel with the fish painted above it.

Mya was small, but she moved quickly. "My father did not betray you. I knew that's what you would believe, and I cannot blame you. He was forced to serve with General Naing as a boy and feels no affection or loyalty to him."

"But Naing still believes he's an ally."

"Yes, and, because of that, he trusts my father."

"Why don't the others at the monastery know that Ashin Dempo is your father?" Shanti asked.

"It would be viewed unfavorably for him to use his daughter as his assistant. But because my father has helped dissidents and outsiders, he trusts no one else. It is not out of ego, but to protect the lives of others."

"You've done this before."

"Yes." Mya didn't elaborate.

This tunnel wasn't as long as the previous one. It sloped gently downhill, its walls painted like the walls of the other one—skulls, battles, gruesome creatures gnashing their teeth. Yeah, Connor had lived through that day once or twice.

Ahead, he saw the entrance. "Shanti, douse the light."

They made their way in darkness to the gate, which Mya unlocked. "If we run into anyone, I will talk for us. Do not pull out your weapons. I will say we are taking a sick monk to see a physician."

"Shanti, be ready for anything."

They stepped out into the night.

S hanti followed close to Connor, doing her best to behave like a Buddhist nun as they made their way down a dirt path toward the river. Above them, a half-moon hung lazily in the sky, its light enough to keep her from tripping on rocks and tree roots, the night full of the sounds of frogs and insects.

After a hike of maybe five minutes, they left the jungle behind, the world opening around them. Boats and structures made of bamboo and fabric dotted the riverbank, people walking here and there. They'd spent so much time avoiding people that being out in the open like this put Shanti on edge. What if they noticed her boots and Connor's? Or her handbag? Or the cuffs of their jeans sticking out beneath the robes?

Then again, if monks had cell phones and laptops these days...

A group of four soldiers walked toward them, rifles over their shoulders. Adrenaline shot through Shanti, made her heart race. She kept her gaze on the ground, tried to conceal her face. The soldiers greeted them, Mya answering.

The seconds ticked by, Shanti barely able to breathe.

They walked on, their voices fading.

"The boat is over here." Mya led them down the muddy bank to a small wooden skiff. "Climb in. I'll untie it."

Connor helped Shanti step into the boat, the small craft rocking precariously, throwing her off balance. "Sit in the center."

He sat in front of her, while Mya pushed the boat away from the riverbank before stepping in with bare feet. The skiff floated out into the river, was caught by the current, and began to glide downstream, Mya at the rudder.

Shanti let out a breath. "I was afraid those soldiers would recognize us."

"People see what they want to see," Mya said.

Connor was back in military mode. "Where does this river lead?"

"It flows into the Naf River, but I can take you only so far as Myar Zin. Then I must return. The water grows too rough after that and would destroy the boat."

Myar Zin.

Shanti knew that name. That was Sareema's village. More than three hundred people had been murdered there. "That was a Rohingya village."

Shanti hadn't realized they were in that part of the country. They really were close to the border now.

"Yes, and you must take care. We've heard that there are Border Patrol and Tatmadaw in the area, both on land and on the rivers."

Shanti's heart sank. "So, business as usual."

Connor grinned at her over his shoulder. "You wouldn't want life to get boring, would you?"

They flowed with the river, passing a herd of elephants that had come down to the river's edge to drink. A baby stood between his mother's front legs and sloshed its little trunk back and forth in the water, playing.

Shanti saw Connor watching, the smile on his face putting an ache in her chest. He had sacrificed so much for his country. He deserved happiness, a chance to live a life that didn't give him nightmares, a future without violence.

She wished that life could be with her. But Connor had been clear.

He didn't do relationships.

What are you going to do when this is over?

She didn't want to think about that now.

They had floated downstream for a couple of hours when the river began to bend gently northward. Mya used the rudder to steer the skiff toward the riverbank.

"Wait." Connor raised the rifle, looked through the infrared scope, then lowered it. "It looks clear."

"This is Myar Zin." Mya stepped out of the skiff. "There are farms owned by Buddhist families not far away, so you must avoid going there. They are good people, but they have been led to believe that you are their enemy. The Rohingya village stood just through those trees."

Connor jumped to the sand, then helped Shanti. "Thank you, Mya. Please thank your father, too. I'm sorry I doubted him."

"He asked me to tell you, soldier to soldier, that he hopes you find true peace one day. To you, Shanti, he asked me to say that there is no greater cause than justice."

Shanti swallowed the lump in her throat, what Dempo and Mya had done for her and Connor overwhelming. "You may have saved our lives. Thank you."

Mya smiled. "Myanmar is a beautiful country, but we have suffered under many empires. We are a young democracy, and like a hot-headed young man, we make grave mistakes. My father and I love this land. We would see it grow into a just and enlightened nation. I am sorry you have been caught up in our struggle."

Shanti pressed her palms together, touched them first to her forehead and then to her chest, and bowed. "*Namaste.*"

From downriver, came the sound of an engine.

"Border Patrol. Go quickly!"

"What about you?" Connor asked.

Just like he had with Pauline, he was thinking of Mya's safety, not just Shanti's. Shanti loved that about him.

"Take my rudder with you." She handed it to Shanti, who found it heavier than she had imagined. "I will tell them I lost it and that it drifted downriver. Hide quickly, or all of this will have been for nothing!"

Pack on one shoulder and rifle on the other, Connor pushed Mya and the skiff out into the current and then ran for cover. "Let's go."

Rudder in hand, Shanti ran beside Connor, ducking down behind a dense growth of ferns, the two of them watching as a motorboat came around the bend, four men with rifles standing inside.

They drew up alongside Mya, idled their engine, greeted her. They spoke for a moment and then tied her skiff to their boat and started upriver. Mya glanced over her shoulder in Shanti and Connor's direction as the boat disappeared around the bend.

Shanti exhaled, relief washing through her. "She'll be okay. Now what?"

"You know the drill. We make camp, get some sleep. The sun will be up soon. I want us gone before that village wakes up. Then we make for the border."

～

CONNOR WAITED until the boats were out of sight and then led Shanti farther away from the river, alert for any sign of the villagers Mya had warned them about.

"Look." Shanti stared at the ground. "It's been razed. They're erasing it."

There was just enough moonlight to show a wide, flat area, charred bamboo that had once been huts piled up to one side. The bastards had cleared the scorched remains of the village away, erasing any sign that hundreds of Rohingya families had once lived here and been brutally murdered.

"This was Sareema's village. They burned her sister alive. They raped her and beat her and caused her to lose her baby. Now there's nothing left. People died here. I don't want to make camp here."

"Yeah, neither do I."

It was too open, too exposed. Though there were some trees, the land here had been cleared to make fields for farming. That left them with almost no cover.

He was overdue to check in with Cobra. "Let's find a spot that's more out of the way, and I'll call in. They might have something for us."

"Maybe we could just follow the river. Mya said it runs into the Naf."

"Yes, but it might meander twenty additional miles along the way. We want to get to the border as efficiently as possible."

They went back to the place where they'd hidden from the Border Patrol, Connor stepping out of the tree cover to call in.

"Where the hell were you?" Shields asked. "Twice today, you just disappeared."

He gave her the short version of the story. "Do you have

our location now? What's our best chance for cover, and what route should we take to reach the border?"

"There's not much cover. It's mostly fields. Your best bet is to head due west right now, if you can, before all the farmers and villagers wake up."

"We got about five hours of sleep this afternoon and real food, so we're good."

"Luxury! You're sixteen klicks away from the river. We've got the fishing boat there with a team ready. The plan is to slip across the border and meet you in the water while SEALs in a couple of RHIBs create a distraction downriver."

"Good copy, Cobra. We'll reach the water. You be ready to fish us out. I don't want to lose her to some damned current."

"Copy that, O'Neal."

He ended the call, walked back to Shanti, who sat where he'd left her, watching him. "On your feet. We're heading west to the border, hoping to make good time before the villages in the area wake up. Keep the robes on. We might need them later."

She stood, shouldered her handbag. "I'm ready."

He chuckled, kissed her forehead. "You are amazing."

Walking near a river at night came with its own risks. Elephants weren't the only animals that came down to the water to drink.

They followed the river until it bent northward then slipped into a stand of trees and made their way around a small village heading due west. Then the moon slipped behind clouds, and the world went dark, Connor unable to see the tip of his rifle barrel. There were no streetlights, no headlights from cars, nothing to show the way.

Yeah, he was going to demand that NVGs make it into their emergency gear.

Despite the risk, he took out the flashlight once again, but it flickered out within a half hour, the batteries spent. He would add spare batteries to his list of changes.

More than once, Connor raised his rifle just to use the scope, trying to pick a safe path. "Let's slow down. I don't want—"

Shanti cried out.

Connor turned to find her on the ground, her foot trapped in a jumble of tree roots. He dropped his pack, knelt to see. *Fuck.* "Can you pull it out?"

She nodded, her teeth clenched. But when she tried, her eyes went wide with pain, and she sank against him, stifling a scream in his robes. "I can't! It hurts too much."

"It's okay."

It wasn't okay. They'd gone maybe six of those sixteen kilometers and had a lot of distance to make before dawn.

"I'm sorry. I'm so sorry."

"Hey, it's not your fault." He cupped her face between his palms, saw panic and desperation in her eyes. "You couldn't see. We were moving too fast. It could've been me. I'm still going to get you home whatever it takes. Do you hear me?"

She nodded. "I trust you."

He made short work of sawing through the roots then put the tool away and took Shanti's ankle into his hands, doing his best to be gentle.

She winced. "It really hurts."

"I believe it. It's broken. Your tibia snapped right above your ankle."

"How am I going to walk?"

"You won't. I'm going to carry you."

He pulled out the first aid kit and took out the flexible SAM splint. "I have to leave your boot on, but I think I can make this work."

He set her foot down in the center of the splint. "This might hurt."

"Oh, good, because it totally doesn't hurt now." She still had her sense of humor.

He wrapped one side across the top of her foot and around her ankle, then did the same with the other half, going in the opposite direction, her gasp of pain cutting at him.

Goddamn it!

When the splint was in place, he took out a rolled bandage and wrapped it around the splint to hold it fast. "I've got morphine, acetaminophen, and ibuprofen for pain. The morphine will take it all away, but it might make you sick or knock you out."

"No morphine. Let me try to walk." She struggled to stand.

"I don't think that's a good idea." He helped her up.

The moment she put weight on her leg, he thought she was going to pass out. He caught her, lowered her gently to the ground.

"I can't. I'm so sorry. I didn't want to be a pain in your ass. I've tried so hard to keep up and not make problems for—"

"You're not a pain in my ass, Shanti. You're the best time I've ever had. I'm going to call this in, and then we'll get moving again.

SHANTI WATCHED while Connor called Cobra from the riverbank, the pain in her ankle not nearly as sharp as her regret. She should have been paying better attention. She should have seen. If she had just taken that one step differently...

Now she was going to slow the two of them down. After

everything Connor had done for her, now he had to freaking carry her.

He strode back to her, knelt, his gaze searching the world behind her. "Cobra has been working with DEVGRU to drop a team in to help with our exfil, but we might make it to the river before they get their shit together. China is standing by Myanmar, which makes our situation a political landmine."

"DEVGRU?"

"What you civilians call SEAL Team Six."

"Oh." Wow. "Am I worth that?"

"You're a prosecutor with the International Criminal Court and a US citizen." He grabbed his pack. "Let's ditch the robes. They're just going to get in the way now. I'll lighten my pack, strip it down to essentials, and you can carry that while I carry you."

Connor worked quickly, putting the things he didn't feel they'd need inside the robes, tying it all into a ball and throwing it into the river where it couldn't be found. Neither of them wanted Ashin Dempo or Mya to get into trouble because of them. Then he stuffed the contents of Shanti's handbag into his backpack, consolidating their gear.

"Okay, you stand on your good leg, and I'll get the pack adjusted for you. Hold onto me for balance."

When that was done, he walked around in front of her and lifted her onto his back.

"I'm heavy."

"Not as heavy as the Unit buddy I carried for half a day once. He probably had eighty pounds on you."

On they went, through stands of jungle and farmers' fields, Connor breathing hard, his heart thudding beneath her hands as she held on to him. They moved on for maybe an hour when the first rays of light stretched across the sky, giving Connor more light, enabling him to go faster—and bringing the world to life around them.

Smoke from cookfires. Barking dogs. The bleating of goats. Voices. And behind them, back toward the mountains, the whirring of helicopter rotors.

Connor stopped in a grove of trees at the top of a ridge, set her down, and went for his water bottle, drinking deeply. Sweat trickled down his temples and beaded on his forehead. "If we have to, we'll shelter in place and take the last few miles tonight. If I see a good spot to set up camp, that's what we'll do."

He lifted her onto his back again and started downhill, taking it slowly, Shanti keeping her eyes peeled for people or anything else that might give them away.

"There's a dirt road ahead," she whispered. "I see what looks like an army vehicle. There are soldiers."

"I see them." He stopped behind an outcropping of rocks, lowered her to the ground, and raised his rifle. "Yeah, that's definitely—"

A bark.

A dog came up behind them, wagging its tail, meaning no harm.

"Shh!" Shanti held out her hand for the dog to sniff, hoping to quiet it.

"Shit." Connor drew his knife. "I don't want to do this, but I—"

A group of five little girls carrying water buckets came around the corner.

Shanti willed herself to smile, but the girls had seen Connor's weapons and ran back toward their village, screaming.

"Son of a bitch!" Connor sheathed his knife, pulled out the sat phone, and made a quick call. "We've been compromised. A group of kids saw us and my rifle and ran away screaming. It's going to get very ugly here in a minute. If you have an emergency exfil plan, now would be the time. Copy that."

"Do they have a plan?"

"They're working on one. Come on. We need to get out of here."

From behind her, came the sound of men's shouts. The girls had roused their village, and the men were coming.

In a moment of clarity, Shanti knew it was over. She slipped off the backpack, pushed it toward him. "Go! You can make it. I can't."

"No, Shanti, I won't leave you here."

"You can't run with me on your back forever. You'll be outnumbered. Those villagers are going to tell the soldiers we just saw. I remember what you said—that they want me alive, but they'll kill you. Please go! I won't let you die for me."

"Those villagers could kill you before the Tatmadaw gets here. And the soldiers—they'll rape you, Shanti. They'll torture you. They'll make you wish you were dead. You've seen what they can do. They'll throw you in a cell—"

"And I'll *survive* just like Sareema did." She could see from the despair in his eyes that he knew she was right. "Go, now, Connor, or they'll have *both* of us. I couldn't live with myself if they killed you. I love you, Connor."

If this was the last time she saw him, she wanted him to know.

His eyes went wide for a moment, then he ducked down and kissed her. "I'm not abandoning you. Be ready for anything."

"Run!"

He took his pack, turned, and disappeared down the hillside, leaving Shanti alone.

Her relief was short-lived, her mouth going dry as the villagers rushed over to her, hoes, axes, and sticks in their hands, rage on their faces.

On a sudden inspiration, she pointed away from the direction in which Connor had run. "He ran that way. He's a bad man. He hurt me. I'm a tourist."

They would find out the truth eventually, but if she could buy him some time...

The head man walked up, knelt, listened while she repeated what she'd said, making up a story about how he'd abducted her. His English was poor, but he understood enough. For a few precious minutes, it looked as if they would take care of her. Women brought her tea. A healer looked at her ankle. A group of men charged off in the direction she'd pointed, running after Connor.

Then the crowd parted, and a soldier appeared.

He walked up to Shanti, looked at a photo of her on his cell phone.

He smiled, said something to the villagers. The blow came fast and hard as he backhanded her across her face, knocking her over, her head striking something hard.

And then ... nothing.

21

Connor watched through his scope as two soldiers carried Shanti upright between them, her head lolling as if she were unconscious. They dropped her unceremoniously in the dirt, one of them laughing as he groped her breasts while another reached between her thighs. They weren't searching for weapons. This was assault.

Rage hammered in Connor's chest, the lust to kill rushing through his veins.

You can't help her if you lose your shit.

He drew a deep breath and another, put his emotions on lockdown.

There were six of them and one of him, but he had the advantage. They believed he was in the wind, running scared, and that Shanti was alone.

I'm right here, princess.

He had scoped out his shots across this hillside, knowing he could fire at most twice from each location before they spotted him. He had to make every shot count—without turning himself into a target.

Her eyes were open now, her face twisted with pain.

One of them jerked her to her feet, her weight coming down on her broken leg, her cry shredding Connor's heart.

Focus.

An officer walked up to her, shouted something in her face, and struck her.

Connor couldn't fire now. If he did, he would risk the round over-penetrating and hitting Shanti, too.

Step to the side, either side, you fucking son of a bitch.

The officer walked to the front of the truck, reached inside for the radio.

Connor exhaled, checked his sight picture, fired.

BAM!

The officer dropped to the ground in a red mist.

Quickly, Connor lined up another shot.

The soldiers forgot Shanti for the moment, letting her fall to the ground again as they scrambled for their weapons.

One raised a rifle, aimed in Connor's general direction.

BAM!

The soldier fell to the ground, a round in his head.

Connor kept low and ran twenty meters to his right, dropped to a knee in a dense stand of bamboo, sighted on the man nearest Shanti.

BAM!

He ran again, this time taking cover behind an outcropping of rock.

Three down, three to go.

One of the soldiers ran for cover.

BAM!

Connor ran to his next position, raised his rifle—and saw that one of the two remaining soldiers had Shanti now. He hid behind her, using her as a shield, his pistol pointed at her temple. He wasn't much taller than Shanti, making the shot tougher.

The soldier shouted something, his gaze searching the hillside for Connor.

Connor wished he had time to circle behind these two, but he didn't. He was sure they'd gotten off a call to their commander and that enemy QRF were now inbound. He could handle six guys, but he couldn't take on an entire army.

The two soldiers had apparently decided to get the hell away from here, one opening the door to jump behind the wheel, the other backing toward the driver's side passenger door and dragging Shanti with him.

Connor aimed at the one climbing into the driver's seat.

BAM!

The soldier toppled to the ground. The remaining soldier stopped where he was, pistol still aimed at Shanti's head. But fear was making him reckless.

He shouted at Connor, panic on his face, the front of his pants wet. Had he pissed himself? "I kill her! Come down!"

Connor moved farther to his right, trying to get a clear shot.

Damn it.

Seeing no alternative, Connor stood, arms raised. "I'm coming out."

The soldier's head jerked around, and he pointed his pistol at Connor, releasing Shanti and taking a step in Connor's direction. He seemed to realize that this was a tactical mistake. He fired at Connor, a single panicked shot, but missed.

Connor flipped the rifle over his shoulder, kept moving, aimed—and fired.

BAM!

Shanti collapsed onto the ground with a cry.

Connor ran to her. "I'm here, princess."

"I knew ... you would come for me." Her left cheek was badly bruised, and she seemed dazed.

"What did they do to you?"

"Hit me... I struck my head... on a rock, I think."

He checked her, found a bloody goose egg on the back of her head. There was nothing he could do about that now.

You shouldn't have left her there. You should have picked her up and run.

He ignored that voice, focused on the moment. "We're taking the vehicle.

Villagers were watching from the cover of trees, the males moving closer. Connor needed to get her out of here—now.

He scooped Shanti into his arms, carried her around to the front passenger seat, and buckled her in, grateful to see that the keys were still in the ignition. Then he ran around the front of the vehicle, stepped over dead bodies, threw his rifle and backpack at Shanti's feet—and climbed behind the wheel.

From the distance, he heard the thrum of helicopters.

Shit.

He started the engine, gunned it. "Talk to me, Shanti. Hey, what's your name?"

"You know ... my name. You just said it."

"Good enough."

With one hand on the wheel, he pulled out the sat phone. "Shanti is injured—broken leg and a probable concussion. We've got a vehicle, and I'm driving as fast as I can. Where the hell am I going? The entire fucking army is bearing down on us."

Shields gave him directions, using old satellite images

superimposed on their location, the helicopters drawing closer. "Left just ahead and then straight on. You'll have to cut across a couple of fields, but that will take you to the river. Team One is inbound in a blue fishing boat. DEVGRU is cooking up a distraction, trying to get those helicopters off your ass."

That would be nice. If the helicopter opened up with a machine gun, they could take out the engine—or kill them both.

Connor took the left, saw the river up ahead. "Hey, Shanti, are you with me?"

Her head came up, and she looked around, clearly confused and in pain.

"See that? There's the river. Just ahead."

Okay, that was a bit of an exaggeration. They had maybe three hundred meters of fields and sand between them and the riverbank. But that's why God had invented four-wheel drive.

"We're going home?"

"Hell, yes, we are. Stay awake, because you're going to have to swim."

"I can swim."

God, he loved her.

"That's what you told me. Hang on. It's time for a little off-roading."

SHANTI FOUGHT TO STAY CONSCIOUS, her face throbbing where the soldier had struck her, pain splitting her head in two. "Is there a boat?"

What was happening? It was hard to pay attention.

"Yes, there's a blue fishing vessel. Swim straight for it. I'll be right there. When we get to the boat, we're safe. You're almost there."

Blue vessel. Swim. Almost there.

Darkness dragged at her, tried to suck her down.

Another helicopter buzzed overhead, so close she could see soldiers with weapons staring down at them. It flew straight ahead of them, and for a moment, she thought it would set down in their path.

Then it abruptly gained elevation and veered to the south.

Connor chuckled.

"What's funny? Where's it going?"

"Remember the DEVGRU guys? They're making trouble somewhere nearby."

DEVGRU. SEAL Team Six.

Shanti must have drifted for a moment because the next thing she knew, Connor had stopped their vehicle.

"Unbuckle, princess. I'll come help you out. The river's right here." He hurried over, slipped a strong arm around her, and lifted her onto her good leg, bending down to grab his backpack and rifle.

She hopped alongside him, one strong arm steadying her.

"We're attracting some attention. Border Patrol. We need to go faster."

But Shanti struggled to keep up with him, black spots dancing in front of her eyes.

Connor hurled his rifle into the river, shouldered his pack, and then scooped her into his arms—and ran.

A splash of water. Cold enfolding her, jarring her awake.

"Okay, Shanti, show me how you can swim. The fishing boat is headed straight for us. So is Border Patrol. We need to get to the fishing boat before Border Patrol reaches us, or it's all over."

Shanti kicked and cried out, pain shooting through her right leg, the resistance of the water pushing her foot back. She gritted her teeth, used only her good leg and her arms, and moved into the river, swimming as hard as she could.

"You're doing great." Connor encouraged her, kept pace with her.

The grinding sound of boat engines drew nearer.

She focused on the blue fishing vessel, the one headed straight for them, the one with the big, redhaired Scot standing at the prow with a rifle in his hands.

"Swim harder, Shanti!"

But the black spots were back, the world going gray, boats and guns and river fading into a dream.

"Shanti, you've got to swim now."

Shanti looked into the eyes of a man she'd only seen in photos. "Uncle Abani?"

"Yes, I'm your uncle. I'm glad we get to speak at last. You've made us all very proud, Shanti, but you can't give up—not now. This fight is not over."

"I'm so tired."

"Yes, but you have important work to do. Swim, Shanti. Swim."

Shanti raised her head above the surface, coughed up water. She looked around, expecting to see Uncle Abani. But Connor was there.

"Shanti!" He took hold of her, turned onto his back, and swam with her in one arm as if she had been drowning.

Had she?

And then the boat pulled alongside them, strong hands lifting her out of the water, laying her gently back on a stretcher.

"They're on board," Dylan shouted. "Go! Go! Go!"

"She's got a broken right tibia." That was Connor. "I think she's got a concussion. She's lost consciousness several times, and she's in a fair amount of pain."

"Shanti, I'm Doc Sullivan. I'm going to give you some morphine. Let's get an IV going in case she's got internal bleeding."

"Two Border Patrol vessels coming up hard to stern." That was Malik.

And they were moving.

"I'm cold," she managed to say.

A blanket.

Connor took her hand. "You did it, princess. We're about to cross the border. You're going home."

CONNOR HELD SHANTI'S HAND, watched the pain leave her face as the morphine autoinjector did its work, adrenaline still thrumming through his veins.

Leaving her had been the hardest thing he'd ever done. It had gone against every instinct he had—to protect, to defend, to keep her safe.

But she'd been right. Between villagers and those soldiers, he'd been outnumbered at least a hundred to one. He would have fought and died, taking civilians with him, and Naing would have her now. She'd bought time for him to reclaim the tactical advantage.

He still didn't know exactly what had happened after he'd gone. There'd been ten unbearable minutes when she'd been out of his sight. When he'd next seen her, she'd been battered and unconscious.

The image of the soldiers groping her and striking her

filled his mind, rage rekindling in his gut. But then he'd known they would hurt her. She'd known it too, and she'd been willing to endure whatever pain and suffering Naing and his men could dole out rather than watch Connor die.

I couldn't live with myself if they killed you. I love you, Connor.

Good God.

She'd told him she loved him. He'd seen in her eyes that she'd meant it. He'd been so stunned by her words, and the situation had been so dire, that he hadn't told her he loved her, too.

Does it matter what you feel?

The two of them didn't stand a chance. She would be going back to The Hague, and he was headed to Denver, where he would probably lose his job and find himself working security at a mall. She deserved better than that. Besides, they'd just been through one hell of an experience together, and she'd been dependent on him. Her feelings might change after she'd been home for a while.

"I thought you'd lost the lass to the river," McManus said.

"Yeah, I did, too."

One minute, Shanti had been right beside him. The next, she had disappeared below the water. He'd dived for her, but hadn't found her until her head popped up a good ten feet downriver where the strong current had taken her.

It had scared the living *fuck* out of him.

Two Navy SEAL RHIBs drew up on either side of them, and two corpsmen boarded with a litter.

"We've got her."

But Connor didn't want to let her go. "I'm staying with her."

Everyone except for McManus, Segal, and Isaksen

climbed onto one of the two RHIBs, which were heading toward a US Navy amphibious assault ship that was hanging out in Bangladeshi waters in the Bay of Bengal. From there, they would fly in a Chinook to Dhaka. The other three would take the little boat back to Cox's Bazar and catch a separate helicopter to Dhaka with Shields and the geek team. They would all fly with Shanti to the Netherlands—provided the ship's surgeon thought she was stable and strong enough for the flight.

"Hey, *cabrón*, go catch us some fish," Cruz teased McManus.

"Go catch the clap," McManus fired back.

Isaksen and the SEALs were ribbing each other.

"Vikings make the best seamen," Isaksen said.

The SEALS laughed—and flipped him off.

Connor sat beside Shanti, holding her hand while the Doc and the corpsmen checked her vitals and did their best to keep her comfortable as the RHIB bounced its way over the waves.

Twice she opened her eyes and asked for him, looking terrified and confused. "Connor?"

"I'm right here. You're safe now, Shanti. You're going home."

The boat ride to the ship took about an hour. The ship's surgeon and Tower were waiting for them.

"Let's get her below," the surgeon said.

Tower clapped Connor on the shoulder. "You go, too. I'd like them to look at that graze wound on your temple."

Connor didn't object because that meant he could stay close to Shanti. While corpsmen did X-rays of her leg, gave her IV fluids, and checked her for a possible head injury, another corpsman examined both of his graze wounds.

"Those are good stitches. How long have they been in?"

Connor had to think. "Five days."

"And you lost consciousness?"

"For about an hour."

"No CT scan?"

"Not in the jungle."

"You might want to get that checked out when you get home. The shoulder wound is healing well. It looks like you got lucky twice."

From the other side of the curtain, Connor heard Shanti's voice.

"Connor?"

That's all it took.

"Thanks." Connor stepped down from the exam table and pushed his way through the curtain. "I'm right here."

"Where are we?"

"We're on a navy vessel. As soon as you're cleared, we'll be taking a Chinook to Dhaka and then flying back to The Hague."

"Another helicopter?"

He couldn't blame her for being sick of them. "This one won't crash."

"I can't believe we're going home. I was so afraid the soldiers would kill you."

"I'm a hard man to kill. What happened after I left you?"

She told him how she'd tricked the villagers at first into believing that she was just a tourist and how they had helped her—until the soldier had walked up with her photo on his cell phone. "He struck me. I think I hit my head on a rock. After that, it's just bits and pieces."

"You are the bravest, most beautiful woman I know."

"I saw my Uncle Abani—the one who was killed in the genocide."

"Your uncle?"

"One minute I was swimming, and the next he was there, beside me underwater, telling me to keep going." Tears filled her eyes. "He said my family was proud of me but that I had to fight because I still had work to do. Then I was under the water, and he was gone. I kicked for the surface—and then you were there."

"I thought I'd lost you. God, Shanti, I thought you'd drowned. One minute you were there, and the next..." *Shit.* "I've never been more afraid in my life."

"Do you think my uncle was really there?"

"What matters is that you thought he was there, and it woke you up."

"What happens now?"

He brought her up to speed. "You'll be back in The Hague late tonight."

"Do you remember what you promised me?"

A night of unlimited kisses.

He stroked her cheek. "I haven't forgotten, but I might not be able to keep that promise. We'll probably be leaving The Hague for Denver after you deplane."

"So soon?"

"Yeah. I'll have a lot of questions to answer when I get back."

"Are you in trouble?"

"We'll see. I broke some big rules.'"

"You don't have to tell them what happened between us, do you? I won't."

"I won't volunteer information, but I won't lie."

Sadness filled her eyes, her cheek bruised and swollen. "I'm not ready to say goodbye, Connor. I love you."

He had to say it. He felt a moral obligation to tell her. "You've been through a real ordeal. Adrenaline has a way of messing with people's emotions. When you get home and life goes back to normal, you might not feel what you feel today. You deserve a guy who can share your life, not a soldier who's gone all the time and can't function in the real world. A month from now—"

"Don't tell me what I deserve or what I feel. I want *you*. A month or six months won't make a difference. Besides, there is no normal after this. This changed me. *You* changed me."

Her words touched him, resonated with him. She had changed him, too. But he didn't say that. "Give it time, princess."

But she wasn't finished. "You were right, Connor. You are a warrior. We need people like you who can stand up to dictators and warlords if we're going to build a better world. I'd be dead if not for you—or locked in a prison cell in Yangon. Now I can prosecute Naing. I know you don't do relationships, but I thought we at least mattered to each other. We do, don't we?"

"Of course, but..."

Tell her. Tell her how you feel.

The moment passed, Connor's inability to put what he was feeling into words leaving hurt and the agony of uncertainty on her face.

"Will I see you again?"

He didn't want to let her down. "I don't know."

22

D rowsy from pain pills and exhausted, Shanti slept much of the way to The Hague, lying back in one of the reclining chairs on Cobra's fancy jet, Doc Sullivan checking on her from time to time. The navy surgeon had set her leg, put it in a boot, and had given her crutches, the anesthetic he'd injected into the break long since worn off.

Connor sat beside her, brought her water and fresh ice packs for her cheek, and helped her get to the restroom on her crutches, keeping a professional distance, treating her like a client once again.

God, it hurt.

She didn't want to get him fired, so she played along, doing her best to hide her feelings for him—and her heartache at having to say goodbye.

When you get home and life gets back to normal, you might not feel the way you feel today.

His words had stung, and yet she could see in his eyes that he cared about her, that this hurt him, too. No, he hadn't told her that he loved her, but she couldn't believe a man could be so caring and so damned good in bed if he didn't feel something for her.

You're being ridiculous.

He'd told her he didn't do relationships. What had she expected?

When he left to use the restroom, Elizabeth sat in his seat. "I'm sorry for what you've been through, Shanti. We all are."

"I'm sorry you lost two men." Remembering, she reached for the plastic bag a corpsman had given her to hold what remained of her belongings and drew out the family photo she'd taken from John Hatch's luggage. "This got wet in the river. Sorry. I thought his family might want it."

Elizabeth took the picture. "You carried this all the way back from the crash site? Thanks. I'm sure they'll be grateful."

"What went wrong?"

Elizabeth told her how the Indian pilot, who'd sold himself out to Naing, had been dating one of Pauline's support staff, the woman who kept her calendar. "When he learned from her that you weren't coming to camp that day, he knew to watch for Cobra transports at the Cox's Bazar airport. He was a pilot, and people were used to seeing him there. He had access to the terminal and tarmac. He and his buddy shot John Hatch and Robert Davis in the hangar— and you know the rest. I ruled the Indian pilot out in my assessment because he'd piloted the helicopter the day those guys fired the grenade at you. I shouldn't have done that. I was wrong, and I'm sorry."

"Pauline wasn't the leak." That was a relief.

"No, she wasn't, but she is horrified. She fired her clerk."

"Do the men's families know?"

Elizabeth nodded. "Notifying them was Corbray's job, not mine—thank God."

Then it was all too much for Shanti—the abduction, the pilots' murders, saying goodbye to Connor. Her eyes filled with tears that she couldn't hold back. "I'm sorry."

"For what?" Elizabeth reached for a tissue. "Damn, girl, you were unstoppable until you broke your tibia. You've earned our respect. Am I right, guys?"

"Hell, yeah," Malik said.

"You're one tough chick," Cruz said.

"There are blokes a-plenty who wouldna be able to do what you did, lass."

"You're a badass, Ms. Lahiri," Mr. Tower said from behind a newspaper.

Shanti hadn't realized the others had been listening.

Elizabeth leaned in and hugged her, whispering in her ear. "Don't worry. Connor is crazy about you. Give him time."

Shanti's pulse skipped. Had she said something to give them away?

Elizabeth seemed to read her mind. "I've never seen him act like this about any woman—ever."

Then Connor was there, glaring at Elizabeth. "Fishing?"

Elizabeth released Shanti, got to her feet. "She was upset."

He narrowed his eyes at her. "Right."

"You should know that we got your Hot Wheels out to the camp hospital. Pauline was grateful." Then Elizabeth spoke in a whisper for their ears only. "This is going to be a *very* interesting debriefing."

~

THEY LANDED in The Hague shortly after midnight.

"Everyone, take a break and stretch your legs." Tower stood, glanced at his watch. "We're refueling and heading on to Denver."

Connor stood, helped Shanti to stand. "How are you feeling?"

"I'm okay." She looked like she might cry, every emotion she was feeling there in those amber eyes—love, gratitude, dread, grief.

"Ms. Lahiri, you've got my deepest apologies for the way this went down. It's been an honor to serve you." Tower held out his hand.

Shanti skipped the handshake and hugged him. "You all worked so hard to keep me safe and get me home again, risking your lives. I can never thank you enough."

One by one, she said goodbye to the staff, giving each of them a hug.

Connor had thought he'd get a moment alone with her. He wanted a chance to set things straight. He'd hurt her earlier, and he hadn't meant to.

Armed hostiles he could handle. Emotions? Not so much.

Fuck.

"We've got paramedics here to drive you to the hospital, Ms. Lahiri. Your boss wants you to be checked out by someone other than a navy surgeon. You can just wait in your seat. Also, your parents are here."

"They are?"

Everyone smiled at her surprise—everyone except Connor.

This was happening too fast. In his head, it hadn't gone like this. He'd been able to kiss her, hold her, say a decent farewell, maybe even find the courage to tell her how he felt about her. But it just wasn't happening.

Airport staff arrived at the plane's rear exit with a special lift to enable the paramedics to transport Shanti on a stretcher, the others heading for the front exit.

Connor stayed put.

"O'Neal, let's get out of the paramedics' way," Tower said.

"I haven't said goodbye." Shanti's gaze met his, anguish in her eyes. She sank into his arms, the feel of her precious. "I will never forget you. Thank you. You saved my life so many times I lost count."

"You saved mine, too, remember?" It was the truth, but that wasn't what he wanted to say to her. "Take care of yourself."

He would have said more, he would have kissed her, but Tower stood there, watching. Connor let her go, every fiber of his body objecting.

She pressed something into his hand. Her business card. "Stay safe."

He willed himself to smile. "You, too."

And for the second time in as many days, he turned his back on her and walked away when that was the last thing in the world he wanted to do.

His heart thundered in his chest, everything in him screaming for him to turn around, to go after her, to say what he'd left unsaid. He willed his feet to keep moving. Down the stairs to the tarmac and toward the terminal.

"Good job, O'Neal," Tower said. "There was a time or two when I wasn't sure we'd get the two of you back alive."

"I bet." Connor glanced back, saw the paramedics wheeling the stretcher out of the plane and onto the lift platform.

Christ!

He felt the tug of her from across the tarmac, every step taking him farther away from her. He willed himself to move on, to let her go. She needed time to heal. They probably both needed time to sort through everything that had happened.

If you don't get a grip, you're going to get yourself fired.

They entered the terminal, the airport almost empty.

He looked to his right, saw the paramedics push Shanti through an entrance farther down the terminal.

Two people ran to her—a tall man with dark hair and a woman with blonde hair.

"Shanti!"

They hugged her, their joy at having their daughter back palpable.

"A happy ending," Tower said. "You gave them that."

"We all did." Connor tried to feel a sense of satisfaction, but everything in the world that mattered to him was leaving by the door at the far end of the terminal. When the door closed and Shanti disappeared from view, he felt it in his chest.

SHANTI SPENT the night in the hospital, her mother remaining by her side while her father stayed in her apartment. In the morning, she saw an orthopedist and a neurologist who did a CT scan on her head, gave her discharge instructions, and sent her home.

It felt strange to walk through her own front door. Bram and her friends from work had sent flowers, and her father had gotten her flowers, too, so the place smelled like roses and lilies. "Thanks."

It was a relief to be out of the jungle, to be safe, and yet...

God, she missed Connor.

If he'd just given her some sign that he cared about her...

You knew it would end like this.

And she'd let herself fall in love with him anyway.

Her mother made them cups of *cha*, and they sat together in her living room, Shanti taking up the sofa so she could elevate her leg. Like a true Bengali, her father asked her about little things at first—the weather in Bangladesh, her flight home, whether she'd heard from her brother yet.

"Enough, Dev," her mother said. "What happened? One day, we get an email from you, saying you're busy at work. A few days later, the State Department calls to tell us you've been abducted, the helicopter has crashed, and you are missing in Myanmar. We didn't even know you were in Myanmar. God, Shanti, I've never been more afraid. I think it took ten years off my life."

Shanti told them the story, leaving out the sexy bits— her visits to the camps, the soldier's cell phone with its damning evidence, the abduction, and Connor being shot.

"I thought he was dead, but then I saw he was still breathing. His gun had fallen to the floor of the helicopter, so I got a hold of it and hid it. I told myself that I would kill, if necessary, to save his life. I don't know if I could have pulled the trigger."

"My sweet, brave girl." Her father poured her more *cha*. "You never should have been placed in that position."

She told them about the helicopter crash, the wild gaur, and the long trek home—the tree house camp, the bombed remains of the *mandir*, the cobra that had almost bitten Connor, the rope ladder and bridge, the World War II plane fuselage with the skeletal remains of its crew inside, and Ashin Dempo and Mya.

"We didn't trust them at first, but they put their lives on

the line to save ours. Mya led us out to the river while her father was in the Great Hall with General Naing."

She told them about the remains of Myar Zin and their trek toward the border and how she'd broken her ankle. "Connor carried me for miles on his back until we were discovered."

By the time she got to the part where she'd told Connor to leave her, her mother was in tears. "Oh, Shanti. You told him to leave you *alone*?"

"If he had stayed, they would have gotten both of us. He would be dead, and I would be in prison. This way, he escaped and turned the tables on them. He rescued me from Naing's men and got the two of us to the Naf River."

"Thank God for him," her mother said again.

"I had trouble staying conscious. I guess I passed out in the water." She swallowed the lump in her throat. "And then he was there, Dad—Uncle Abani."

She told them what her vision of Uncle Abani had said. "I was drowning, but he woke me. I pushed myself to the surface and coughed up water—and then Connor was there. He held me the rest of the way to the boat. He said he thought he'd lost me. Was Uncle Abani truly there? Was that his *atman,* his soul?"

Tears filled her father's eyes. "Who can say? But as this vision of him saved your life, I call it a miracle."

"I wish we'd gotten a chance to meet Connor and thank him," her mother said.

"So do I." She couldn't hold it back any longer, tears spilling down her cheeks. "I love him. I know he cares about me, too, but... I think some part of him believes he's not good enough for me."

"It's probably just the situation, sweetheart." Her mother

took her hand. "You both went through a lot together. It's natural that you would feel close to him."

"That's what he said." But it wasn't what Shanti wanted to hear.

"You are very different people," her father said. "He works as a fighter, and you work for peace. I always imagined you with a scholar or an attorney. I'm grateful to him for getting you home alive, but, Shanti, he lives a life of violence."

"If there weren't people like him who were willing and able to fight, people like me wouldn't be able to do our work."

Her father's expression became troubled, and she could tell he was struggling with that idea. "I suppose that's true. When did my daughter become so wise?"

"That's what he taught me."

And now Shanti would have to get used to life without him.

23

Connor and the rest of the Cobra team reached Denver in the early afternoon.

"Debriefing at zero-nine-hundred hours," Tower said as they disembarked.

Connor carried his gear to his Ford F-150 and drove through traffic to his condo in LoDo, regret sitting in his chest, cold and heavy as lead.

Shanti.

He'd thought about her all the way home, dreamed about her when he'd slept, everything in him wishing he'd had the guts to tell her how he felt. He'd hurt her. He'd seen that in her eyes. He told himself it was better this way, that the two of them were just high on adrenaline, that they would both get over it.

Keep telling yourself that.

He went through his post-mission routine—laundry, grocery shopping, checking his gear, making a list for the debriefing.

A pair of NVGs. More MREs. Spare batteries.

Then he called his folks, let them know he was safe. The

State Department had told them he'd been shot down, and he knew they must be worried.

"They going to give you any time off after this one?" his father asked. "Seems to me you deserve it. We would love a visit. It was Christmas when we last saw you, son."

"I've got lots of apples," his mother added. "I'll make apple pie and homemade ice cream."

"Yeah, we'll see."

When Cruz texted him to say that the guys were heading to the Pony, Connor joined them, tossing back one whiskey after another, and rebuffing the hot blonde who hit on him. She was pretty and clearly wanted a quick fuck—but she wasn't Shanti.

"Another time maybe." He left after that, took a cab home.

Alcohol made for a bad night's sleep, nightmares about Shanti being swept downriver jolting him awake twice.

As Shields had predicted, it was an interesting debriefing.

"Why the *fuck* would you leave a defenseless client alone and allow her to be taken by the enemy?" Tower asked.

It had been Shanti's idea, but the responsibility for the decision rested solely on Connor's shoulders. "It was a tactical retreat."

"A tactical retreat?" Corbray asked. "You're going to have to explain that, man."

Connor told them how the dog had found them, the little girls following behind. "They saw my rifle and knife, and their screams brought villagers down on us. We knew the villagers would get the soldiers whose vehicle we'd just seen. We were caught between the two groups."

"And Ms. Lahiri was incapable of walking," Tower said.

"If I had tried to run with her on my back, they would

have taken both of us. I would most likely have been killed on the spot, and Ms. Lahiri would have become Naing's prisoner. By leaving her, I was able to choose my ground, take the soldiers out one by one, retrieve her, and commandeer their vehicle. She was out of my sight for about ten minutes. It was one of the toughest decisions I've ever had to make."

And the longest ten minutes of Connor's life.

"You're damned lucky they didn't rape her—or kill her." Tower was pissed.

Connor couldn't blame him. "It wasn't luck. She managed to convince the villagers that she was a tourist and that I had hurt her. They helped her at first."

"She is one smart woman—and brave," Corbray said.

They had no idea.

"Eventually, one of the villagers brought a soldier, who recognized her. He struck her, and her head hit a rock. I didn't see this. Ms. Lahiri told me afterward."

Corbray and Tower didn't ask whether he and Shanti had gotten intimate—and Connor sure as hell didn't tell.

"Unconventional but tactically sound," Tower said at last. "Outstanding work, O'Neal. Truly top-notch. Also, the British government is grateful for the location of the Blenheim. They're working to get permission to repatriate the remains."

Connor set the dog tags he'd taken from the crash on the table. "Their families might want these."

Tower picked one up, examined it. "I bet they will."

The meeting moved on, Corbray taking over. "We're putting together a team for a small security operation on behalf of the State Department in Nairobi—a diplomatic mission."

"Let's do it." Connor needed a distraction.

"Not you, O'Neal," Corbray said. "You're over your operational-hours limit for the month. You've got the rest of the month off."

Fuck.

"You just ruined his day," Shields teased.

Connor drove back to his place through a city that ought to have felt like home but didn't. Nothing seemed the same —not Denver, not the office, not his condo. He told himself it was just re-entry, just the same struggle he always had. But he didn't believe it.

This was about Shanti.

Get a fucking grip.

He sent her a quick email, asking her how she was feeling—and went for his bottle of whiskey. He started to pour himself a drink.

It won't help. You know that. You've done this before.

He stopped. It was September 7, and he had the rest of the month off. He couldn't spend that entire time drinking.

He cleaned his condo, watched ESPN for a while, hit the gym, a storm raging inside him. Desperate, and with nowhere else to turn, he packed a bag, threw it into his truck, and headed north to Ault.

SHANTI'S PARENTS stayed for a week, buying groceries, making meals, doing her laundry, keeping her company. She slept a lot—something the doctor had said she might do. When she was awake, she checked her phone obsessively for email from Connor. She was happy to hear he hadn't gotten in trouble and that they'd given him some vacation.

"I'm at my parents' farm for a few days. They don't have

good internet so you might not hear from me for a while," he wrote. "How is your head?"

"I still have bad headaches most days, but I'm walking with a boot now. The bruise on my cheek and the bump on my head are healing."

She signed her emails, "Love, Shanti." He signed his simply, "C."

Then came Sunday morning, and it was time for her parents to fly home.

"Take care of yourself, sweetie." Her mother hugged her tight, then lowered her voice to a whisper. "If this Connor fellow you're heartsick over feels the same for you, it will work out. Look at your Dad and me."

"Thanks, Mom. And thanks for your help."

"Good work, my angel." Her father kissed her forehead. "You've always wanted to make the world a better place, and you are doing just that."

Then they stepped into the taxi and headed to the airport.

That's when the nightmares started. Twice that night, she awoke, terrified and covered in cold sweat, dreaming that Connor had disappeared in front of her, leaving her alone in a dark tunnel with no way out.

The next morning, she went back to work, her coworkers standing up at their desks and applauding as she hobbled by.

Bram walked with her to her office, bringing her quickly up to date about their progress cataloging the evidence. "I am so grateful that you're home and safe."

"Thanks, Bram."

Shanti threw herself into her job, working late hours, even though using the computer made her headaches worse. She finished organizing all their evidence—survivor and witness interviews, cell phone videos, still images from the videos, satellite data shared by various nations, UN data, reports from Bangladesh—and wrote an extensive brief that would be part of their official request for an arrest warrant.

It wasn't easy, not just because of her headaches, but because she kept forgetting things. She resorted to writing herself notes and found herself leaning on her clerk much more than usual. "I'm sorry, Makena. I don't know what's wrong with me."

"Don't worry, Ms. Lahiri. We all know you've been through something terrible."

It had been terrible, and yet this was harder.

We call it re-entry... When the adrenaline wears off, that's when the nightmares and the self-doubt set in.

She understood now—or at least she thought she did.

Was he suffering, too?

God, she missed him.

Despite the nightmares and headaches, she pushed herself, one goal in mind—to see Naing arrested and behind bars so that the killing could stop.

After two weeks of this—headaches, nightmares, sorting through images of rape and murder—she found herself at an emotional edge.

"Maybe you're not ready to be back at work. I want you to see a doctor," Bram said one day when he'd caught her at her desk, in tears and rubbing her temples.

"I'll see a doctor when we get the warrant," she told him.

Finally, on the last day of September, Shanti stood in front of the judge and presented the case that had nearly taken her life.

"Your Honor, for these crimes against humanity, the Office of the Prosecutor requests a warrant for the arrest of General Min Thant Naing."

Judge Pekka Karvonen, a Finnish judge, didn't hesitate. "Granted."

The relief was so intense that Shanti had to grab onto the table.

Judge Karvonen wasn't finished. "Ms. Lahiri, your commitment to this case has been outstanding. This court is aware of the great personal price you paid to be able to approach this bench and make this request. You are to be praised."

"Thank you, Your Honor."

Then the hearing was over.

There was cake and champagne in the prosecutor's office, but Shanti didn't feel up to celebrating, her headache so severe she thought her brain might explode.

"What's wrong?" Bram asked.

"My head. I feel strange, and my vision... It's disappearing."

"We're going. Come."

He took her in an official ICC limo to the ER, where they diagnosed her with a migraine and post-concussive syndrome, gave her pain medication, and sent her home with strict orders to rest and stay off the computer for the next few weeks.

"You need to take care of yourself now," Bram told her on the drive to her apartment. "You've done enough."

Shanti's last thought as she drifted into a drug-induced sleep was of Connor.

❧

CONNOR CLEARED the breakfast table and helped his mother with the dishes.

"Thanks, hon." His mother wiped the counter, started the dishwasher. "It's sure been nice having you home."

"It's been good to see you, too."

Three weeks was the longest he'd been home since he'd joined the army. He wasn't sure what he'd expected when he'd come here or even why he'd come. If he was looking for something, he sure hadn't found it.

Still, it had been nice to see his mother, to hang with his old man, his brother, Ryan, and his sisters, Kate and Tara, and their kids. He'd helped his father with the farm work, the physical exertion burning off some of his restlessness. But it hadn't made him forget Shanti.

His phone buzzed with a message from Corbray.

```
The ICC just issued an arrest warrant for
Naing. Thought you'd want to know.
```

"News?" his mother asked.

"The International Criminal Court put out an arrest warrant for General Naing."

"That's the man who was after you on this last mission, right?"

"That's him." He kissed his mother on the cheek. "Thanks for breakfast."

He fired up his computer, sent an email to Shanti, knowing she must be relieved.

"You did it, princess," he wrote. "You made it happen. Congratulations."

He stupidly waited for a reply, hoping to hear from her, her absence like a hole in his chest. When nothing came, he shut down his computer and went out to help his father, who was harvesting pumpkins.

"Need some help?"

"Sure." His father handed him a pumpkin and pointed to the cardboard containers on the back of the trailer he'd hitched to his tractor. "We got frost coming in."

"Since when do you grow pumpkins?"

"Since I discovered that having a pumpkin stand and a corn maze makes good money come Halloween."

"A corn maze?" Connor noticed that the stalks in the nearest cornfield were still standing. "Who cuts that?"

"I got a fellow out of Kansas comes in and uses GPS and a mini-tractor to get the job done. This year, it's an elephant. I've got a drone photo if you want to see it." His father pulled out his smartphone and pulled up the image.

"GPS? Drone photos? You've gone high-tech." Connor took the phone, grinned. "Well, look at that. An elephant."

And instantly, his mind was back on Shanti again.

It was hot, thirsty work, the two of them taking a break on the bumper of the trailer, drinking iced tea from a thermos.

"What's eating you, son? You come home, work your butt off, and don't say a word. You're shook up about something. Is this about the helicopter crash?"

Connor chuckled. "Dad, that was my fourth helicopter crash, and it went well."

"Then what's up? Talk to me. Your mother is worried."

Connor had never talked about his missions, never talked about what he'd had to do, but he found himself telling his father about the boy in Syria and what had happened in Myanmar with Shanti, leaving out the sex. His parents were pretty old-fashioned when it came to that stuff.

"I wanted to tell her I loved her, but I couldn't. I ... I can't help thinking she deserves someone better, a man who's made something of himself."

"Let her decide what kind of man she wants. Correct me

if I'm wrong, but last I heard less than ten percent of the soldiers who try out for the Unit actually make it."

"Yes. About ten percent."

"You have made something of yourself, one hell of a something. You've done more for your country than most people, and we're awful proud of you. If Shanti loves you like she says she does, she already knows that."

His father wasn't getting the point.

"Shanti is an educated woman, a high-powered attorney. She works for peace. Even her name means 'Peace.' Her family was nearly wiped out in a genocide before she was born. Her entire life has been about stopping violence. I fight and kill for a living. This isn't like you and Mom, where you met in high school, lived in the same town, and both grew up farming."

His father chuckled. "Well, you've never done things the easy way."

That much was true.

"Maybe it's time for you to find a new line of work. You've done your part. Let someone else take it from here."

"If I don't work in private security, what the hell do I do?"

His father grinned, as if he'd known this was the problem all along. "If you knew you couldn't fail, what would you do?"

"I don't know. I've always wanted to go to college and get a degree."

"Then that's what you should do."

Connor shook his head. "I'd be in school with a bunch of kids, and when I graduated, I'd be forty-two."

"You know what's going to happen if you don't go to college?"

"What?"

"You'll still be forty-two, but you won't have a degree. It's not too late to follow your dreams, son. You only get one shot at this life."

"When she left us, Mya, the monk's daughter, passed along a message. He told me that he hoped I'd find true peace one day. Hell, Dad, I don't even know what that is. The only time I've felt at peace ..."

The realization hit him like a bolt of thunder, drove the breath from his lungs.

"The only time I've felt truly at peace was with Shanti." And suddenly nothing else mattered. "I'm heading back to Denver after dinner."

His father nodded, took another drink of tea. "Let's get these pumpkins in before lunch. I think your mama's making fried chicken."

"Dad, thanks."

His father stood, drew him into a sweaty bear hug. "You're a damned hero, Connor. No father has been prouder of his son than I am of you."

∼

OCTOBER 3

Shanti was asleep on the couch when a knock at the door woke her. She stood, hobbled across the room, and looked out the peephole to see...

Oh, my God!

She opened the door. "Connor!"

He stood there looking handsome as sin in a denim jacket, T-shirt, and jeans, a day's growth of beard on his face, a duffel bag at his feet. "Hey, princess."

She couldn't say who moved first, but in the next instant, she was in his arms, laughing and crying at the same time. "I can't believe you're here."

He lifted her off her feet, held her close, buried his face against her throat. "It's so good to see you."

And for a time, they stood there, holding each other.

He set her back on her feet. "Can I come in?"

She laughed, wiped the tears from her face. "Yes! Sorry. It's cold out in the hallway."

"I emailed to tell you I was on my way."

"I haven't been checking email. The doctor says screens are bad for people recovering from a concussion."

Connor carried his duffel inside, glanced around. "Nice place."

She shut the door behind him. "Can I get you something?"

"All I want right now is you." He pulled her into his embrace again, kissed her long and deep and slow. "God, I've missed you."

"I've missed you, too, so much." Then it hit her. "How did you find me?"

He grinned as if her question amused him. "You've met Shields, right? She contacted Bram, had a little chat, and here I am."

"Ah, yes. Of course." She should have known. She'd have to thank Elizabeth later. "Come and sit down."

They settled themselves on her sofa, Shanti's pulse still racing. "I can't believe you're here. This is the best surprise ever."

That made him smile. "Sorry it took me so long. I had some shit to figure out."

He took her hand, rubbed his thumb over her knuckles, his brow furrowed with concern, his gaze moving to the faint, yellow bruise on her cheek. "How are you feeling? I heard you're on medical leave."

"I'm better now that I'm resting and not on the computer

all day. I still get headaches, but they're not as bad. My leg is healing, and I'm getting around just fine."

"Congratulations on the arrest warrant. That's an amazing accomplishment. I heard the British journalists were freed the day the warrant came out."

"I couldn't have done it without you, but, apart from the journalists' release, the reaction has been super disappointing."

"Why do you say that? The bastard is an outlaw now."

"Myanmar won't take him into custody. As long as he stays in his country, he's untouchable. I wanted to do something to help the Rohingya find justice, but all I was able to do was get that warrant. Bram says it sends a message, but it's not much of a message if Naing is free to keep killing. I had wanted to do more than that, to put him behind bars so the world would see that no one escapes justice."

"The ICC can't just go get him?"

She shook her head. "Myanmar isn't a signatory to the Rome Statute, so the court doesn't have the authority to take him into custody."

"Damn. You know, I had that bastard in my sites at the monastery. He was there in the courtyard, and I had a clear shot. I should have taken it."

"No, it's better than you didn't. His country would have rallied around him, and he would have been a martyr. Now, he's an international pariah."

"Bram told Shields you've had nightmares."

Good grief! What else had they talked about?

"They're always the same. We're in a tunnel, like the ones beneath the monastery. You disappear, and I'm alone. It's dark, and I can't get out. I panic and... Then I wake up. Post-traumatic stress, I guess."

He nodded. "Sounds like it."

"The organization is connecting me with a therapist."

"Good. Go. Take care of it."

"Are you still on vacation? I thought you had to go back to work today."

It was the first of October, wasn't it?

His gaze met hers, his blue eyes warm. "I quit."

She gaped at him. "You ... you *quit*?"

"I'm done, Shanti. I did my part, and I'm done. No more fighting or killing."

Shanti couldn't say why, but the news put a lump in her throat. "You really quit?"

He tucked a strand of hair behind her ear. "It's time for me to do something else. I've got a good amount of money in savings. I'm going to sell my condo."

Hope kindled behind Shanti's breastbone. "What do you plan to do?"

"I want to use my GI benefits, go to college, get a degree."

"That's wonderful. Do you know what you want to study?"

He shook his head, grinned. "No clue. Elephants. International relations."

It was a big change for him, but he seemed different, more relaxed, happier.

"What brought this about?"

"You did, Shanti." He hesitated as if trying to find the right words. "Remember Dempo's message for me?"

"He said he hoped you found true peace."

"I thought about it long and hard. Hell, I've barely thought about anything else." Connor leaned forward, cupped her face between his palms, looked into her eyes. "The only real peace I've found is with you. *You* are my peace, Shanti. I love you."

Joy washed through her, her heart swelling until it was

almost too big for her chest, tears filling her eyes. "Oh, Connor. Say it again."

"I love you, Shanti."

"Again."

He chuckled, held her close. "I love you, Shanti. Hey, mind if I stay here with you while we figure this out?"

"Oh, my God, yes! You still owe me a night of endless kisses, remember?"

"I haven't forgotten." He stood, scooped her into his arms, his voice dropping to a sexy purr. "Want to get a head start on that?"

She wrapped her arms around his neck. "I think that's a good idea. It's going to take time, you know—all those kisses and other things."

"*All* of the other things." He started down the hallway. "And Shanti?"

"Yes?"

"I brought condoms."

She laughed all the way to the bedroom.

EPILOGUE

June 5

C onnor stood at the bar in the rented ballroom of the Ithaca Marriott drinking and shooting the shit with his brother and his Unit and Cobra buddies, music thrumming through rented speakers.

"To the friends who never came home—the true heroes." He raised his glass.

"To the true heroes."

"Cheers."

He tossed back his first whiskey in months.

Ryan, his younger brother, refilled his glass and made another toast. "To my brother, the bravest man I've ever known."

"To O'Neal!" Nick Andris raised his glass.

Andris had fought beside Connor in the Unit and gotten Connor his job at Cobra. His wife, Holly Andris, worked as an intel expert for Cobra and had come from the CIA, like Shields.

"Given the situation, I've got more questions about those

five days you and Ms. Lahiri spent alone in the jungle," Tower teased.

Laughter.

Across the room, Shanti danced with Taj. She was wearing Connor's favorite blue sari, her hands, wrists, feet, and ankles painted with henna, Connor's name woven into the intricate designs on her skin. Oh, how he'd love to peel off that sari and enjoy her decorated body. The only downside of this whole getting married thing is that they hadn't slept together since his parents had arrived in Ithaca.

Thank God that would end tomorrow night.

Connor grinned. "You can ask, Tower, but I'm not going to answer. I don't work for you anymore."

"Jungle love." Cruz nodded. "I want an assignment like that."

"Hell, yeah." That was Jones.

"Where do I sign up?" Isaksen said.

"This is your fault, Tower," Corbray grumbled. "We need to hire more female operatives."

Howls of laughter.

McManus didn't look happy with that idea. "You think a lass can do the work we men do?"

Shields plucked the olive from her drink. "Shanti did—apart from the shooting."

"Och, well…"

"What's wrong, McManus? Cat got your sexist tongue?" Elizabeth walked off, a teasing smile on her face, henna on her hands and wrists, too.

The women had held a henna party this morning, while Connor, with the help of his dad, Devesh, Ryan, Taj, and the Cobra guys, had set up the party tent and the four-pillared frame for the canopy that would cover the wedding platform.

"I hear you got into Columbia University," Tower said. "Congrats."

"Isn't that an Ivy League school or some shit?" Corbray asked.

"Can we *not* talk about that tonight? I've got other things on my mind."

"You nervous or something?" Tower asked.

"Hell, no. Marrying Shanti is the smartest thing I've ever done."

She and Connor had lived together now for eight months, first in The Hague and then in their new place on the Upper East Side of Manhattan, near the United Nations Plaza where she worked. His life with her was good, better than he'd imagined life could be. He had no doubts, no second thoughts, no regrets. But he wanted the ceremony to go well. He wanted this to be special for Shanti and their families.

He had worried that his parents might not approve of a secular ceremony with Hindu elements, but they had taken it in stride. His father and Devesh had hit it off from the start, talking about the economics of farming and acting like old friends. His mother and Shanti's mother, Susan, got along well, too, despite having little in common beyond an unrelenting desire for grandchildren.

Which reminded Connor...

"Hey, Tower, when is that baby due? Aren't *you* the one who should be nervous?"

Tower's wife, Jenna, was very pregnant. She sat with Shields and Holly, the three of them smiling and laughing together.

"She's due in the middle of August—and, yeah, I *am* nervous."

"I'm still trying to wrap my head around that—you a

father." Corbray shook his head, chuckling. "How times have changed."

That was the truth, and Connor couldn't be more grateful.

But he'd had enough of this.

"If you boys will excuse me, I want to spend some time with my bride."

$\sim$

SHANTI SLOW-DANCED WITH CONNOR, a bit tipsy from champagne and more than a little turned-on. "I wish we could sneak away from the party. I want you naked. I miss you. It's been five long days."

"Only five? It feels like a month." He kissed her—and inspiration struck him. "Hey, I could get us a room here in the hotel. We could be quick, discreet."

Warmth rushed to her belly. "You want to pay for a room for the night just to get it on for fifteen minutes? Brilliant. Let's do it."

"I'll go first. I'll text you when I've got the keycard. You slip away and join me at the elevator."

Shanti watched him leave, wetness gathering between her thighs, the muscular mounds of his ass looking incredible in his dress pants, his shoulders broad. She couldn't wait to get her hands on him—all of him.

Taj walked up to her, a drink in his hands. "Where's Connor going?"

"Oh, I, uh, don't know. The restroom?"

"There are restrooms over there." Taj pointed with a nod of his head.

"Maybe he has to make a phone call. The music is pretty loud."

Taj seemed to buy that. "When I heard you'd gotten together with a guy who'd been a soldier, I didn't like it. I knew he'd saved your life, but I couldn't see you with a man like that. He's nothing like I imagined. I think he's perfect for you."

"Thanks, Taj. I'm so glad you feel that way. He makes me very happy." As much as she appreciated what Taj had said, she hoped her brother would walk away. If he saw her head in the same direction as Connor, he'd put two and two together.

Not that it mattered. The whole not-sleeping-together thing was for the benefit of Connor's family, not hers.

But Taj kept talking. "I think he's cool."

Shanti stood on tiptoe, kissed her brother's cheek. "He likes you, too. I'm going to see if there's any cake left."

She walked away from her brother—and her cell phone buzzed. She left the ballroom by a side door and hurried down the main hallway toward the reception area.

Connor stood near an elevator. "I can't wait to get you alone."

Shanti fought to keep her hands off him in the elevator, knowing there were security cameras, secrecy adding to her arousal.

When the door to the room closed, he dragged her against him, kissed her hard, backed her across the small space to the bed. "I want to be inside you."

"God, yes." It couldn't happen fast enough.

He'd had lots of practice with saris now and knew where she hid the safety pins, removing them quickly before pulling the silk from the waistband of her petticoat, spinning her in a circle, and dropping the sari onto the floor.

While he freed his cock, she took off her panties, got onto the bed on her hands and knees, and tugged her petticoat up to her waist, baring herself to him completely. *"Now!"*

He grasped her hips with one hand and teased her clit with the fingers of the other, his cock nudging against her entrance. "You are so fucking hot."

He knew her body well, knew just how to make her come fast, how to make her plead, how to make her scream. What he was doing felt so good, and it just kept getting better, pleasure building inside her, clever fingers the source of her bliss.

In this position, all she could do was take it.

He nudged her knees wider apart, entered her with a slow, deep thrust, moaning as their bodies came together. "God, Shanti."

And then he was moving, thrusting deep and hard, his fingers still busy with her clit. It felt good, so good… the ache sweet… carrying her higher… tension drawing tight inside her.

She shattered, coming with a cry, ecstasy carrying her away. When her climax had passed, he took hold of both of her hips and drove into her hard, groaning as he came inside her. They collapsed on the bed, laughing.

Connor settled onto his back, his pants still down, and drew her into his arms. "I don't know about you, but I feel a hell of a lot better."

"Oh, yeah. *So* much better."

"My baby girl—a bride." Shanti's mother kissed her cheek. "Look at you."

Shanti had decided to wear a sari of white lace and silk, one that combined the traditions of both of her countries.

The *pallu*—the part that would drape over her shoulder—was translucent with white lace flowers. Her blouse, which stopped just below her ribs, had little cap sleeves of matching white lace.

"Do you think Connor will like it?"

"Oh, honey, he is going to go out of his mind when he sees you. That man loves you more than life itself. I get choked up even thinking about it."

Shanti reached for her veil—an elbow-length veil of silk tulle with lace flowers across the bottom. She would pin it just above the beautiful bun her mother's stylist had made for her.

"Hold off on that for a minute." Her mother took the veil, set it back. "I think your father wants to speak with you."

A knock.

Her father stepped inside, his gaze moving over her. "My sweet girl. Don't you look beautiful? I wish your grandparents had lived to see this."

Shanti wished that, too. "Don't make me cry, Daddy. It will wreck my makeup."

He sat, motioned for her to sit beside him, a good-sized wooden box in his hands. "These belonged to your grandmother's grandmother and so on, going back to the Eighteenth Century. They would have gone to my sister, but ... I have saved them all this time for this special day."

Shanti opened the box—and stared, the breath leaving her lungs in a rush. "Oh!"

On a lining of red velvet sat a necklace, bracelets, a hair ornament, and matching earrings, all of them made of gold and set with diamonds, rubies, and little pearls.

"Your ancestors were Barendra Brahmins and very

wealthy. These jewels are all that remains of their ancient wealth."

Shanti's vision blurred. "You want me to *wear* these?"

"How does it go—something old, something new...? These are very old. They are twenty-two karat gold. The stones and pearls are real.

"You'll have to help me." Shanti had never worn anything so valuable—or heavy.

"This is a *maang tikka*." Her mother clipped the hair ornament into her bun and rested the fine golden chain in her part so that the gem-encrusted ornament hung against her forehead. Her father took the heavy necklace and draped it around her throat, fastening the clasp. Her mother slipped the bracelets over her wrists. The earrings were so heavy they came with gold wires that went over and behind her ears for extra support.

"Oh, Shanti, look at you." Her mother put on her veil.

Shanti stood and walked to the mirror, seeing her reflection for the first time. If it hadn't been her face, she wouldn't have recognized herself. She looked like a bride, but not a typical American bride. She was the child of two cultures, of two countries, and both of them shone in her reflection.

Her father kissed her on the top of her head. "When you walk down the aisle today, you walk with all the generations of your family."

Shanti hugged her parents, fighting tears. "Thank you. I love you both so much."

Her mother handed her the bouquet of white orchids. "It's time."

∽

"Let me fix your tie."

Connor endured his mother's fussing with the knot, excitement warring with disbelief inside him. He and Shanti were getting married today. Shanti was going to be his wife. How *the fuck* had he gotten so lucky?

"There. You look so handsome."

"Thanks, Mom." Connor had decided to stick with a tux —black on black—rather than wearing Bengali clothes.

"All right, son. Are you ready?" his father asked.

"I'm more than ready." Connor entered the party tent with his parents, the plain interior transformed overnight by bouquets of red and white roses that decorated the aisles, the wedding platform, the corners of the silk canopy, and even the walls. A chamber orchestra sat off to one side, string music filling the space.

"This is lovely," his mother whispered.

Dr. Choudhary, a friend of Devesh's from Cornell, was officiating and stood on the raised platform, a low altar in front of him, fire burning in a brazier at its center, plush seats set along the back for the parents.

Connor walked down the aisle with his mother and father, friendly faces turning his way, everyone smiling. He and his parents climbed the stairs to the platform, where they shook hands with Dr. Choudhary, the three of them speaking quietly together. Yes, it seemed an auspicious day for a wedding. Yes, Connor was excited. Yes, it was fun to have a cross-cultural celebration.

The song finished, and the chamber orchestra started a piece by Bach—the music Shanti had chosen for her entrance.

Barely able to breathe, Connor waited.

The flaps were drawn back, and there she stood.

Connor's heart gave a hard thud, his pulse drowning out the music.

Princess.

It was the only word his brain could manage.

Shanti walked between her parents, looking like a vision of heaven, the sight of her making his knees weak. She wore a white lace sari, a veil hanging down her back, the skin of her hips and belly peeking through lace. She glimmered with gold and jewels at her forehead, her throat, her ears, her wrists.

A vision.

She walked gracefully up the stairs and came to stand before him, her gaze locked with his, the longing and joy in her amber eyes a mirror for his own emotion.

"You are so beautiful." He took her hand, kissed it.

She smiled. "You look hot."

Dr. Choudhary began to speak, but Connor barely heard a word he said, the world around them fading, Shanti the only thing in his universe. When it was time, his parents handed him a garland of white and red flowers, which he draped around her neck—a symbolic way of welcoming her to their family. Her parents did the same, but he had to bend down so Shanti could get the garland over his head.

More words, Dr. Choudhary's voice flowing around him like water.

Then Connor took her hand in his, ready to lead her around the fire seven times, while Dr. Choudhary recited seven blessings.

"May you be blessed with abundance and comfort."

"May you be strong and help one another in all ways."

"May you be blessed with prosperity and peace."

"May you be always happy."

"May you be blessed with a joyful family life."

"May you live in love and harmony, fulfilling your promises to each other."

"May you forever be the best of friends."

With one final step, they came to stand back where they'd started. They exchanged vows and rings, both of them promising to love, honor, and cherish for the rest of their lives.

And then, at last, Connor got to do what he wanted to.

He drew his princess close and kissed her.

≈

September 4

SHANTI SHUT OFF THE ALARM, rolled over, and kissed Connor's bare chest. "Wake up, sleepyhead. It's your first day of school."

His eyes flew open. "Shit."

Shanti couldn't help but smile. The man who'd taken on an army was nervous about starting classes. "Take a shower and get dressed. I've got a surprise for you."

Connor took her into his arms, rolled her beneath him, kissed her. "I love you."

He said those words often now.

"I love you, too. I'm so excited for you. I can't wait to hear all about it when I get home this evening."

Their four-bedroom condo was a ten-minute commute to United Nations Plaza, where Shanti had taken a job as an attorney for the UN's refugee resettlement program, and only twenty minutes from Columbia University. They would never have been able to afford the place if it hadn't been for the money she'd inherited from her grandparents. Now, they had a home in the heart of the city, a place where they could put down roots, where they could raise a couple of kids one day.

While Connor showered and shaved, she went out to the kitchen and found the recipe for chocolate chip pancakes that she'd gotten from his mom. By the time he joined her, she'd gotten the pancakes off the electric griddle and had set them on the table with real maple syrup, butter, and coffee made just the way he liked it—hot, black, and strong.

His face split in a wide grin. "Chocolate chip pancakes? You're the best."

"Today is a special day. We need to celebrate."

She watched while he took his first bite. She wasn't much of a cook and hadn't made these before.

He chewed, nodded. "Mmm. Perfect."

She took a bite. "Oh, these *are* yummy."

They talked about little things—the bus schedule, the weather, the arrival of the new dishwasher tomorrow.

Then it hit Shanti. "A year ago, today, we were running through the jungle. It was the day we found the old temple ruins, remember?"

Had that really been a year ago? How their lives had changed in the course of that time. How *they* had changed.

"Hell, no, I haven't forgotten that—Stone Porn Temple." He grinned when she started to object. "I know. I know. It's sacred art."

They went through Connor's schedule together. He'd opted to major in Peace and Conflict Studies and had won a full scholarship thanks to his high test scores and the brilliant and very personal entrance essay he'd written about the impact of combat on soldiers and their families.

After breakfast, he cleaned up while Shanti showered and dressed. She was wearing a skirt suit and carrying a briefcase, while he was wearing jeans, a T-shirt, and carrying a backpack full of books and notebooks.

All too soon, it was time to say goodbye.

"Have a wonderful day—and try not to notice all the eighteen-year-old women running around campus in tight jeans."

Connor wrapped his arms around her. "You have nothing to worry about—ever. Everything I want is here with you."

They kissed, sweet and slow.

Shanti pulled out her phone. "I need to take a photo to send to your mom. Stand by the door with your backpack."

He gave her a look that said this was stupid. "You're kidding me, right?"

"No, it's your first day of school."

"Okay, fine, but I'm not in kindergarten, you know."

He stood there, looking tall and strong and handsome— her hero, the man who had saved her, the love of her life.

"Smile." She took a couple of shots. "See you this evening. Have a wonderful day. You can do this. I know you can."

"Thanks for making me believe that I could be more than I was." He kissed her again then turned and walked out the door.

Shanti watched him go, a lump in her throat. Then she texted the photo to his mother along with a little message.

First day of school. A new beginning.

THANK YOU

Thanks for reading *Hard Asset*. I hope you enjoyed this Cobra Elite story. Follow me on Facebook or on Twitter @Pamela_Clare. Join my romantic suspense reader's group on Facebook to be a part of a never-ending conversation with other Cobra fans and get inside information on the series and on life in Colorado's mountains. You can also sign up to my mailing list at my website to keep current with all my releases and to be a part of special newsletter giveaways.

ALSO BY PAMELA CLARE

Slow Burn (Book 2)

Falling Hard (Book 3)

Tempting Fate (Book 4)

Close to Heaven (Book 5)

Holding On (Book 6)

Chasing Fire (Book 7)

Historical Romance:

Kenleigh-Blakewell Family Saga

Sweet Release (Book 1)

Carnal Gift (Book 2)

Ride the Fire (Book 3)

MacKinnon's Rangers series

Surrender (Book I)

Untamed (Book 2)

Defiant (Book 3)

Upon A Winter's Night: A MacKinnon's Rangers Christmas (Book 3.5)

ABOUT THE AUTHOR

USA Today best-selling author Pamela Clare began her writing career as a columnist and investigative reporter and eventually became the first woman editor-in-chief of two different newspapers. Along the way, she and her team won numerous state and national honors, including the National Journalism Award for Public Service. In 2011, Clare was awarded the Keeper of the Flame Lifetime Achievement Award for her body of work. A single mother with two sons, she writes historical romance and contemporary romantic suspense at the foot of the beautiful Rocky Mountains. Visit her website and join her mailing list to never miss a new release!

www.pamelaclare.com

51335831R00180

Made in the USA
Lexington, KY
02 September 2019